Praise for Mar

'The king of the British hard-boiled thriller'
— *Times*

'Grips like a pair of regulation handcuffs'
— *Guardian*

'Nick Sharman is like black coffee at 4 o'clock in the morning: very black, very bitter' — **Derek Raymond**

'Reverberates like a gunshot'
— *Irish Times*

'Definitely one of the best'
— *Time Out*

'The mean streets of South London need their heroes tough. Private eye Nick Sharman fits the bill'
— *Telegraph*

'Full of cars, girls, guns, strung out along the high sierras of Brixton and Battersea, the Elephant and the North Peckham Estate, all those jewels in the crown they call Sarf London'
— *Arena*

Other books by Mark Timlin

A Good Year for the Roses 1988
Romeo's Tune 1990
Gun Street Girl 1990
Take the A-Train 1991
The Turnaround 1991
Zip Gun Boogie 1992
Hearts of Stone 1992
Falls the Shadow 1993
Ashes by Now 1993
Pretend We're Dead 1994
Paint It Black 1995
Find My Way Home 1996
Sharman and Other Filth (short stories) 1996
A Street That Rhymed at 3 AM 1997
Dead Flowers 1998
Quick Before They Catch Us 1999
All the Empty Places 2000
Stay Another Day 2010

OTHERS

I Spied a Pale Horse 1999
Answers from the Grave 2004
as TONY WILLIAMS
Valin's Raiders 1994
Blue on Blue 1999
as JIM BALLANTYNE
The Torturer 1995
as MARTIN MILK
That Saturday 1996
as LEE MARTIN
Gangsters Wives 2007
The Lipstick Killers 2009

MARK TIMLIN

REAP THE WHIRLWIND

A NICK SHARMAN THRILLER

cmc

This edition published in 2021
The Crime and Mystery Club
Harpenden, UK
www.crimeandmysteryclub.co.uk
fb: Crime and Mystery Club

A CIP catalogue record for this book is available from the British Library.

ISBN
978-0-85730-379-0 (Paperback)
978-0-85730-381-3 (Ebook)

Typeset by Avocet Typeset, Bideford, Devon, EX39 2BP
in Adobe Garamond

Printed in Great Britain by Severn, Gloucester

For more information about Crime Fiction go to crimetime.co.uk

CONTENTS

For Lucy and Schmoo Ramsey

'When in doubt, have a man come through
the door with a gun in his hand.'

Raymond Chandler

By falling, we learn to go safely

Chinese proverb

This is based on a true story.

1

White Light/White Heat
– The Velvet Underground

This all happened between then and now.

It was a short hot summer that year. Just a few weeks, but it seemed longer. Hotter than '76. Reservoirs dried up, hosepipe bans arrived, birds dropped out of the sky, and fluttered into the shade to recover. Good natured shopkeepers put bowls of water outside their shop fronts for thirsty dogs. The general public were advised to share bath water with a significant other. Sadly, I didn't have one. I made do with a punk rock rubber duck with a Mohican and studded collar that my daughter had left in my bathroom. The city was baking, like beef stew in a slow cooker.

At first it looked like a simple job. Just a bus ride up to Holborn. Drop into the office of a legal firm. Leave an envelope with one of the partners, get a signature, then lunch at a little Japanese restaurant I knew, a bus ride home, two hundred sovs in the bin. Job done!

But let's go back to the very beginning. A very good place to start. It was yet another boiling morning. Eighty degrees by eight o'clock, and not a hint of a breeze. The sky was a tight blue skullcap over London, and the sun was a red-hot poker, from which there was little escape. Humidity was up, and the barometer was down. Even with the heatwave, I tried to stay fit. Every morning I did my usual run to Brockwell Park, up to the old house, then back to my office. Well, more like run there, limp back. I was dripping when I let myself in, so I went back to the small shower I'd had fitted after a good result, stripped my wet gear off and stood under cold water for five minutes, dried off, then got dressed in t-shirt and shorts. If anyone happened to drop by and want some private detecting done there was a navy blue, lightweight Cecil Gee suit hanging on the back of the door, with a white shirt, a serious tie, and on the floor a pair of black slip-ons with clean socks tucked in. The Venetian blinds in the window were closed, the door was open just to let the world know I was still alive, I had a Silk Cut in the ashtray, there was a glass of iced coffee courtesy of my new, expensive espresso machine. One of a pair I'd bought after another bit of a result recently. One for home, one for away, and the air was being slowly moved about by a small electric fan. The stereo was softly playing some kind of mod jazz compilation with plenty of Hammond organ. The current account was healthy, and all was right with my world.

I should have taken a holiday, business was so quiet. I could have been sitting by an infinity pool, smoking a blunt the size of a baby's arm, drinking New England iced tea or something similar, served by topless Nubian maidens whose only desire was my pleasure, and only pleasure was my desire. Trouble was, I was so bone idle I couldn't rustle up the energy. That was all about to change when the phone rang. I picked up the instrument. 'Sharman,' I said.

'Good morning,' said a male voice. Husky, with no special accent. 'Are you available for a job?'

'Depends on the job,' I replied.

'An easy one. A distant relative of mine died. Her will is

in probate. The solicitor requires some extra paperwork that I hold. I'm in the south of France on important business and can't get back. All I need is someone to take an envelope to the solicitor, get a signature, and that's that.'

'Where is the solicitor.' I asked.

'Just off High Holborn.'

'Why not put the stuff in the post, or use a courier?'

'I want it signed for, and the receipt returned to me. I favour the personal touch.'

Me too, I thought, but said nothing.

'I'll pay you two hundred pounds,' he added. 'Cash.'

Now he was talking. Cash is king. 'How did you find me?' I asked. Always nice to know.

'A recommendation.' He mentioned a name that I knew.

'OK,' I said. 'Get the stuff to me.'

'Your address is still Station Approach, SW2?' I confirmed that it was.

'Expect a registered delivery.'

'I will Mr…?

'Martineau. M-A-R-T-I-N-E-A-U. Harry Martineau.'

'OK, Mr Martineau. I'll keep a lookout.'

And I did.

The postman bought a bulky registered parcel the next morning. Inside was a brown A4 envelope, sealed with red wax. Old school! On the front, in black ink, was written:

For the attention of:
Mr Leonard Stowe-Hartley
Senior Partner,
Mssrs Gyre & Gimble,
37 Highcross Street, Holborn,
London W.1.

Also enclosed was a smaller envelope containing two hundred quid in brand new sequential twenty pound notes. Plus a handwritten note with the telephone number of the solicitors and Stowe-Hartley's extension. Also inside was a receipt for the papers and a pre paid, addressed envelope with a PO Box number in London for the receipt. Nothing more.

Later that morning I rang, got his secretary, explained my task, and got an appointment to call the next morning at eleven. Perfect for a quick half before lunch. The next day dawned hot again. So hot that *The Sun* newspaper had fried an egg on the pavement outside their office.

Next morning I skipped my run. Then dressed to impress, in a pale blue Oxford button down shirt, a somber tie, a two button, single vent mohair whistle, black socks with pale blue clocks, and black Chelsea boots polished to a high shine. So, showered and shaved, come 9.45 I set off to catch a number 68 bus on Norwood Road.

The bus was empty so I went upstairs to the front seats, just like I did when I was a nipper, with my mum and pretended I was the driver. Both front windows wound halfway down, so I cracked them both, took off my jacket and enjoyed the breeze.

The bus meandered through Herne Hill, Camberwell, the Elephant, over Waterloo Bridge and dropped me off opposite Holborn tube at quarter to eleven. According to my A-Z, Highcross Street was two streets along High Holborn, then two more north. And it was. At five to eleven I turned into one of those streets that hadn't changed for a hundred years or more, lined with four storey terraced town houses painted sparkling white and smelling of old money well looked after. Number 37 was smack dab in the middle of the terrace on my right, and at eleven o'clock precisely I climbed the four steps that led between two columns to the massive front door. Next to it was a shiny brass plate with Mssrs Gayle & Gimble writ large. At least I was in the right place.

In the middle of the black lacquered door was a big bell push with another brass plate that said RING AND WAIT. Figuring I had no choice, I did so. Almost immediately the door opened and a middle aged man in a sergeant's uniform covered with gold braid and medal ribbons stood in front of me. Blimey, I thought. A doorman. How posh. I introduced myself, and he ushered me in, stood me in front of his desk and called through on the telephone. Once convinced I was expected, he showed me to an old fashioned accordion fronted elevator and sent me skywards towards the third floor where I was met by a young blonde in a severe two piece suit who showed me into Stowe-Hartley's office. And very tasty it was too. All dark, polished wood, thick carpet, with a desk as big as my office. Completely clear except for two phones. The air conditioning was on high. It felt like paradise after the street outside.

Behind the desk was the man himself, I supposed, who rose as I entered and stuck out his hand. 'Mr Sharman,' he said. 'Stowe-Hartley. You're very punctual.'

'The politeness of princes,' I replied. 'Or so my old granny used to say,' as I took the extended mitten.

He was a big man, tall, middle forties I guessed, beautifully suited in Savile Row's finest, and a starched white shirt and patterned tie in a Windsor knot. His dark hair was swept back and greased down, and his smile and voice were so sincere I immediately took a dislike to him. Don't ask me why. It was just something about him that made me think of a basking shark waiting to make a kill. 'So true,' he said back. His handshake was firm and dry, and his voice was sincere as hell, but I was still tempted to count my fingers when he let go.

'Do sit,' he said and indicated a comfy looking leather chair in front of his desk. I did as I was told and put the envelope from Martineau on his desk. He broke the wax seal, opened the envelope and pulled out a sheaf of papers. He flicked through, then grinned a shark-like grin and said, 'Excellent. This seems to be all in order.'

'Good,' I said 'Now if you'll just sign this receipt.' I passed that over too.

'Of course.'

He took the proffered linen and made a show of a complicated signature with a massive gold fountain pen. He passed it back. 'Thanks,' I said and stood up. He stood also, and I made my leave, found his secretary in the outer office, who showed me back to the lift which creaked down to the sergeant's lair, and out through the front door to the big, wide world, and a world of trouble.

2

Summertime Blues-Eddie Cochran/ T-Rex/The Who

The sun was at its peak when I got back outside, and the street was whited-out like a negative photo. After the air con in Stowe-Hartley's office, it was almost unbearable, and I took off my jacket, and rolled up my shirt sleeves. Now I knew how that fried egg outside the newspaper office felt. I crossed the road heading back towards High Holborn, and I noticed a man standing on the pavement opposite looking like he was lost. He was about my size and looked like he went to Bertie Wooster's tailor. He was wearing a three piece tan summer suit, a long collared pink shirt with what looked like a tabbed collar, which I immediately fancied, and a matching paisley tie and handkerchief, flopping out of the breast pocket of his jacket, with two tone brown and white brogues. He even had a carnation in his button hole. Like him, it hadn't wilted in the sunshine. How he managed the waistcoat in the heat I couldn't imagine. He was holding a silver topped walking cane. I only looked for a second but there was something about him. Elegance I think, and he made me feel like a badly tied bag wash.

I turned left at the corner of Highcross Street and as I strolled along, I heard a voice from close behind me. I hadn't heard him following. I must be getting old. 'Mr Sharman,' said the voice. 'Nick Sharman.'

I turned, it was the bloke in the tan suit. 'What?' I said. Not original, but there you go. He seemed perfectly affable close up. No obvious weapons apart from the cane. He reached into the inside of his jacket. If he was armed and about to shoot me, then I was a goner, with nothing on me more lethal than a Mont Blanc ballpoint pen. Instead of a pistol he pulled out a leather case, flipped it open and showed me a Metropolitan Police ID. 'Detective Inspector Douglas Spencer,' he said. 'Can we have a word?'

Of course now I know he probably had a leather case in every pocket, under different names, and different identification for every security and police force in the country, but I didn't know that then. And I didn't ever know his real name as far as I knew. Not ever. But, I'm getting ahead of myself.

'About what?' I said. 'Hold on, have you been following me? What's going on?'

'No. I haven't followed you. I just knew where you were going to be this morning. Fancy a drink?'

I was confused. Not for the first time in my life as it happens. But I was also intrigued and wondered what previous misdemeanour was about to jump up and bite me on my arse. 'Alright,' I said. 'Why not? It's a hot day, and a cold drink sounds just fine.'

'There's a pleasant pub, just around the corner,' he said, and led the way. I followed like a lamb to the slaughter. The boozer did indeed look alright. The woodwork was painted shiny black with hanging baskets leaking water from a recent soaking, which I could cheerfully have stood under to cool myself down. Inside it was polished floors, a polished bar, and polished bottles reflecting the low lights. Orange and red. The barman was behind the jump, polishing a glass. There was a CD of Motown greatest hits playing quietly. Air con there too. Happy days.

'What do you fancy? asked Spencer.

'Bottle of Becks,' I replied. Then spotting fresh limes on a shelf behind the bar, I added. 'With a squeeze of lime juice.'

He went to the bar and ordered. I sat on a padded banquette and waited for my drink. Spencer came back with two glasses of beer. Mine had a lime juice top just like I'd asked.

'Told you,' he said. 'Not a bad place.'

I agreed out of politeness as Marvin Gaye segued into Gladys Knight. 'So,' I said. 'What's this all about?'

'I'll come to that. You see there's just one thing we don't know about you, Mr Sharman. We don't know if you're on the side of the angels, or the dark side.'

'We?' I said.

'The security forces. The forces for good.'

'I didn't know I was so popular.'

'I wouldn't go that far,' he replied after taking a drink. 'But you're definitely on our radar.'

'Nice to know.'

'Which is why you're here. We… I recognise you're a shrewd operator. And you were a bloody good copper until you turned to grand larceny.'

Obviously he didn't believe in gilding the lily. He was right, of course, but that's another story.

'So you see, we… I need your opinion on something.'

Just then the penny dropped and I recognised his voice. 'Hold on,' I said. 'It's you. On the telephone. You're the bloke who called me.'

He didn't even have the goodness to blush. Instead he shrugged and said, 'Guilty as charged.'

'And you weren't in France.' He shook his head.

'So there is no deceased old lady.'

'Oh there is. An old dear died in an old folks home. No reason. No sign of foul play, and indeed no sign of fair. Poof.' He threw open one hand. 'And she was gone. According to the postmortem her heart just stopped. Her grandson was most distraught. He approached us and so began my little deception the other day.'

'And my opinion?'

'On the fellow you met today. Leonard Stowe-Hartley .

'The lawyer?'

'The very same. A slippery cove.'

He saw my frown.

'Do you read, Mr Sharman?'

'Sometimes.'

'I do. It's my way of relaxing. Crime fiction mostly. Christie, Wallace. The golden age of British crime writing, and sometimes I slip into the argot.'

'I have a friend who shares your interest,' I said. 'My favourite is Lee Child.' It was his turn to frown.

'I believe he's quite popular.'

'Why do you want to know what I thought of Stowe-Hartley?'

'Going back to the old lady. The home she died in is part-owned by him. And coincidentally he's her lawyer. Or was. Hence the delivery you did today.'

'I see,' I said, though I didn't. 'As a matter of fact I didn't like him.'

'Why was that, pray tell?'

We were back in the thirties.

'Dunno, to tell you the truth. Just didn't like him…'

'Good. I hoped you'd say that. You see, as well as being a slippery cove, our Lenny is rich. There is no Gyre and Gimble, it's all his. Plus he's clever, he's duplicitous, he's ruthless, and he's bloody elusive. And Stowe-Hartley isn't his birth name.'

'Which is?'

'Sidney Hartley. Stowe was his father. So you see, he's a bastard by name and nature.'

'So what exactly does he do?' I asked.

'He's a fixer. An architect. He plans jobs. Criminal jobs, and takes a cut. A large cut we hear.'

'So why not nick him?'

'Because he is as clean as clean can be. When these jobs go off he's in Scotland playing golf, on the beach in Barbados, or on his yacht moored on the South of France. And he's a hail fellow well met. The life and soul of the party as everyone else will testify. Alibied to the hilt. Simple!'

'But that still doesn't tell me where I fit in.'

'Fit, precisely,' he said. 'You are the perfect fit. What we're looking for is someone to put a spanner in his works. A cat amongst the pigeons. And you would be perfect.'

Suddenly, the room seemed colder than the air conditioning warranted. 'Let's get one thing straight from the get go,' I said. 'No matter what you might have dug up about me, I don't kill people for money, or for any other reason.'

He managed to raise one eyebrow like a low rent Roger Moore. 'No no, Mr Sharman. That's not what we want. Heaven forfend. Just a little sand in his shoes. Besides, it's been tried. Twice, as a matter of fact. And both would-be assassins ended up dead. No, just a little abrasion in his life. Come on, with your pedigree it would be easy.'

'Well,' I replied. 'You can forget about that. I don't do dangerous things any more, and that sounds dangerous to me. My life is chasing debts, finding missing persons and delivering writs. That's it. I just want a quiet life.'

'Don't we all?' he said. 'Well, if that's your last word, I suppose I'd better leave you to finish your drink and enjoy your quiet life.' He consulted the expensive-looking watch on his wrist. 'Time I was going. Thanks for yours. Time that is. Oh I nearly forgot.' He reached into his jacket again and pulled out an envelope and slid it across the table to me. 'Another two hundred pounds for your trouble. And don't mention this meeting to anyone, there's a good chap.'

It's been a long time since anyone called me that. 'Fine,' I said, and pocketed the dough.

'I'll take that,' he said, nodding towards the envelope with the receipt inside. 'I'll make sure it gets delivered.'

I passed it over. He picked it up, rose, leaving his beer, and with a good-natured 'Cheerio for now', he left me to finish mine. Which I did. Then I headed for the Japanese restaurant where, as I ate my Japanese sliced steak, my Japanese crunchy noodles and my Japanese hot sauce, and drank my Japanese cold beer, and where the air conditioning was on high too, I figured that I hadn't been fed such a bunch of bullshit for a long time. But I didn't let it spoil my appetite. After all, I thought, as I sat on the bus home, what could he do to me? I didn't have to wait long to find out.

3

In The Jailhouse Now
– Jimmie Rodgers

Two days to be precise.

Two days wondering what the hell this DI Spencer had really wanted from me, and why. It was like a nail in my shoe, or a nagging toothache all weekend. On the third morning, Monday, I had some business to do with a local lawyer about an old case I'd worked on. Nothing dramatic. No dead bodies littered about. I'd put on a suit and presented myself at his office, then back to mine.

Another boiling morning, jacket on a hanger, shoes off, tie pulled down. Another Silk Cut smouldering in the ashtray, the same CD in the same stereo, the same electric fan slowly moving the hot air from one side of the room to the other, and the current account a little fatter, when my buddy Li who ran the tiny Vietnamese restaurant just up the road popped in for a natter. Now, just understand with Li there was no lookee, lookee, Charlie Chan bullshit. Li was shirt for Lionel, and he spoke English better than me. Not that that was anything to go by. So did lots of people. Li was second generation immigrant. His grandparents had done a runner in the fifties to get away from the regime and somehow got here and settled in Herne Hill. Li's father was one of a tribe of kids. He'd married a local girl and Li was the fruit of his loins. The son had gone to catering college, then opened his restaurant in a shop next to the station, barely large enough to swing a proverbial. Li made the wickedest hot and sour soup I'd ever tasted. Hot and sour enough to bring tears to the eyes. But the taste!

'Morning Nick,' he said, as he stood in the doorway, leaning against the jamb. 'Hot enough for you?'

'Too bloody hot,' I replied. 'But not sour.'

That would soon change.

'Me too,' he said.

'You're kidding. With your ancestry out in the paddy fields, I would've expected this sort of weather suited you down to the ground.'

'I'll ignore that possible racist slur on my ancestors and remind you of my mother's delicate constitution regarding heat. She's a child of England's bloody cold.'

'So why do you stand in that tiny kitchen all day sweating your bollocks off cooking red hot chilli curry?' I asked.

'Because I have to earn a crust just like you. But looking around there's not much sign of discreet enquiries, or for that matter, enquiries of any kind.' He was referring to the motto on my business cards. I shrugged. 'Quiet time of the year,' I said. 'But up here.' I tapped my temple, 'it's all action.'

He looked over his shoulder and said, 'Well, I reckon it's going to get noisier in a minute. And action-packed if I'm not mistaken. There's two blokes clocking your place from across the road, and I smell pork. And not of the sweet and sour variety. See ya.' And with that he legged it back the way he'd come. He didn't like cops any more than I did, and certainly had a nose for the boys in blue, even in plain clothes. And he was never wrong. I knew as soon as I saw the pair of them fill the doorway he had just vacated. 'Nick Sharman,' said the one on the right.

'That's me,' I replied, the picture of innocence.

'Good,' said the other one, and they both moved into the room, closing the door behind them. That's when they showed ID, and introduced themselves. The one on the right was DS Burke, the one on the left DI Dixon. I didn't make any jokes about Dock Green.

Burke was wearing a suit well above his pay grade, and a watch with more dials than strictly necessary. You could probably tell the time in Nicaragua, and the metal strap could tug a charabanc. He was polished as a Rolls-Royce, and twice as slippery. Dixon, on the other hand, looked like an old fashioned door kicker in trousers worn shiny in the backside. Put them together and they spelled big trouble. Dixon took the client's seat, Burke turned off the stereo and leant against the wall. Dixon said, 'Yesterday morning, you paid three hundred and sixty pounds in new, sequential twenty pound notes into the Tulse Hill branch of HSBC.' As soon as he said that I knew what was coming. I should have tucked that dough under the mattress.

'Correct,' I said.

'Well, those notes were part of the money stolen from the Knightsbridge branch of the National Bank on the 30th May this year.'

'You don't say,' I said. So Spencer had stitched me right up.

'Oh, I do,' said Dixon. 'Can you explain how you came by them?'

Well I tried. I told them the story from A-Z, and the more I told it, the worse it sounded.

'Very good,' said Dixon. 'And you expect us to believe that rubbish?'

'It's what happened.'

So then we started to go round the Mulberry Bush. There was no Spencer involved in the case. They hadn't heard of

Stowe-Hartley, or some deceased old woman dying under suspicious circumstances in a care home. They wanted an alibi for the bank holiday weekend. I remembered it well. Just me, my DVD player, and a bunch of old films.

'No one to back it up?' asked Burke, speaking for the first time. I shook my head. 'Nicky no mates,' he said, shaking his head. 'Shame.'

I could only agree. 'But I did have takeaways on that Sunday and Monday night,' I said. 'Vietnamese on the Sunday, Pizza Express Monday. They're bound to have records.'

'Vietnamese from the establishment of that young gentleman who just ran up the road?' asked Dixon.

'Correct,' I said.

'Then maybe you do have mates after all,' said Burke. 'But not for the daytimes, they're what matter.'

'It won't wash,' said Dixon. 'Whatever your story, we've got you for receiving. There are officers outside with a search warrant for here, your car, and your flat. Keys please.'

I handed them over, then they told me to stand, nicked me for suspicion of robbery of the bank, and receiving stolen goods, read me my rights, handcuffed me, and took me out to their car. At least they let me put my shoes on.

As we drove away, I saw Li standing in the road watching the sorry saga.

Before we go any further, let me remind you of the robbery in question. It was big news that bank holiday week. No wars, no terrorist attacks, no rock stars OD'd. No female film star got out of a cab showing her lack of underwear. So the robbery at the main branch of the National Bank in Knightsbridge got all the headlines.

What happened was, the bank was cuddled up close to a low rise office block that had an advertising agency as its one tenant. The office was shut for the long weekend. No security apart from an occasional drive-by. After all, who wanted to steal an advertising campaign for feminine hygiene products?

Come the Friday evening about eight, two shiny vans bearing the livery of an upmarket executive decorators that didn't exist pulled up. Witnesses saw maybe half a dozen, maybe more, maybe less, workmen in clean overalls unload ladders, buckets, paint pots, tools of all shapes and sizes. One of them bumped the front door in less time than it would take to unlock it, fixed the burglar alarm, and took the kit inside. Once in situ, they all left, only to return on the Saturday at six am, and the subsequent Sunday and bank holiday Monday at the same hours. There was hardly any noise all weekend, certainly not enough to upset the few residential neighbours.

Inside, they rigged up a huge drill, tough enough to break through concrete, and drilled through from the office basement to the main vault of the bank. Inside were nicely wrapped brand new five, ten, twenty, and fifty pound notes waiting to be distributed to the bank's smaller branches. Three million sterling if you were counting. Every last Lady Godiva was loaded into the decorators vans and spirited off God knows where. Not a trace of the dosh, or the robbers, had been seen since. That is, not until those twenties turned up in my bank, screwed, blued and tattooed. That was me.

4

I Got Stripes
– Johnny Cash

Not much was said on the short drive to Denmark Hill nick. They wanted me on tape. Dixon asked if I wanted a brief. I declined. I figured I'd let this run its own course and end up where it would. But it didn't look like it would end well from where I was sitting in the back seat of a police car that smelt of stale McDonald's.

At least it gave me time to think. Paranoia was on the rampage. I was being set up. But why? Was it some kind of karma? Where had the cash from the robbery come from? Or was it all an elaborate plan to help the cops get Stowe-Hartley? Maybe that money wasn't from the robbery at all. I only had Burke and Dixon's word for it. I sat in the back of the cop car where the air con wasn't working properly, just bubbling some faint memory of a chilly draft from when the motor was factory fresh, watching the pedestrians on the street going about their usual business. Lucky them.

Downstairs at the cop shop smelt even worse than the car. Shit and cheap disinfectant. They took my photo front and side then put me in a bare room with just a table and four chairs, all bolted down. On the table was the recorder. The lights were fluorescent and too bright. But at least it was cooler than outside, although the walls were leaching something nasty and toxic.

The two detectives joined me with coffee, informed me I was still under caution, unwrapped two cassettes and started. We three identified ourselves for the tape, and Dixon asked me again if I wanted a solicitor present. I declined again.

Then they began. I could have done a no comment interview, but where was the fun in that? I was innocent. At least of these charges, and wanted them to know it. This is how it went.

Dixon: 'Mr Sharman, about the money that you paid into your bank that has been identified as part of the cash stolen from the National Bank in Knightsbridge on the spring bank holiday weekend this year. Can you explain how you came by it?'

All around the Mulberry Bush again.

Me: 'I've already told you. I got a call from a bloke calling himself Martineau. He asked me to deliver some papers to a lawyer in Holborn. The fee was two hundred quid in cash. It came in the post with the papers. I did the job and he was waiting for me outside. Flash dresser. I told Burke they would probably have got on. He then identified himself as DI Spencer. Bought me a drink and asked what I thought of the solicitor, then gave me another two hundred to keep quiet.'

D: 'Which you're not.'

Me: 'Then I didn't expect to end up here.'

B: 'And why would the Met care what a scrote like you would think of anyone?'

Me: 'That's rude. And I don't know. He just did. Then he told me this solicitor was a fixer. Architected jobs including the bank job.'

D: 'Alright. The name of the solicitor again.'

I told him. Burke left the room. Dixon and I stayed. Five minutes later Burke came back.

B: 'There's nothing on the solicitor. Clean as. No DI Spencer on the bank job.'

Me: 'Look, I don't know where Spencer came from. I don't know where he went. All I know is, he was there, and everything I've told you is the truth.'

D: 'But most interestingly, how did he get money from the bank? No money has been recovered.'

Me: 'Don't ask me. I'm completely in the dark. Not for the first time.'

D: 'I think we'll leave this for now. Let's see what the searches to your home, office and car turn up.'

All I added before they locked me up again was that, if four hundred quid was my cut from a robbery that had netted three million quid according to the reports I had read at the time, I had to be a low man on the totem pole. Although I read once that the most important figures depicted were the ones at the bottom. Funny the things you remember.

Anyway, after we'd done wasting each other's time, they sent me to a cell where I was fed a cold egg mayo sandwich and a warm cup of tea.

The one good thing was that there was nothing to find at my flat, office, or in my car. Not anymore. At least that was what I thought.

I kicked my heels in the cell all afternoon, then Dixon appeared and told me the search of my flat had turned up another eighteen grand and change in new notes. Same sequence. In the freezer of all places. How original.

So Spencer had really done a number on me. But why? But I had a horrible feeling I would soon find out.

I was released on police bail later that afternoon after agreeing to surrender my passport, which the cops already had from the search.

They kicked me out at six o'clock, handing me back only my keys and a copy of the interview cassette. What I was supposed to do with that, Christ knows. It was hardly Abba's greatest hits. Luckily, I had my Oyster card to get the bus home, which was full of commuters sweating their bollocks off. The inside of the bus smelt nearly as bad as the cop shop. I was sweating mine off too when I got back to my flat, which looked like a bomb had hit it, so I spent the evening putting Humpty back together again and decided to leave seeing what they'd done to my office until morning.

5

Dinner with Drac
– John Zacherle

But first I needed to speak to my old best of enemies, Detective Inspector Jack Robber.

I called him on my land line as the cops had also nabbed my mobile. Not that there was anything incriminating on it. Not as far as I knew, but I hadn't known about the cash. I hoped the most interesting would be the Russian ladies looking for a date, a free ten quid go on the *Mirror* bingo, and a special offer on blue jeans from the Levi's site.

He answered after three rings. 'Robber.'

'Hello Jack, it's me, Nick.'

'Oh Christ! What the hell do you want?' I knew he'd be glad to hear from me.

I explained what had happened and he laughed out loud. 'Jesus, but you attract trouble like shit attracts flies. Burke and Dixon. I know them. One's Burke by name, Burke by nature. The other one couldn't find his dick in a light fog. Burke and Hare more like.'

'They found me.'

'You're easy to find.'

It's always nice to be compared with shit and a copper's penis.

'So what do you want, as if I didn't know?' he asked.

'If you hear anything...'

He laughed out loud again. 'What are you like? The National Bank job. You are coming up in the world.'

'It's not funny, Jack.'

'It is from where I'm sitting.'

'So will you listen out?'

'Course I will. I wouldn't miss out on this for the world. We'd better meet. Same time, same place. Tomorrow.'

My heart sank. That meant seven thirty at the Dog and Dart public house in Loughborough Junction. Or, as I called it, the dog it was that died. A boozer that stuck to the old school idea of the perfect pub. No music, fruit machines or karaoke. Where the idea of fine dining was two slices of white doorstep bread, a slab of orange cheese, and a pint of bitter, and the most miserable landlord unhung. 'No Fackin' Kids' Robber would growl. That probably meant anyone under forty. So, while all around, pubs were going sport, gastro or being converted into flats, the Dog and Dart proudly faced the past.

'I'll be there,' I said.

'And bring money. But nothing that can be traced.' He laughed again and cut me off. Always nice to catch up with an old friend. I knocked up a quick fried egg sandwich for my dinner, then made yet another mistake in a week that seemed to be full of them. I phoned my ex-wife and asked to speak to my daughter. 'She's not here,' came the reply.

'Where is she?'

'She's horse riding.'

'Blimey. When did that start?'

'A while back.'

'I didn't know anything about it.'

I think she wanted to say it was none of my business, but

didn't. Instead she said pointedly, 'If you called more often, she might have told you herself.'

She was right, of course. 'So why didn't you consult me?' I asked.

'Why should I?'

I was halfway in a hole, and should have stopped digging. 'What happens if she falls off and hurts herself?'

'She's a big girl now, Nick. Children grow up faster these days. And she has an experienced rider with her.'

'And I suppose it's expensive?'

'We can afford it.' By we, she meant her and Louis, her new husband.

'So that's it, I suppose,' I said, retiring hurt from the fray. 'Tell her I called, will you? And ask her to give me a bell.'

'I will,' she replied, and cut me off without another word.

I spent the rest of the evening drinking and smoking in front of the TV. Not the most productive use of my time I'll admit, but I couldn't think of anything else to do.

6

Early In the Morning
– Bobby Darin

I'd made my plans for the next day, but then plans can be changed.

At exactly seven thirty by the alarm clock next to my bed, someone started hammering on the front door and ringing both flat bells. Thankfully my downstairs neighbours were hardly there, otherwise my shaky relationship with them would only get worse.

I got out of bed, pulled on a pair of jeans, ran my fingers through my hair, grabbed my keys, and barefoot, headed down one flight of stairs to the flat door, then down another to the street entrance.

I pulled it open, and I should have known, there stood Burke and Dixon.

'What?' was all I said.

'Did we get you up? asked Dixon.

I didn't bother to reply.

'My word Sharman,' said Dixon. 'You are popular.'

'How so?'

'There's a big cheese from Special Branch come all this

way to see you.'

'Why?' I was still half asleep.

'They don't tell the likes of us.'

'Most amiable fellow,' said Burke. 'Name's Smyth. With a y.'

'Better not keep him waiting,' said Dixon, and gestured towards the car that was parked outside. The back door opened, and out stepped Martineau/Spencer. I might have guessed.

He pushed open the gate and headed up the garden path. Just like the one I was being led up, I thought.

He was immaculate in a grey Prince of Wales double breasted suit, a white pin-through collared shirt, and a fat flowered tie, complete with diamond tie pin. Only he'd left his stick behind. 'Good morning,' he said, pulling another leather case from his pocket, and flashing it in my direction. I didn't bother to look closely. It was either as real or as fake as the police ID he'd shown me before. 'Mr Sharman. We meet at last. So sorry to bother you at this unholy hour, but I've got more appointments this morning.' He didn't even have the manners to wink.

I said nothing. I was going to let this comedy play itself out, then maybe I'd know what the hell was going on.

He turned to the two police detectives. 'Well chaps,' he said, 'I think I'll take this from here. Wait in the car for me if you'll be so kind. I won't be long.'

Burke and Dixon looked a bit pissed off at this turn of events, but said nothing. Just turned and walked back towards their car.

'Shall we go in?' said Smyth or whatever. 'You look a trifle *déshabillé*. Maybe a pair of socks…'

7

Truth Hurts
– Bullet For My Valentine

He came in, and I closed the street door.

After much fro-ing and to-ing, and after you-ing, I led the way up to the flat and parked him on the sofa in the living room. The room still smelt sour from the previous evening even though I'd left the windows open when I went to bed, but there had been no breeze, just the oppressive remains of the day's heat. There were empty glasses and a full ashtray on the coffee table which I'd left for the morning, but then I hadn't expected an early wake up call. I didn't bother to apologise for the mess, just loaded a tray with everything and dumped it in the kitchen next door. I went back and asked if he wanted coffee, though I didn't care if he did or not, but I was dying for a cup. All very civilised, but I could cheerfully have throttled the bastard. He answered in the affirmative, and when I asked how he took it, he told me, 'black as the Squeaker's heart.' Whoever the Squeaker was.

I left him where he was and went to the bathroom where I cleaned my teeth, took a piss, had a quick wash, and combed my hair.

Then back to the kitchen, where I fired up the coffee machine, put on some milk to heat, found clean socks balled up on the tumble dryer and pulled them on.

When the coffee was brewed and poured, I put the mugs on a tray and went back to where Smyth, as I'll call him from now on, was waiting. I gave him his drink, then sat on the armchair opposite him. 'So to what do I owe the pleasure of this rude awakening?' I asked.

'I apologise again but I do need to enlist your help. Just like I told you at our last meeting.'

'I told you no then and I meant it.'

'But circumstances have changed. You're in serious trouble.'

'Trouble of your making.'

'But no one but you and I know that. Delicious coffee, by the way.'

'Glad it's to your liking. I could always tell those two dunces cooling their heels downstairs the full story.'

'And, of course, they'd believe you over me. From their demeanour, and their comments about you this morning in their car, I doubt that very much. Now, where was I?'

'You were about to tell me why you've stitched me up over the last few days.'

'Yes, of course. You remember I mentioned bringing in someone to put a spanner in Stowe-Hartley's works? A scorpion in his Waldorf salad. A cat amongst his pigeons.' Enough with the idioms already, I thought.

'I remember,' I said.

'Well, you are that spanner, that scorpion, that cat.'

'Just me, against this ruthless, cunning master criminal and his cronies. Your words remember?'

'Precisely.'

'So why not just kill him?'

'Bold words. In fact, it's been tried. Twice. Like I told you both assassins ended up in body bags.'

'Lovely. That makes me feel much better.'

'It's up to you.'

'But why me?' Pathetic, or what? 'No thanks, again. But just tell me where you got those notes that you paid me with. Money from the raid that no one else has seen since the day they were nicked?'

'Bit of a cheat there, old boy,' he replied. 'A sleight of hand you might say. Or computer keyboard. You see they weren't part of it at all. We sort of added those numbers to the original intelligence sent out to banks and building societies, anyone who might be interested, knowing somehow they'd turn up with your name on them. Bit of a foul ball. Sorry about that. But needs must when the devil drives.'

'In this case who exactly is the devil? And the answer's still no. And what bright spark hid the cash in my freezer? Any fool who watches cop shows on TV knows that's the first place to look.'

'That, I must admit, was my scheme. I wanted to make it easy for, as you put it, the likes of those dunces sitting waiting in their car for me. And it's just as well you didn't fancy a frozen lasagne for breakfast.'

I was getting even more pissed off with every word. 'Take it as read,' I said. 'No way.'

'Sorry, but I don't think you have any options,' he said. 'We have your passport, your bank accounts have been frozen, and although you missed the morning papers, you'll be all over the *Standard* this afternoon, as the first significant arrest after the bank job. You'll be famous, not for the first time, and I'm sure Stowe-Hartley will be in touch. You see, Mr Sharman, you've been extremely lucky not to end up in jail after all your exploits in the past. You stole evidence, and in doing so, several of the ungodly got away scot free. You were a disgrace to the uniform you wore, and a traitor to those who wear it with pride.' I couldn't argue with that.

'Well, now the chickens are coming home to roost,' he went on. 'You've sewn the wind, now you must reap the whirlwind. Just trust me, if you don't do as I ask, I'll guarantee you one thing. You'll go on trial, and go to prison. A cliché I know, but you know what happens to ex-coppers in the shovel.'

I did, and it didn't help when he ran the forefinger of his right hand across his neck. 'I just wonder where it all went wrong for you.' Like I said before. Totally fucked.

I didn't answer the unasked question from his last remark, just asked, 'What's in it for me?'

'Your freedom, which I can arrange at any time, the chance to be the model citizen you now claim to be, and the eternal thanks of Her Majesty's security forces. Plus a little payment for your time and inconvenience. And talking of money,' he went on, and reached inside his jacket, hauled out a thick envelope, and dropped it on the coffee table with a thud. 'There's five hundred pounds in there for expenses etc. We'll sort out some increment for your time later.'

When he saw my face, he smiled. 'Don't worry, these notes are kosher. Nothing on the wanted list. And there's a mobile phone. Just press any button and you can get me twenty four hours a day.'

'I'll think about it,' I said. But I knew it sounded as weak to him as it did to me. I had no bloody choice, and he knew it.

And bold as I liked to pretend I was, in fact, and I'll only admit it to you, he was telling the truth, and the truth bloody hurt.

'You know what they say?' he asked. 'When you come to a fork in the road. Take it.'

Wise words.

8

The Big Beat
– Fats Domino

He left then, I got dressed and made more coffee. I sat back down in the living room and thought about what had just happened. It wasn't that Smyth or whatever he was calling himself today had shafted me, it was more about what he'd said about me going to what he'd called the dark side. He hadn't actually asked what had turned me from being a copper to being a crook. But he might well have.

It was simple.

I had a friend once. More than a friend, more like a brother. His name was David, never Dave. Always David. We first met when we joined the Met at the same time, trained together at Hendon, then we were both stationed at Kennington nick. After being puppy-walked by more senior constables, we were teamed up and walked the beat in tandem, when coppers still did that.

We had a fine old time. Up Westminster Bridge Road from the nick, past Lambeth North tube station, turn right into the Cut market, past the Spanish Patriot pub where we were on the pool team, into Waterloo station to ogle the female office staff, whom we called secretary birds, down the east side of the Cut again, then took a right into the Blackfriars Road and back to the station, then home.

In fact, home was the section house at the Elephant. Living was easy with free uniforms and good cheap food in the canteen. You might say we carved a swathe. We got free food in cafes and restaurants too, and free drinks in the pubs that liked having coppers for customers, and indeed, some which didn't.

There were plenty of pretty girls who gave themselves for free as well. And we tasted some illegal substances from time to time. Good days.

We got up to some larks, no danger. But we were good coppers on the whole. I'll tell you a true story. One deep December morning we got a call out to the local Peabody estate. Bad smells reported by neighbours. Not good, especially when the temperature was below freezing. The kerbs were crusted with dirty snow, and you could see our breath in clouds as we walked over.

After giving the bell and knocker some stick, David bent and pushed open the letter box. He flinched. You could smell the death stink a mile off, and there was a strange humming sound from inside. We forced the door and went into a hoarder's paradise. Newspapers, magazines, old records, bits of electrical equipment, all sorts. The kitchen was a roach's paradise, the sink piled high with mouldy dishes, and the noise we could hear was flies. Hundreds, maybe thousands of the bastards. The three bar electric fire was on full, and had been for a long time. Lying on a sofa in front of it was the skeletal, mummified remains of an old man. At least, we thought it was a man. Could've been either sex given the state of the body. David waved his hand in front of his face. 'Now I know where flies go in the wintertime,' he said.

By the sofa was an ordinary shopping bag. Tesco's as a matter of fact. I picked it up. Inside was a treasure trove of banknotes, thousands of them. Some notes too old to be legal tender. We could've had them away easily. But no, we handed them in at the station. Didn't even take a drink. No one claimed them, and they ended up in the widows' and orphans' fund. We took some stick for that from older coppers. But I think we did the right thing.

Or maybe, I'm justifying what happened later. I'm good at that.

Then circumstances between us changed. I got a girlfriend, then got married and we had a baby. Family life and a big mortgage sort of puts a kibosh on the strongest bromance.

I cleaned up my behaviour, David didn't. The booze and drugs got stronger. He lost his flat and moved back into the section house.

One afternoon, on one of my days off, David phoned me at home. He wanted to see me, he said he was desperate. But then he'd always been a bit of a drama queen. What I did then was unforgivable. I took the phone off the hook, and went back to my family.

Two hours later, I put it back. It rang almost immediately. It was one of our sergeants. David had been found hanging in his room.

I went to the section house then, but didn't go inside. I stood in a doorway opposite and smoked a cigarette. It was raining. The private ambulance, just a polite name for the meat wagon, was parked outside, its cellulose bible black, and the raindrops on it reflected the street lights like jewels.

The coroner's men, bareheaded and wearing long black coats, brought the stretcher out. I watched them drive away, dropped my cigarette end, ground it out, and went home.

I can measure my downfall from that day. The day I let my best friend down.

I went to his funeral. Dress uniform, tall hat, white gloves, whistle in my breast pocket on a silver chain. His family asked me to be a coffin bearer, but I couldn't. You should have seen the looks I got. And I deserved every one. That's the story, and I never forgave myself. Not to this day. Eventually, of course, I got my comeuppance.

I did well as a copper for a bit. Got promoted to detective constable at Neasden, passed some exams, took a Metropolitan police advanced driving course including defensive and offensive tactical manoeuvres, served as a uniformed sergeant in Islington, was licensed as a firearms officer for side and automatic weapons. And finally ended up as a detective sergeant back in south London. Fast tracking they call it now. Dunno what they did then. A big mistake as it turned out. An embarrassment.

You see, I got in with some bad people. Of course, being a plain clothes copper you'd expect that. But not on their payroll. And I came by a nasty habit. The extra money went straight up my, and several young ladies' nostrils. But nothing's for nothing, and I found myself owing a great deal of money to several people one just did not owe money to. So I was forced to rob the evidence cupboard at my own nick of several grams of A1 cocaine to pay off the vig, as I believe it can be called. After that, I was shot in the foot because I went on a raid hungover and still stoned from the night before. Totally my fault, and I got away with an honourable discharge, a lost pension, and a limp that reminds me who I am. Pretty lightly to be honest.

On the way, I lost my wife and child. To a better man as it turned out. At least one who didn't stay out for days at a time, and come home stinking of booze and someone else's perfume.

So that fucker Smyth got me bang to rights. And it didn't get any better.

9

Zorba The Greek
– Herb Alpert & The Tijuana Brass

After a bit, like I'd planned, I decided now was the time to face the bomb site that I was sure the cops had left of my office.

But first I needed food. I walked down to the high street and over to Georgio's, our local Greek greasy, or greasy Greek. The food was lousy, but it was cheap and there was plenty of it. The perfect recipe for a hangover cure. I went for the full English: sausage, bacon, fried egg, mushrooms (tinned), tomatoes (tinned), baked beans, and two white toasts. Washed down with Georgio's coffee, thick and black as sludge. Or the Squeaker's heart, as Smyth had said.

There was also a full Greek on offer, which added chips and a stuffed vine leaf. You probably got a knife in the back as a bonus. I kept mine to the wall just like Wild Bill Hickok. But look what happened to him.

When I was halfway through my dish fit to put before a king, Georgio came out from behind the counter and headed my way. He was a sight for sore eyes. Rotund, bald, handlebar moustache, wearing a Greek international football shirt stretched by his enormous belly, and pink shorts that exposed legs hairy enough to make a gorilla jealous.

'Nicky, my friend,' he said when he got to my table. 'How's your bad luck?'

'That's just it mate,' I replied. 'Bad luck is right. If I didn't have bad luck, I'd have no luck at all.'

'I know the feeling,' he said, pulling up a chair, and easing his bulk on to it. 'Man, with a wife like mine, there's no end to it.'

Georgio was constantly moaning about his wife, his mother-in-law, and his dozen children who ate him out of house and home.

'How is Mrs Georgio?' I asked.

'Don't ask.'

'And the kids?'

'Still hungry,' he said.

'How many now?'

'Still twelve, I think,' he said. 'I lose count. She's addicted to having kids. No sooner is one off the tit, than she wants another. I get confused. I went home the other night, saw one in the front room, told him to get ready for bed, turns out he belongs down the road. Just visiting. I don't know what to do.'

'With all this, and you're moaning,' I said, gesturing around the cafe, where the heat was even more intense than outside from the burners and chip fat bubbling in the kitchen, and the lone ceiling fan, black with twenty years' or more cigarette smoke turned lazily, and hardly shifted the air. 'You don't know when you're well off.'

'Well off!' he said. 'I'm nearly skint. And that bloody mother-in-law of mine. She spends my money like it grows on trees. The old bitch. Anisede! What kind of fucking name is that? She don't even spell it right. Fat old cow. Swanning round in tart's clothes that cost a fortune, and me with holes in my underwear.'

Not a pretty thought whilst eating.

'And always flashing her saggy old paps. Who'd want to suck on those?'

'Georgio. I got food here.'

'Sorry, Nick. But once I get started.'

'Do you know she had a fancy man once? Dumped her by email. Couldn't face her ugly mug to do the deed. Not that you can see it all, what with her moustache and all. She's got a better beard than me.'

I had to smile, despite it all. 'You could go back to Greece,' I said.

'Go back?' he said. 'The state it's in. This EU is no good for my country. It's broke and getting broker. The house I bought for our retirement, up in the hills. The geezer down the road. Same kind of house, but maybe a few more olive trees. Tried to sell it for two years. When he finally got a buyer it had lost half its value. What does that say for mine? We should get out of Europe, and so should you.'

'I don't know if we can, or you. Anyway, how could you bear to leave all this behind?'

'You're so right,' he said. 'More coffee?' I declined, paid my bill and left.

The office was just like I'd guessed. Drawers open, papers all over the shop, and the business half of the computer gone. Luckily the coffee machine and the stereo still worked. I turned on both, and I got busy as Brother Ray Hit the Road Jack, and the espresso brewed. A couple of hours later I'd got the place organised, and, with nothing else to do, I headed home.

10

Roadrunner
– Bo Diddley

On the way I stopped off at my local corner shop for a bottle of JD and the afternoon edition of the *Standard*. I knew something was up as soon as I walked through the door. My friend Mehmet didn't give me his usual grin, and said nothing as I bought the booze and the paper. I opened it outside. I hadn't made the front page, but I was all over page three. I read the piece leaning against a lamppost. It was worse than I thought it would be. I was pictured as a super thief, even though the word 'alleged' was used often. There was also a sidebar resume of my previous misdemeanours.

At least, the ones that they knew about. Some of the worst were still deep, dark secrets.

I dumped the paper in the first rubbish bin I came to, but kept tight hold of the bourbon.

When I got home, I microwaved some cheesy thing, then made a phone call. Jesus, but it was still hot, and my shirt was sticking to my back. Although the cops still had my phone with my stored numbers, they'd left my old address book. My Filofax. Remember them? I flicked through the index to G.

The call was to a bloke called Len. Len Goodman. He ran a second hand car showroom and garage in Balham. He'd used me to collect some outstanding debts, although I hadn't heard from him for months. I called his direct line.

He picked up straightaway. 'Goodman,' he said.

'Hello Len, it's Nick Sharman.'

There was a short pause before he spoke again. Just enough for me to know I wasn't going to like what I was about to find out. 'Hello Nick. Long time.'

'Yeah. All your punters paying up these days?'

'Generally.'

'Good. Listen Len, you put someone on to me a few days ago. How come?'

'He just wanted someone who you'd worked for as a referee.'

'Well, I've got to tell you, mate, he got me into a lot of trouble.' There was another pause.

'I'm sorry, Nick. You too?'

'Me too what?'

'Your tax. Are you, like a bit iffy with your tax returns?'

'No, I pay my tax. What's my tax got to do with anything?'

'That bloke. Martini, or whatever he's called.'

'Martineau,' I said. I didn't mention Spencer or Smyth, why complicate things further.

'He's with the Inland Revenue. He said if I got in touch with you, tell you he wasn't strictly kosher, he'd go through my books like the proverbial.'

I sighed. 'And I suppose he had all the correct credentials?'

'A pocketful.'

'Of course, he did. I don't think he's with the Revenue. I don't know who he's with. He's a fucking ghost. I do know that.'

'So what trouble are you in then?'

'Go get an evening paper and you'll find out.'

'You're in the papers. Christ, it must be serious.'

'It is.'

'And it's my fault. I'm real sorry, Nick.'
'Not your fault. He's a clever bastard, I know that.'
'Anything I can do…'
'No. It's too late for that.'
'No hard feelings.'
'No. If he hadn't used you, he would've used someone else.'
'Sorry again, Nick.'
'Forget it.'
And with that, I finished the call.

11

The Pub With No Beer
– Slim Dusty

The afternoon moved on towards evening, and warmed up even more, I tried to stay cool, calm and collected. Which amazed me, as I knew all of this was not going to end well.

About four, the landline rang. It was my daughter, Judith. 'Dad, it's me,' she said.

'Hello, love.'

'Dad, what have you done? You're in the paper. Mum wouldn't let me see, but I looked it up on the web.'

The blessed web, I thought. What would we do without it? 'It's nothing, love,' I said. 'I've done nothing.'

'That's what you always say.'

Which was true, but I didn't need to hear it from someone her age. Laura had been right, she was growing up fast. 'This time it's true, I swear. Someone has put my neck in a frame, and they're tightening the screws.'

'Who?'

'Long story. I'll explain when it's all over.' I hoped it wouldn't be at visiting time in Brixton Prison.

'Promise?'

'Of course.' I thought it was about time to change the subject. 'And by the way, what's all this about horse riding?'

'I was going to surprise you.'

'What. And come round on horseback like Dale Evans?'

'Who?'

'Annie Oakley?'

'Who?'

I gave in. 'Like a cowgirl?'

'Yes. I know how much you like cowboy shirts.'

'And cowgirls. Do you ride Western?'

'No English. Though they've got a Western saddle at the school. They said if I'm good they'll let me.'

'Then, be good.'

'I'll try. You too.'

'Always.'

'I've got to go. Mum's back.'

'Go on then.'

'Love you.'

'Love you back.' And with that she was gone. I hung up the phone, and nearly cried.

I stayed in jeans, t-shirt, dark summer jacket, and black winklepicker boots, and hit the highway for Loughborough Junction at seven. It wasn't a long run and I parked three or four car lengths from the Dog and Dart.

When I went in, it was just as it had always been. It was deserted. Quiet as a mouse, a dead one. The lights were dim, but did nothing to hide the sticky marks on the bar, and the brasses on the pumps were dull. The smell of the place was similar to Denmark Hill nick, but with the added piquancy of over-cooked vegetables. It was so quiet I half expected to see tumbleweed roll across the tattered carpet. Funny that I thought, when Cowboy Bob's bar and disco round the corner where the crack squirrels played was rammed every night. Surely the mystery of the Dog in the night time.

I went up to the jump. The till was open and empty; either business was as bad as usual, or they'd just been robbed. I favoured the former. Still nothing stirred so I called out, 'Service.'

A minute later the landlord showed himself. He'd seen me many times before, but there was no sign of recognition. No welcome. Like I said, a right horrible place. I ordered a bottle of Becks.

'No Becks,' said the landlord. I should have remembered. Although there was a poster advertising Becks on the wall, there was never a drop to drink. 'A bottle of whatever lager you've got, then.'

He pulled out a brown bottle from the cooler with some cyrillic style lettering and a name I didn't recognise. I declined a glass and took the bottle to a far table and lit up a Silkie to disguise the odour. They say smoking will be banned in pubs soon. Some fat chance!

12

Too Much Monkey Business
– Chuck Berry

Robber was ten minutes late and I hadn't touched my beer. He was always late, just to show who was boss. When he came in, he went straight to the bar, not looking right or left. He knew I'd be there. He conversed with the landlord, received some brown foamy liquid in an old fashioned dimpled mug, paid, and headed towards me.

Like the boozer, he didn't change either. Same old brown suit, run-down shoes, wrinkled shirt, tie pulled down, and top button undone. He didn't appear to notice the weather. His reddish hair was beginning to show a hint of grey, and his moustache could have done with a trim. Sometimes it's comforting when people and places don't change.

He dropped into the chair next to mine, took a swig of beer, swallowed, then said, 'I shouldn't even be talking to you, on bail. Let alone drinking with you.'

'I'm not drinking,' I said back. Not this muck.

'Maybe you should. Anyway, I am. How much?'

'How much what?'

'How much have you got for me?'

'Yeah. Nice to see you too, Jack.'

'Bah!' Was all he said in reply. Then. 'Just tell me.'

Now, you've got to understand that Jack Robber wasn't a bent copper. Certainly not like the way I had operated when I was on the force. He just did favours for certain parties for a small remuneration. Parties like me.

'A couple of hundred', I replied.

'Good.'

'I hope you're worth it,' I said.

'Aren't I always? Now give.'

13

Police And Thieves
– Junior Murvin

B ut first I filled Robber in on what had occurred that day. When I'd finished he asked, 'So who is this geezer?'

'Christ knows.'

'Right,' he said. 'There's two DI Spencers in the Met.' He fished in his inside pocket and pulled out a couple of photos. 'Either of these him?'

I looked and shook my head.

'Was the ID he showed you kosher?'

'It looked the part. It fooled me, the Revenue ID fooled my mate Len, and the Special Branch ID fooled Burke and Dixon.'

'Well, that's not the hardest thing in the world. Smyth, you say.'

'With a y.'

He took out a notebook and pen from another pocket, opened it, and scribbled a note. 'What about the dough he hid at your place?'

'It wasn't part of it. Somehow he added those numbers onto the list of stolen money that was circulated to all interested parties. A sleight of hand as he called it.'

'Clever bastard. Fucking spook, you betcha life.'

'Yeah, I'm looking out for black helicopters in the back garden.' He ignored that.

'But how did he know you would pay it into your bank? And how did he know it was your bank?'

'Well,' I said. 'I must have been on his radar for a while. I'm a law-abiding citizen these days. An open book. I pay my taxes and my TV licence. But you can be certain if I hadn't, he'd've found some other way to sick the minions of the law onto my tail.' Christ, I was beginning to talk like him.

'It must be love,' said Robber. 'And what about this other villain, Stowe-Hartley? Sounds like a brand of biscuits.'

I had to smile. 'He's a solicitor. Real name Sidney Hartley. According to Smyth, he owns the firm Gyre and Gimble.' I gave him the address. 'There is no Gyre, no Gimble. And he owns an old folks home too. And Christ knows what else.'

'Weird mixture. Master criminal and public benefactor.'

'Money laundering?'

'Could be. Stranger things happen. What's he look like?'

'Tall, dark and sleazy.'

'I'll check him out'. More scribbles.

It seemed to me I was giving out more info than I was receiving. Maybe Robber should be paying me.

'Do that', I said 'But I don't have a mobile. Those bastard coppers nicked it off me.'

'Less of the "bastard coppers". You'll hurt my feelings.'

'Sorry. I'll get a new one tomorrow, and text you with the number.'

'Do it.'

'So what else have you found to earn two hundred quid?' I asked.

'Early days. But we do know that nothing from the robbery has turned up. Not even what they found at your place, apparently, if your mate is telling the truth. Red faces all round. Police 0, thieves 1. Like I said, early days. Now, show me the dough.'

I'd split the monkey Smyth had given me, folded two hundred quid and passed it over. 'Not going to come back and bite me on the arse is it?'

'Not as far as I know.'

'Better not, and that's a promise.'

14

Havana Bound
– The Pretty Things

That said it all really.

I stayed a bit longer as Robber bought another pint, and a ham roll that seemed mostly thick white fat covered in lumpy, acid yellow mustard. He loved it.

'So, how's business?' I asked.

'Same shit,' he replied. 'Nasty one today. Pulled one out of the river. Bloating and floating. Black skin, blue eyes he'd been in so long. Stank like a khasi.' He sniffed his fingers. 'Thank Christ for non-latex gloves.'

'Accident? Murder? Suicide?'

'Who knows? Bleedin' nuisance is all I know.'

'Enough to put you off your supper.'

'No fucking chance,' he said, and sunk his teeth into a bit of fat protruding out of the roll.

And that said enough, so I left, and left my untouched beer on the table. I stood outside in the gloaming and smoked another cigarette, then got in the car and drove home. Air conditioning on full.

It was just getting dark when I got there, and had to park a bit up the road from the house because a big, black, continental looking SUV stood in the space I usually called my own. Loads of chrome, and blacked-out windows all round. I should have sussed out something wasn't right. My bad guy radar seemed to be on holiday lately.

There's no residents' parking on our street at the moment, so we don't suffer too much from parking wars at my end. At the bottom, where most of the massive old Victorian mansions are divided into four, five, or even six flats, it's a different matter. Still, I felt a bit miffed as I got out, slammed the door and set the alarm from my key fob. I walked down towards the garden gate, when the back door of the SUV slid open, a huge figure emerged, grabbed me by the lapels of my jacket and literally threw me into the vehicle. I landed on my back on the carpet, more shocked and surprised than hurt, when the figure jumped after me and slid the door to behind him, with a bang.

15

Drive, He Said
– Pere Ubu

The geezer who'd picked me up like I was a little kid was big. Big, black and bald. And built like the proverbial. He had muscles on muscles. Biceps so vast they stretched the sleeves of his black suit almost to ripping point, and quads that filled his trousers the same. He even had muscles in his face that moved under his skin so when he spoke he resembled Dizzy Gillespie taking a solo. And he was sweating cobs. The inside of the SUV was cool. They must have been running the A/C. But even so, the geezer was soaked, and the atmosphere stank like a hog's privates.

'Sit up,' he ordered, and gestured with the automatic pistol that had magically appeared in his left hand. 'Empty your pockets.'

I pulled myself up onto the back bench seat and, for the second time in three days, I did as I was told.

He looked at the phone Smyth had given me and tossed it to the bloke in the driver's seat. 'Kill it,' he said. The driver took off the back, took out the battery and tossed it into the passenger-side well. So much for 'call me any time'.

Next my wallet. It contained cards and the remains of the cash I'd got that morning. He pocketed the money and threw the wallet back. Car keys he let me keep. Mont Blanc ballpoint, he threw back, notebook he kept. 'The watch,' he said. I took off my Rolex and he studied it with a grunt. 'Real?' he asked.

'Twenty five quid in Thailand,' I said back.

He grunted again, and tossed it at me. I put it back on, and thought that if he couldn't tell a real Roller from a fake, he was more stupid than he looked.

'The boss wants to see you,' he said. 'Wants to know what your game is.' I said nothing. There was nothing much to say.

'Drive,' he ordered, and the driver turned the ignition key.

16

Death Cab For Cutie
– The Bonzo Dog Doo-Dah Band

We took off down the hill towards the main road. Right at the lights, and on towards West Norwood. Then the driver turned left. Hard left, and the black guy put up his left hand, the one holding the gun, to steady himself against the side of the car, the barrel of his pistol moved off me, and I took my chance. I grabbed my Mont Blanc ballpoint and shoved it hard into his right eye. As hard as I could. I guessed if these two got me to Stowe-Hartley I wouldn't be coming home, except in a box. The black guy screamed then. Not deep like his voice, but high pitched, and he kept on screaming.

I jumped up from the back seat and reached round the driver's headrest, and got hold of his head. I pulled it back hard and let my fingers find his eye sockets. He screamed too, let go of the wheel and grabbed at my hands. All I could think of was that I hoped the black guy wouldn't shoot me in the back. The car lurched right, hit a parked vehicle whose alarm went off with an electronic screech, then bounced back to the left lane, hit the kerb and turned over once, twice, before ending up on its roof. Both front airbags went off with twin explosions, and the air was full of talcum powder. And the black guy kept on screaming.

17

There's A Moon Out Tonight
– The Capris

Luckily, I'd ended up on top of him as we'd been tossed about in the crash. Face to face. Close enough to kiss. Except the shaft of my pen still sticking out of his face might've got in the way. His gun was nowhere to be seen.

My feet were against one back window, and luckily again, I was wearing hard heeled boots. I kicked back against the window, once, twice, three times and the glass exploded outwards. I had to get out. The engine was still running, and I could smell petrol. Lots of petrol. It may have been safety glass, but as I squeezed through the gap I felt fabric and skin tear. I hit the tarmac, rolled, got up and ran to the pavement and into the shadows. There was no one about, but I could see curtains starting to twitch, so I ran up to the first left hand turning, and took it.

There was a huge red full moon lighting my way. I slowed to a walk, turned up the collar of my jacket. And remembering my sunglasses in my top pocket, put them on. As I reached the first house, the sky lit up, followed by an explosion, and an orange mushroom cloud appeared above the rooftops, blotting out the moon, followed by a number of sharp cracks which would be the ammunition in the pistol exploding, and I hoped that no Good Samaritan had tried to help the passengers in the SUV.

I kept walking, as I heard the sound of sirens, and a helicopter appeared, its spotlight quartering the area. But by then I was just another pedestrian making my way home. I couldn't catch a bus or even duck into a boozer, the state of my clothes, that I could see in the streetlights were heavily bloodstained. So I kept on walking, head down. There weren't as many CCTV cameras then as there are now, but I didn't want my boat on anyone's laptop. And by Christ, my legs and chest stung. And the heatwave just wouldn't break.

18

Codeine
– Eric Clapton

When I got into my road, I walked up slowly, on the opposite side to mine, blimping parked cars for occupants. Nothing. The street was deserted. No strangers lurking in the shadows or belted raincoat-wearing individuals leaning on a lamp post pretending to read a newspaper like someone out of a Le Carré novel, waiting for me to return home.

I went up to my flat, and into the kitchen. Under the bright ceiling lights I checked my clothes. t-shirt, jacket, jeans, all ruined. I undressed, found a garbage bag, and dumped them all in the kitchen bin. I'd sort them out later. I was well pissed off. Not only that I'd allowed myself to be kidnapped, but I was very fond of that jacket. Paul Smith as it happened, and not cheap.

Then I checked myself. The safety glass had ripped my legs and chest. I hobbled into the bathroom, got under the shower and let the warm water rinse the blood away. I felt the wounds, but there didn't seem to be any glass embedded in them.

I got out of the shower and patted myself dry with an old

towel that would soon join my clothes in the rubbish.

When you're in my line of business, you can get hurt, so a good first aid kit is a must. I dug mine out and doused my legs and chest in disinfectant, then, using the largest plasters I had, I patched myself up. I followed that with a handful of super strong, probably highly illegal, painkillers that a pal of mine had brought home from Mexico, washed down with a hit of JD straight from the bottle, and suddenly all was right with the world.

But not with the couple in the SUV. *C'est la guerre* as the French say. If you play with fire you might end up getting burnt. Literally.

I got dressed again in fresh clothes, and figured it was time to go and see Madge.

19

Lady Be Good
– Count Basie

Now, let me tell you about Madge.

I met her two years previously. Another summer, but not so hot. One Saturday morning I was on my way to Mehmet's for milk, bread, a paper, cigarettes and booze, when I saw her. Elderly. Grey hair, wearing a light mac, looking at the postcards in the shop window advertising all manner of delights, from cleaning jobs to French lessons. And we all knew what they were. She was holding the handle of one of those push me, pull you, tartan shopping trolleys. From out of the pocket at the front, I could see a brown handbag or purse. Twenty yards or so from her, a couple of young likely lads, one white, one black, both on bicycles far too small for them, were giving the bag the eye. I went into the shop, did my business, keeping a watch on them through the open door, and when I left I stopped by her and said, 'I think you're being watched'.

'I know,' she said back. 'I can see them reflected in the window.'

Smart woman.

'I think it's time they went,' I said, and turned and gave

them my dirtiest look. It seemed to hit home, as after a second they turned their bikes and pedalled off.

'Thanks for that,' she said. 'But there was really no need.'

'Better to be safe. And you really need to keep hold of your purse.' I nodded at it in the trolley.

'I know.'

'Still, no harm done. Which way are you going?' She pointed in the direction I'd come from.

'Me too,' I said. 'Can I walk you?'

'Certainly,' she said. 'It's been a while since a young man did that. Unless, of course, you're going to steal my bag.'

'I don't think so,' I said, offered her my arm and we set off.

'What's your name?' she asked, as we ambled along. 'Nick,' I replied. 'Nick Sharman.'

'And what do you do, Nick Sharman?'

'I'm a private detective,' I replied, fished in my pocket and handed her one of my cards. 'I've got an office up by the station.'

'Fancy,' she said. 'That sounds interesting. And dangerous.'

'Not really. Just the odd lost dog. That sort of thing.'

She frowned as if she didn't believe me.

'And you are…?' I asked.

'Madelaine,' she replied. 'Madelaine McMichael. But my friends call me Madge.'

'Then I hope I can call you Madge,' I said.

'Charmer.'

When we reached the corner of Palace Road, I said, 'This is me.'

'Me too.'

'Well, let's go on,' I said.

When we reached the first right turn, she gestured at the corner house opposite. 'Here we are,' she said.

It was a huge Victorian mansion, as estate agents had started to call them. Dark and foreboding. A real House of Usher job.

'You've got a flat there?' I asked. She shook her head.

'A room?' I had a horrible vision of her all alone with just a Baby Belling to cook on.

'No, it's all mine. My husband, John, he's dead now, bought it years ago. He was in the navy.'

'Smart man. These used to be dirt cheap, but not anymore. I'm sorry to hear he's dead. Do you live alone?'

She nodded.

We crossed the road, pushed through the gate and up the path, where the house frowned down on us. The garden was overgrown, and the house itself looked like it could take some TLC, but it looked solid, and worth a packet.

I walked her to her door and said, 'I hope your security is up to scratch. I know someone who could give it a once over. And he won't rip you off.' I don't know why I bothered. I just liked her style. And I'd get to like it better as time went on.

'That's kind,' she said. 'I'll think about it. Would you like to come to tea tomorrow?'

I was surprised at the invitation, but didn't show it. 'That would be great,' I replied.

'Four o'clock. If the weather holds, we can have it on the veranda.'

'That's a date,' I said. 'It's been a pleasure to meet you, Madge.' As she didn't say anything, it looked like we were going to be friends.

Instead, she stretched out her hand for me to shake, then added, 'The pleasure has been all mine.'

20

The Cat – Jimmy Smith arranged by Lalo Schifrin

The next day, Sunday, I pitched up at Madge's front door just as the clock on our local church chimed four. For politeness sake, I was wearing a pale grey summer suit, grey cotton tab collar shirt, and a bright red tie. I was carrying a bunch of flowers from an Esso garage, and from Mehmet's shop a box of chocolates, and a bottle of something cold, wet, and white.

She answered promptly, only saying, 'First a young man walks me home, then brings me flowers. I'm flattered'.

She led me down a long wood-panelled hall that felt cool after the afternoon sun. A single flight of wide stairs led up, and through the banisters a furry feline face peered down at us. The cat had a coat of many colours, black, white, and gold that shimmered in the half light. 'That's Schmoo, my cat,' she explained. 'She's a little shy. I got her from the RSPCA. A rescue cat. She had a bad start in life. I try to make it up to her now.'

'That's kind,' I said.

I'd had a cat once, just called Cat, but he moved out and

into a house with an Asian family, so he could enjoy their chicken curry. I still see him in the street. He's about the size of a small London bus now, but he still waddles over so I can tug his ears, his favourite form of petting.

After the cat had looked at us, and we'd looked at the cat, Madge led me into a huge reception room complete with a fireplace laid with newspaper and logs, and a pair of French windows leading to a veranda and the back garden.

'Nice digs,' I said.

'I'm glad you approve. Shall we go outside? You can smoke there, but not indoors, if you don't mind.'

'You know I smoke?'

'I saw you buying a packet yesterday through the window.'

'Good spot.'

There was a large metal table and four chairs on the veranda. The table was set for tea. I sat and lit a cigarette. She sat opposite me.

The garden was long and wide, with a lawn that needed cutting, and ended in a wilderness. Just before the undergrowth began was a tumbledown shed and a swing and slide that had seen better days.

She saw me looking. 'Those were for the children. Gone now. One to America, the other to New Zealand. As far away as possible, it seems.'

'I'm sure that's not true.'

'Well, that's as maybe. But it's sad to have grand children you've never met. How about you?'

'Grand children, no,' I said. 'But I have a daughter. She lives with her mother and her new husband. Forest Gate. Not quite New Zealand, but still I miss her.'

'I'm sure.' She clapped her hands. 'But enough of that. Let's have tea. I hope you've got an appetite. I've been baking.'

'I skipped lunch especially.'

'Good. I'll see to it.'

'Do you need a hand?'

'No, it's all ready in the kitchen downstairs. I won't be long.'
She got up and bustled into the house.

I sat back and lit another cigarette.

21

Tea For Two
– Frank Sinatra/Art Tatum

A few minutes later she came back empty-handed. A kitchen crisis, I thought. Tea's off.

'You can help me now,' she said. 'This way.'

I got up and followed her back into the house. What I'd taken for a cupboard door in one wall was now open, and she leant in and gave something a tug, and with a mechanical whirr a box appeared in the opening complete with two trays. One full of plates of sandwiches, scones with cream and jam, and a Victoria sponge on a dish, the other with a teapot, complete with cosy.

'A dumb waiter,' I said. 'You don't see those every day.'

'No. Come on, grab a tray.'

I did as I was told and we parked the trays on the table outside. Madge played mother with the tea in china cups, milk and sugar for me, lemon for her.

The sandwiches were many and various. Ham, egg mayonnaise, cucumber, smoked salmon, tomato, on brown and white bread, cut into quarters with the crusts removed. Right posh. Just like the Ritz Carlton. The cake was moist and sweet, the scones were so light, they almost floated away, and the tea was strong, and plenty of it.

We scoffed the lot, apart from the cake, and when only crumbs remained of the sandwiches and scones, and the teapot was down to leaves, she said. 'It's getting chilly. Let's go inside and light the fire. The wine's on ice.'

'Good idea,' I said.

'You can bring the dishes,' she said.

I did the necessary, and dumped the trays back in the dumb waiter, then sat as Madge collected the cold wine and two glasses from the kitchen.

22

Pistol Packing Mama
– Gene Vincent

She twisted the bottle open and poured two glasses, and I sat on the sofa. Schmoo the cat was sitting on the arm, looking suspiciously at me. 'I don't think he likes me,' I said.

'She,' Madge corrected me. 'All tortoiseshell cats are shes.'

'You learn something new every day,' I said.

'And if she didn't like you, she wouldn't be in here. Now light the fire, please.' She pointed out a box of foot long matches on the mantelpiece. I got up, lit one, bent down and put the flame to the newspaper in the grate. It caught and started to lick at the logs, and I sat back down and tasted the wine. 'Not vintage,' I said. 'But the best Mehmet's had in stock.'

'Tastes fine to me,' said Madge.

The fire caught and started to spit sparks. 'Where do you get the logs?' I asked.

'An old friend has a farm in Essex. He drops a lorryload off every autumn.'

'Handy.'

'Now, Mr Sharman...'

'Nick, please.'

'Nick. You mentioned security.'

'Yes. You should be well prepared.'

'I've been here a long time with no trouble.'

'I hate to be the bearer of bad news but things are getting worse. Look at those two lads yesterday. They would've knocked you down and pinched your bag without a second thought.'

'So what do you suggest?'

'I have a friend. He owes me several favours. I can get him to do you an estimate. Rock bottom price. In fact, if you can do better I'll pay for it myself. And I'll oversee the job.'

'Why?'

'Why what?' I asked.

'Why are you bothering with an old lady like me?'

'I don't know. You remind me of someone, and anyone who can make cakes like that, and cares for a stray cat…'

'Someone nice, I hope. The person I remind you of.'
'Absolutely.'

'Alright.'

'Can I just have a quick shufti around? Just the ground floor. To give my mate some idea.'

'Of course.'

'Don't worry, I won't pinch the family silver.'

'I didn't think for a minute you would.'

I got up and went out into the hall. There were two other large reception rooms on the ground floor, with windows overlooking the street. The windows themselves were old-fashioned push up frames, with simple slide locks that could easily be opened from the outside by pushing a knife up through the gap between the top and bottom frames, and sliding them open. Just as I thought. Easy. The room on the right was the dining room, with a long table shining with wax, six chairs, and another door leading to another dumb waiter. All mod cons in 1910.

But it was the room opposite that was the eye-opener. It was huge also, with floor to ceiling bookshelves crammed with what looked like the entire works of crime writers from Conan Doyle to Michael Connelly, from the eighteenth century right up to date. I recognised most of the authors, although I had not read them all. The room was a real reader's haven. In the centre, was a high table with two gooseneck reading lamps, and two leather captain's chairs.

I went back to the sitting room where I'd left Madge. She'd switched on a standard lamp behind her chair, and on her lap was a large tapestry bag with knitting needles sticking out.

'Blimey, Madge,' I said. 'I'm impressed by your library.'

'Those books are my weakness,' she said. 'In fact, the garage is full of boxes of them. One day I'll get around to fitting shelves in there so I can show them off.'

'Are they worth much?'

'Some of them. But it's not the money, it's what's on the pages.'

'Even so. Your security really isn't up to scratch, so with your permission I'll talk to my friend.'

'If you think it wise.'

'I do. And no charge for the advice.'

'Let me think about it.'

'Sure,' I said, and sat back down, and took a hit of my drink.

'Do you look after this place all on your own?'

'I have a lady who does. A young Polish girl. Two days a week. She's a marvel.'

'Good,' I said, took another drink and relaxed. The fire was burning bright, and the cat looked me straight in the eye from her perch.

'I think she likes you,' said Madge. 'Give her a knuckle on her cheek. She loves that.'

I felt a bit foolish, but did as I was told. The cat pushed back hard with her head until her skull rattled, and started to purr. 'Told you so,' said Madge. 'If she likes you, it's good enough for me. I'll take you up on the offer.'

'Good,' I replied. 'Otherwise, I'd worry.'

'But I have managed so far. I have my own security measures.'

'Yes?' I said with a query.

'Yes,' she replied, stuck her hand into the bag and pulled out what looked exactly like a nickel plated, pearl handled Colt 1911, seven shot automatic pistol.

23

Gun Fever
– The Techniques

People often say 'my jaw dropped', but don't mean it. Let me tell you, mine did. I couldn't believe what I was seeing. 'Is that for real?' I asked, after a moment.

'As real as real can be,' said Madge, with a smile. 'It's one of a pair.'

'Where's the other one?'

'Upstairs, in my bedroom, under my pillow.'

'Where else?' I said. 'I hope your cleaner doesn't see it.'

She smiled. 'She's Polish. The Polish have a history of violence.'

'Does she give it a quick once-over with a duster?'

She smiled again, then worked the slide, popped a shell into the chamber and cocked the pistol.

Her smile turned into a laugh, and I joined in. 'Christ, you're a bloody marvel, Madge,' I said.

'I try to be.'

'Where did you get it... them?'

'I told you my husband was in the navy. He was an admiral. When the fleet docked in San Francisco, the mayor held a big dinner for the commanding officers of the ships. Everyone got a pair.'

'God bless America. Are they legal?'

'They've never been registered. Not over here.'

'Just as well with the way things are. Can I look?'

'Of course.'

I got up and walked over to her chair. The Colt looked huge in her tiny hand, but she spun it round like an expert, and offered it to me butt first. I took it and gently lowered the hammer. Accidents can happen. It felt heavy, but snug in my hand. 'You're a woman of many parts, Madge,' I said.

'Like I said, I try to be. Now, sit down Nick, I've got a proposition for you.'

'I'm all ears,' I said, handing the gun back, and resuming my seat. 'Tell me all.'

24

See That My Grave Is Kept Clean
– B.B.King

'You see, Nick,' said Madge. 'What it boils down to is that I'm bored. Bored stiff. Yesterday, when you came along on your white horse to help an old lady in distress, I was ready for those boys. You didn't notice, but I had this in my hand.' She reached into her knitting bag again, came out with something that resembled a shotgun cartridge. She tossed it to me, I caught it one-handed and looked closer. It was a can of Mace, a sort of pepper spray, made in the USA, and highly illegal here. Just like her pistols. And a bastard to be sprayed in your eyes.

'God bless America,' I said again.

'You saw my library,' she said.

I nodded.

'I love those books, crime fiction and true crime. Trouble is, with the former, I always guess who done it from early on, and with true crime, it's obvious.'

'Why didn't you write one yourself?'

'I tried. But then I knew who done it from word one, and I lost interest.'

'Fair enough.'

'Anyway, you came, and being a detective I looked you up on the web.' She nodded in the direction of a computer set up and printer on a table behind the door. 'You've led an interesting life.'

I couldn't argue with that.

'Especially when I went on the dark web.'

'What do you know about the dark web?' I asked.

'Nick. I used to be in the navy too. That's how I met my husband. Intelligence. Naval intelligence, if that's not too much of an oxymoron for you. More like a headless chicken farm. But I know a lot about a lot of things.'

'I'm still listening.'

'I just thought that if you ever need a sounding board in one of your adventures, or if you ever need a bolt hole, or somewhere to keep anything illegal, then feel free.'

'Madge,' I said. 'Do you know I might hold you to that.'

And I did, which is why I telephoned her that night after my adventure with the pair in the SUV.

And I did get my mate to set up a state of the art security system at her house. A cat proof one. After all, if she was going to hold stuff for me, I had to know it was safe.

The afternoon became the evening, and my bottle of wine vanished, and Madge produced a bottle of very decent red, which from the age and the label probably cost ten times or more than Mehmet's had. The cat was sleeping and the fire was ruby red ash, and Madge and I were talking like old mates.

She was telling me about her husband and his adventures on the seven seas, when I asked how he'd died.

'Cancer,' she said. 'Leukaemia. A right bugger.'

'Sorry,' I said. 'I shouldn't have asked. Naturally nosey. The job you know.'

'Of course. Don't apologise. It's been years. But I can still tear up.'

'Then forget I asked.'

'No. People don't. At first they do, then they stop. The world keeps turning. I love talking about his life. His death is as much part of his memory.'

I didn't say anything. I could see she was looking inward, and there was nothing I could add.

'It wasn't so much the cancer that killed him. His immune system was down the drain. He kept getting these shocking infections in his chest. Of course, he'd been a smoker. Cigarettes were dirt cheap in the service. And liquor, of course. Funny thing… ironic thing, was that he gave up smoking years before he got sick. Then, with the chemotherapy the doctors told him to abstain from alcohol. He just stopped. Fantastic willpower. I poured everything alcoholic in the house down the drain. Didn't make any difference. He just got sicker. Wasted away. Terrible thing to see. He had the most terrible coughing fits. So bad I thought he might have a heart attack. They gave him antibiotic after antibiotic. No good. Just prolonged the agony. I knew he wanted to die, but didn't want me to be on my own. The children came and went, and they had their own lives to lead. He told them straight. Don't hang around, for his sake. Harsh, I know, but that was him. We had another cat then. Name of Lily. She somehow knew he was dying. Wouldn't leave him alone. Followed him round like a little dog. Slept on him, or as close as she could get. They were like a little gang. I was almost jealous. She was inconsolable when he finally went. Wailed through the house. We mourned together. She gave me comfort too. She died a few years later. I didn't replace her for ages. Not that she was replaceable, if you understand.'

I nodded, and could see the fire reflected in the tears in her eyes.

'Madge,' I said. 'I didn't mean to upset you.'

'Fiddle dee dee,' she replied. 'Just an old woman's foolishness. He had a saying. His granny's: "It's not the cough that takes you off, it's the coffin they take you off in".'

'I know that one,' I said. 'My granny's too. She had a million of them. All full of doom.'

'Now is there anything left in that bottle?'

I told her there was, and replenished our glasses, and drank a toast to absent friends.

25

Grocer Jack (Excerpt From A Teenage Opera) – Keith West with The Mark Wirtz Orchestra

So that was Madge. And, believe it or not, she did help me with a case shortly after. One I couldn't have solved on my own without her help.

The client was John Coffey. He was well known in the manor, a self-made millionaire who owned five south London supermarkets. Streatham, East Dulwich, Norwood, Camberwell, and his headquarters in Brixton on the main road to Clapham Common. He was no Tesco, but he was very successful, and was well-liked, good to his staff and customers as far as the local word went. His stores were simply named Coffey Shops, before coffee shops started to take over our high streets. I'd spent many a hard-earned sovereign on food and wine in his establishments over the years without a complaint.

I got a call from his PA, who simply asked me to expect him at my office first thing on the first Monday in October, the same year as my first meeting with Madge.

I breakfasted at the greasy Greek that day, and was in my office by eight thirty. John arrived at nine precisely in a shiny black chauffeur-driven Mercedes saloon. Latest model. That year's plate.

He was an imposing figure as he walked across the road towards me. Tall, with military bearing. His hair was short, curly, and he wore a double breasted dark blue suit well. His shoes were polished to a mirror shine. He looked important and knew it. So important that I stood and opened the door for him.

'Coffey,' he said when he came in, hand outstretched.

'Nick Sharman,' I replied, and took his hand. His grip was firm, but he didn't squeeze too hard. No power games there.

'Come in,' I said.

He did, and I indicated the client's chair. He sat, carefully setting his trousers in their crease.

'Coffee?' I asked.

'That's me,' he replied with a grin. 'Black. That's me too.' That's when I decided I liked him.

I'd already put the coffee machine on, and poured two mugs. Mine with milk. 'Sugar?' I asked.

'Just as it comes.'

I delivered the beverages, and sat in my chair. 'So, Mr Coffey, sir. You wanted to see me.' He had that way about him that made me call him 'sir'. Not many blokes do.

'John,' he replied. 'Just call me John.'

'John, it is. So, John, what can I do for you this morning?'

He took a sip of coffee, put the cup and saucer down on my desk and began. 'You know me?' he said.

I nodded.

'And you know what I do?'

'Everyone knows you,' I said. 'I've been in your shops.'

'I know,' he replied. 'I've seen you. And, of course, in the papers.'

'Maybe the less said about that the better.'

'Maybe. But that's for another time. In retail, as in the army, there's such a thing as acceptable loss. In my business, it's shoplifting, breakages, and staff pilfering. It's part of the game. There's no point in worrying about it. But this summer our losses have been too high. Now, we're coming into the busiest part of the year. Christmas. And I want the losses stopped. That's where you come in.'

'Really. What about security on site?'

'I have a security team. Four at each store, eight hour shifts. Ex-military, prison officers, police. All good men. We open seven till eleven. I tried twenty four hour opening, but it was too much aggravation. So now, it's lights out just as the pubs shut. Safer for all concerned.'

'Cameras?'

'At all the stores. At Brixton, inside, on the warehouse doors, and the car park.'

'Looks like you've got it covered.'

'Obviously not,' he said.

'Police?' I asked.

'They're good,' he replied. 'They come when we call. We support them. The superintendent's ball. Open days. Sports days. We fed and watered them and the fire brigade and ambulance people during the riots. But they can't be with us day in, day out. And anyway, coppers around the place isn't good for business.'

That made sense. 'That makes sense,' I said. 'What sort of stuff are you losing? Surely a few packets of bacon isn't a major crime.'

He shook his head, as if at my *naïveté*. 'I see your scepticism,' he said. 'It's not just a few packets of bacon. But have you seen the way the price of pork has shot up recently?'

I had to admit I hadn't. He continued my lesson in retail. 'Joints of meat. Steaks. Electrical goods. Spirits. Even though they're locked in cages. DVDs. You'd be amazed how it mounts up.'

I agreed that I would.

'It's my main branch that's taking the losses. Brixton. That's where we get wholesale deliveries, keep the bulk, and transport the rest by van to the other shops.'

'Nothing goes astray *en route*?'

'Drivers and mates. Long term staff. Checked out and in.'

'But you did mention staff pilfering.'

'Peanuts,' he said. 'People got to stick it to the man. Human nature. My staff are well treated. I let a little go. No, this is serious.'

'So who's in charge of the warehouse?'

'My partner. Tony Harvey.'

'Is he in the frame?'

Coffey smiled. 'A history lesson, Mr Sharman.'

'Nick.'

'Nick. Tony and I were in the army together. Lance jacks. Nothing glamorous. Queen's Own. Infantry. Cannon fodder. We were best mates. Took leave together. He stayed with me in our house in Brixton. You see, my nan and gramps came over after the war. Not on the *Windrush*, but not far behind. Nan was a nurse, and everyone expected gramps to work on the buses or the tube. Racial stereotyping. But he had a job in the National Bank head office waiting when he got off the ship. The male staff had been decimated by the war, and he'd worked at their branch in Kingston. Jamaica, that is. They offered him a head clerkship in London. Amazing for a black man in the 1950s. He took it, and bought a house in Brixton. A big one. He'd never have got a mortgage if he hadn't worked in a bank. They were hard to get in those days. Not handed out like lollipops as they are now. Then dad and mum and I joined them. Mum was a nurse too, and, funnily enough, dad did drive a bus. The number two that stops outside the pub opposite your office.'

I knew the route. I'd taken it often.

'It wasn't always easy' he continued. 'We got our fair share of blackies, coons, niggers, jungle bunnies. That was the one that amused my father most, as we had never ventured closer to a jungle than Clapham Common. Broken windows and paint on the brickwork. We just got on with it. Replaced the windows, painted over the 'DARKIES GO HOME' graffiti. It would have been worse if we'd been cramped together in a rented flat, like lots we knew. I promised once I got back, and made something of myself, I'd help my community. And I meant both black and white. I wasn't born to work in an office,' he went on. 'I wanted adventure, so I joined up, then it all went bad. Mum, dad and gramps were killed in a car crash. The hand of God. Nan lasted less than six months. Died of grief. She left me the house. I couldn't live there. Not then. I sold it. Got a pretty penny. Enough to buy me and Tony out. We'd always talked about setting up in business together. We got a stall in the market, stocked it up, got a couple of rooms in Electric Avenue. Shared kitchen and bathroom. We worked like dogs, got a shop in the arcade. Everything a pound. We were amongst the first. Then a corner shop with green grocery, then bigger shops, then supermarkets, and when Sainsbury's moved out of Brixton, I bought the premises lock, stock and barrel. Turned out the land with freehold was soon to be worth a mint. Funnily enough, Nan's house came back on the market years later. It had been converted into bedsits. I converted it back, and my family and I still live there. There you have it. Long story short. I don't usually tell my life to strangers.'

'I've got that sort of face, I've been told. So you obviously trust him?'

'With my life. Brother in arms.'

'I know the feeling.'

'You were military?'

'Police.'

'Of course. Once we got a bit successful, I gave him half of the business. It was just my luck. My bad luck that I had the cash to set it up. It cost me three loved ones. He would have done the same in my place. He shares in the profits. He lives in a flat above the warehouse free of charge, though God knows I've told him to invest in property enough times. He says he'll wait until he retires, if he ever does, and buy a cottage in the country with roses round the door for him and his wife.'

'Fair enough. But you have to understand there's just me.' I gestured round my tiny office.

'You seem to have succeeded on your own before. And I like to support local businesses. What are your fees?'

'Two fifty a day, plus reasonable expenses.'

The look on his face made me think I could've asked for more. 'That seems fair,' he said. 'If you want the job, I'll get my office to get you a cheque for a week or so in advance. Would that suit?'

I decided then and there to give it a shot. After all, I wasn't busy, and Christmas was coming and a week or so in advance was very tempting. 'I'd have to take a look round,' I said.

'Of course.'

'When?'

'Well, there's no time like the present, unless you have something else to do.'

'My calendar is clear,' I said.

'Then, let's go.' And we did.

26

Oh Lord Won't You Buy Me
A Mercedes Benz – Janis Joplin

I ushered him out, pulled down the blinds, locked the door, and joined him in the back of his car. It smelt of leather, money, and influence. I reckoned he could have easily afforded a Rolls-Royce, but maybe he didn't want to show off his wealth too much. Black man with too much money. Still not a good look in our part of the world.

The Mercedes ran smoothly through the end of rush hour streets, and soon we were in the car park of his flagship store in Brixton. We got out and returned to the real world.

We walked through the store towards the back. John was greeted by every staff member, who to a man and woman wore their COFFEY SHOPS t-shirts or sweats, and called him either Sir, Boss or John, depending on their seniority or length of service I imagined, apart from a burly bloke standing by the front door, next to a Christmas tree groaning with fairy lights. He wore a blue faux police uniform with SECURITY written in white on the back and on each upper arm. John cheerfully replied to each one. They pretty much ignored me, which suited me fine. The shop was busy, the shelves were full, and the tills were ringing. Not much to worry about there. The halls, or rather the shelves, were decked, if not with boughs of holly, with tinsel and paper decorations, and carols were being played through the public address system. A bit early for all that I thought. But then, I wasn't a retailer.

At the back of the store was an open door marked STAFF ONLY, and we passed through into the warehouse area. It was busy in there too. The place was full of metal shelving right up to the ceiling packed with everything a Saturday shopper would need from kitchen roll to baked beans. People were scurrying around pulling stuff off the shelves and into trolleys, and a couple of forklift trucks were running about squeaking warnings to the pedestrians. Once again everyone was wearing a corporate shirt. There were choruses of Good mornings which John replied to with a wave. The back of the warehouse was open to another parking area that was full of suppliers trucks and smaller vans once again marked COFFEY SHOPS. There was another door further down with a sign reading CANTEEN, and I could smell bacon cooking. Obviously breakfast was served. Good staff relations, I thought. He took my arm and propelled me through the workers, up a flight of stairs to a glass fronted office that sat above the warehouse with a view of the place from all four directions. Inside was a young woman at a desk complete with three telephones, a computer and a printer. Further back was a larger desk, clear except for piles of paper invoices. Behind it sat the man John wanted me to meet.

Now if John was black, his partner was as pale as a ghost with wispy blond hair going thin on his nut. John looked at the girl and said. 'Julie, give us a moment please.'

She smiled, nodded, stood up and left the room. Before she went, she asked, 'Coffee?'

John shook his head. 'Maybe later,' he said.

She smiled again, and left, closing the door behind her.

John introduced me. 'Tony, this is Nick Sharman. He's the investigator I told you about. Nick, my partner Tony Harvey.'

He looked at me like he might examine something Schmoo the cat had dragged in from a garbage tip, and made no move to get up and shake hands. 'Really,' he said with a sneer. 'I told you I didn't think this was a good idea.'

So much for me, I thought. 'It's my decision,' said John, and I knew then who was the more equal of partners, although Harvey might own fifty per cent.

'Your funeral,' he said.

'John,' I said, and I could tell Harvey didn't like me being on first name terms, 'if this is awkward…'

'It's my decision, I said,' said John, and this time there was steel in his voice. 'And it stands. Come on Nick, I'll show you round downstairs.'

With that, and a dirty look from Harvey to me, we left. Maybe I'd get a coffee in the canteen.

27

Shop Around
– The Miracles

John led me through the warehouse, pointing out matters of interest, then back to the main shop, and through a corridor to what he told me was the security office. Inside, in front of a bank of a dozen monitors, was another security guy. 'Good morning, Chas,' said John. 'Meet Nick, he's giving our security system the once-over.'

Chas didn't seem miffed by me intruding on his bailiwick, instead turned, offered his hand, and said, 'Welcome aboard. Want a cuppa?'

'Sure,' I replied.

'Help yourself,' and he pointed to a table covered with mugs, sugar, and a vacuum flask.

'I'll leave you two to chat,' said John. 'Show Nick the ropes.'

'Will do,' said Chas.

'Just one thing,' said John, and he went to a big metal cupboard. He opened the door and pulled out a plastic wrapped sweat shirt. 'Extra large should do,' he said and gave it to me. 'Just to make you feel at home.' Then he reached into his pocket and brought out a card. 'My private number,' he said. 'Any time.' And with that, he wished us both another good morning, and left.

I made myself a cuppa and looked over Chas's shoulder at the monitors. 'Four outside, one in the warehouse, and seven in the shop,' he explained. 'And you can zero in on any one.' He touched a button, and the twelve screens became one. Then a fader to zoom in. 'See.'

I saw.

'Trouble is, it would take twelve days solid to see everything in real time.' Which could be a problem, I thought. But all seemed serene, and after a few minutes I drank up and went for a wander. A few minutes later my mobile rang. It was John. 'Sorry to abandon you,' he said. 'I had to have a chat with Tony.'

I thought that that probably didn't end well. 'No problem,' I said.

'Perhaps you could go to the warehouse tomorrow first thing and just melt in?'

'That works for me.'

'Do you need a lift?'

'No, I'll make my own way back. Give me time to think.'

'Fine. Check in with me as and when.'

'Will do, John. Good to meet you.'

'The feeling's mutual. I think we'll get along.'

With him yes, with his partner no way. 'Hope so.' And with that we made our farewells and finished the call.

28

Too High For The Supermarket
– The Uninvited

I rolled down to Brixton bright and early the next morning for my first full day on the job. I parked up in a space marked 'STAFF' and all dressed up in my COFFEY SHOPS hooded sweat shirt and reported to Harvey in the warehouse. He made a big deal of looking at his watch. Obviously, he thought nine ack emma was no time to clock in. But if he thought I was turning up at six thirty he had another thought coming. 'It's not here that stuff's going walkabout,' he said. 'Nothing gets past me. Everything's military style, triple checked. If you want to catch thieves, better look inside.' He motioned at the front of the building.

'Fair enough,' I said. 'That's where I'll be if you need me.'

His look said hell would freeze over first. 'By the way,' he said, as I left, 'John let the cat out of the bag yesterday, telling Chas who you were. And the staff aren't happy having a stranger checking on them.'

That was putting it mildly. The workers were as close mouthed as the *Cosa Nostra*. To say I got a cold reception was nothing but the truth. By lunchtime, I felt like something found floating in a toilet bowl that just wouldn't flush. Even when I went for a cup of coffee, around eleven, I found myself the only one sitting at a table for four.

And that's how it went for the next couple of days. I'll be honest, I'd never felt more hopeless. Now, I can find a missing person, collect a debt, serve a writ, and check up on the faithfulness of a husband or wife, but finding out who nicked a pound of pork and onion bangers was beyond me.

What pissed me off most was the fact that, on the Wednesday morning, when I went by my office, there was a cheque for fifteen hundred smackers from John Coffey's personal bank account waiting for me on the welcome mat. At least I had the good grace not to cash it. I might be a lot of things, but a fraud I ain't.

So it was with a heavy heart, and an uncashed cheque in pocket, I bearded the man himself in his Streatham den on the Thursday morning of that week.

29

Grits Ain't Groceries
– Little Milton

He sat me down opposite his desk, and I said, 'John, this isn't working.'

'How so?'

'I'm getting no help from your staff. They don't trust me. Neither does your partner. He didn't want me around from the get-go. And in his shoes, neither would I. It's not good for worker/management relations.'

'You must've had tougher assignments.'

'Sure. But normally a few days' research, or a week sitting in my car, pissing in a bottle, or even a few sore heads, does the trick. None of those works here.'

'I see.'

I could see he was disappointed in me, and that hurt. Don't ask me why, it was just that I liked the bloke.

I took out the cheque. 'Thanks for this,' I said, 'but I can't accept it. Can we tear it up, and call it quits?'

'If that's how you want it.'

'No, it's not. I hate being beaten. Especially in the case of the purloined potato chips, as Holmes might have called it. Hardly my finest hour.'

'It's up to you.'

Suddenly, I had a thought. 'John. Do you by any chance have a job for a nice middle aged lady whom no one would suspect was working undercover?'

He thought for a moment. 'I might. Can she work a rotisserie?'

'I'm sure this particular lady can work anything.'

'Well, my girl who cooks the chickens is off sick. Could she fill in?'

'Well, I haven't actually asked her, but I'm sure she'd be game. It's smack dab by the front door if I remember right.'

'You do.'

'Perfect to keep watch on anything flying out.' I put the cheque back in my pocket. 'I'll hold on to this, if that's OK.'

He nodded.

'Right. I'll shoot off and give her a tug and let you know what's what by close of play.'

'Good. If she accepts the job, tell her to report to the floor manager.' He wrote a name on a Post-it note. 'Tell her I authorised the hire. I often do.'

'Great. And John...'

'Yes.'

'Not a word about who she is.'

He made a zip-like movement over his mouth. 'Trust me.' And I did.

30

Do The Funky Chicken
– Rufus Thomas

I turned up at Madge's uninvited that afternoon with a bottle of something decent that didn't come from Mehmet's corner shop, and a picnic basket from a posh deli that had recently opened in Dulwich Village that I'd read about in the *Sunday Times* colour supplement. It cost me dear, but I didn't care. Cast your bread upon the waters was my motto that day.

'Nick,' she said when she answered the door. 'What a pleasant surprise.'

'Maybe you'd better hear what I've got to say before you say that.'

'Sounds ominous.'

'Tea and sandwiches,' I said, handing her the basket.

We went inside, and she plonked the basket on the table and opened it. 'What have we here?' she said, opening the first carefully-wrapped parcel.

'Smoked salmon, duck pate, Brie and cranberry, shrimp with mayonnaise, cream scones and jam. Just like my mother didn't use to make.'

'My, my, what did I do to deserve this?'

'I hope it's what you're going to do.'

'Are you propositioning me?'

'You could say that.'

'Then I'll go and put the kettle on.'

Over our tea and sandwiches, I told Madge my problem. 'Can you work a rotisserie?' I asked when I'd finished.

'Of course. It's just a chicken roaster.'

'If you say so.'

'And I'm to look out for bad guys.'

'Just look, don't touch. Leave that to me.'

'A proper Hetty Wainthropp,' she said.

'Who?'

'Elderly female detective. Heard of her?'

'No,' I said, shaking my head.

'She's on television.'

I shook my head again. 'Must be my night for choir practice. Anyway, I thought Miss Marple was your favourite.'

'Hetty's more down to earth.'

'Then I must try and catch the repeats. You start tomorrow at nine. I'll pick you up at quarter to. No mention of me, though. You report to...' I checked the piece of paper John had given me. 'Mavis Hampton, and I hope that's not rhyming slang.'

'Save it for choir practice,' she said.

'Now about payment.'

She gave me one of her old fashioned looks. 'Don't be silly. This is pro bono,' she said.

'Does that mean gratis?' Another look.

'How about lunch at the Ritz?'

'You must be getting well paid.'

'Rate for the job. How about it?'

'Only if we get, how do you say it? A result.'

I had to laugh. 'Even if we don't.'

'You're the boss, boss.'

'And never forget it. I'll pick you up tomorrow at eight forty five, and drop you off, then collect you again at five fifteen. No public transport for the staff of Sharman investigations.'

'Sounds like a plan.'

And then we opened the bottle, and spent a most convivial evening together.

31

Back At The Chicken Shack
– Jimmy Smith

As promised I picked her up at eight forty five, and let her out in a side street at the back of the supermarket. No one saw us. I made sure of that. 'I'll be here at quarter past five,' I said. 'Make sure no one sees you with me.'

'Aye aye, captain.'

I spent the day just hanging out at home. Playing old vinyl, drinking tea, and watching daytime TV.

I was bang on time at the pick-up spot and Madge arrived ten minutes later wearing, you guessed it, a COFFEY SHOPS sweatshirt. 'Looking groovy,' I said when she dropped into the passenger seat.

'Not my choice of apparel,' she replied. 'But needs must...'

'How did it go?'

'Dozens of birds consigned to their maker. Hot and sweaty. Not my choice of a career move either. I ate vegetarian for lunch. I felt guilty about the poor creatures.'

'Not that. I meant any signs of the bad guys?'

'Maybe. Give me some more time.'

'Not even a hint?'

'Not yet. I don't want to rush my fences.'
'OK, Hetty. Fancy some supper?'
'A lovely idea. Just as long as it isn't chicken.'
'Trust me.'

32

Experiment In Terror
– Kai Winding

After a spaghetti dinner in our local Italian, I dropped Madge off at home. I grilled her slightly less than the courgette, tomato, cheese and garlic starter, but she kept closed lips except to eat and drink. 'Sinks ships,' was all she said.

The next morning I picked her up again and took her to Brixton. 'Keep your mobile on,' she said, as she left the car.

She called me about one. I was sitting in my office, listening to Kai Winding's Suspense Themes CD I'd picked up cheap. Good stuff.

'Got them,' she said.

'Who?'

'Come to the shop and you'll find out. Better bring John Coffey if you can.'

'I'm on my way.'

I phoned John's office and told him the news. 'I'll meet you there in twenty minutes,' he said.

I drove down to Brixton, and we both arrived at the same time and parked up next to each other. 'What do you know?' he asked.

'As much as you,' I replied. 'It's all down to Madge. I'll call her.' I did just that, and she said, 'Where are you?'

'In the car park.'

'Is Mr Coffey with you?'

'Yes.'

'Then wait there. Don't come in yet. I'll just lock up my till. Don't want any more larceny.' She cut me off, and a minute later came out of the front doors. She came over and said, 'Hello gentlemen, I have something to show you.' She nodded to John's car and said, 'Better inside.'

We squeezed into the back of John's Mercedes. He told his driver to take a smoke break, and then turned to Madge who was sitting between us and said, 'OK, Mrs McMichael what have you got for us?'

'Good news if you can call it that. I know what's been going on. But the bad news is that I'm afraid your security man Chas is at the bottom of this.'

A sad look crossed John's face and he shook his head. 'Oh no,' he said. 'Not Chas. He's a friend.'

'Sorry,' said Madge. 'It has to be him. He was in the security office with the screens. He must have seen.'

'Seen what?' demanded John.

'I'll show you.' Madge took her phone from the pocket of her sweat shirt and pressed a button. On the tiny screen two hooded figures pushed loaded trolleys through the front door. There was no sign of the other security guard.

'Who else was on security today?' he asked Madge.

'Tom. But he was called to the tills where there was a bit of a kerfuffle. Happens a lot. Like yesterday when Chas was in the security room again, and the same two boys left without paying.'

'Christ,' said John. 'Let's go inside and find out what the hell has been going on.' So we did.

Before I go any further, this is Chas's story as told to Madge and me outside when everything had been made clear, and the job was over, before I drove her home. As he told us, there was a tear in his eye.

Chas Hill had been in the army. By coincidence, in the same regiment as John, but later. He'd served two tours in one of those small wars in the Middle East which we'd fought at that time without any idea of the consequences, and come home to a country fit for heroes, to a welcome fit for heroes, with PTSD, and an honourable discharge with a pension that barely covered basics. His army house was repossessed, and he moved his wife and son in with his in-laws in a two up, two down in Brixton Hill. He heard about John on the ex-military grapevine and approached him about a job. John was happy to have him on board, and hired him for security, and over the three years he worked for Coffey Shops he was promoted to deputy head of security. He also became a friend of John and his family where he was often welcomed as a guest. After one year, with a loan from John, he managed to obtain a mortgage on a small house close to the Brixton branch of the chain.

All, it had seemed, had been well. But it obviously wasn't.

33

It's Over
– Roy Orbison

The three of us went through the front door, and there was Chas at his post. When he saw John he came to attention, then he frowned as his eyes turned to Madge, and over to the deserted rotisserie. 'Where have you been?' he asked.

'Sorry, ' she said. 'Chicken's off.' His frown deepened.

'With me, Chas,' said John, and he marched across the shop floor towards the security camera room, with Chas, Madge and me following him, our little convoy receiving puzzled looks from any staff who clocked us going by.

John ushered us through the door where the other security guard on duty, Tom, another black bloke, swivelled his chair at our entrance. The tiny room seemed claustrophobic with us all crammed in. John grabbed the only other chair in situ and gestured for Madge to sit, which she did.

'Can I have your phone?' he said to Madge.

She obliged, and he pulled up the video on the screen. He peered at it and said to the seated guard, 'Tom, show me the main doors at twelve twenty three.'

Tom pushed some buttons and up popped the video. It ran

on for thirty seconds or so, then there was a tiny glitch, almost too brief to notice unless it was being searched for. The time line at the bottom of the screen jumped back, once again only visible if being closely examined.

Chas's face blanched and he staggered close to collapse. Madge jumped up and between us we sat him down. 'Head between your legs,' she ordered.

He did as he was told and the room seemed to shrink even more, and get warmer.

'I'm so sorry,' gasped Chas. 'After all you've done...' he didn't finish.

'Why, Chas?' asked John.

'They threatened my family,' he said, 'They know where I live.'

'Who?' John again.

'Kids. Young men. They hang around. Black kids.'

'And?'

'They make me load up trolleys. Then when I'm on the monitors they steam in and grab the stuff...'

'But the screens,' John interrupted. 'How the hell did you do that?'

'One of them. Blood. He learned how to fix them at his college.'

Tom sucked his teeth.

I asked. 'You know him?'

'Unfortunately. Him and his crew are a bloody nuisance. Carole's the boss. Then there's Bez and Blood. Always smoking dope. Messing around.'

I think if Madge hadn't been in the room, he'd have used stronger language. 'They're here now. Out front.'

'Are they?' said John.

'What are you going to do, guv'nor?' said Chas. 'I never made a penny. I swear.'

'I should call the police,' said John, but by his tone I knew he wouldn't, and that was when he became my friend. 'But I won't. You're going on holiday. Take the family down to my place in Sussex. When you come back you're going to the Dulwich shop.' He turned to me. 'Nick. What can you do?'

'Nothing,' I replied. 'But I know a man who can.'

34

The Lobster Song – The Naughty Boys of Finchley (The Coastels)

I took charge then. I called Robber from my mobile. He was at Brixton nick. Less than five minutes away. I gave him the bare bones of the story. I told him this was unofficial. He wasn't impressed. I told him he'd have my undying gratitude. Ditto. I told him he'd be helping a soldier who'd suffered for his country. Ditto again. Then I mentioned that John Coffey would be grateful, and he changed his tune. 'Really?' he said. 'Are those blokes there now?'

'Tom,' I said, 'show us the bit of the car park where these kids hang out.'

He pulled up the image. Three hoodies, smoking spliffs by the looks of it. Cool as a trio of cucumbers. That was soon to change.

'They're there now,' I said.

'I'm on my way,' and he hung up.

'He's coming,' I said to John. 'Looks like he's going to be your new best friend.'

'I'll cope.'

It seemed almost at once that my phone rang. 'I'm outside,'

said Robber. 'Leaning against a new Mercedes.'

'Don't scratch the paintwork,' I said.

'Let's go,' I said. 'Not you, Chas. Sorry. Tom, let's go.' I would have normally left Madge if it looked like trouble, which it did, but she was more than capable of handling herself, and, of course, she had cracked the case single-handedly, so I didn't even mention her staying put. Probably just as well for my health.

Once again, our small group headed across the shop. More funny looks. Outside Robber was waiting by the Mercedes talking to John's driver. I was surprised he wasn't giving the cellulose a polish while he waited. 'Round here,' said Tom.

There they were at the side of the shop. The hole in the wall gang. Three black steamers, smoking spliffs, who looked at us as we went into the road with a mixture of contempt and amusement. Like I said, that would soon change.

Robber palmed his warrant card and led the way. 'Carole,' he said. The tallest one, who was leaning back against the shop wall, narrowed his eyes. Robber showed him his brief. 'Detective Inspector Jack Robber,' he said. 'You'd better remember that.'

Carole lifted the blunt to his lips. Robber brushed it away in a shower of sparks. 'Empty your pockets.'

'Fuck off, man,' he said.

Robber grabbed him by the throat and slammed his head back so that it hit the wall with a satisfying thunk. 'Empty your pockets, or I will, and if there's anything sharp, and I cut myself, I'll castrate you. Do you know what that means? I. WILL. CUT. YOUR. BOLLOCKS. OFF.'

I think Carole got the message. He reached into the pocket of his hoodie and produced a decent-sized bag of weed.

Robber grunted and pocketed it. I often wondered what he did with the drugs he took off miscreants. Did he use them, or use them to fit up other poor sods? I know he never passed any on to me.

'Anything else?' he asked.

Carole shook his head and Robber let it pass. This wasn't his *raison d'etre* today. 'Now,' he said, 'it's come to my notice that you three stooges are stealing from Mr Coffey, and have threatened a decorated hero of our country, who has not been well, and his family. Including a young boy.' Carole's head hit the wall again and this time left a blood stain. Skull versus concrete. Concrete two, skull nil. 'That's against the fucking rules. And from now on, these are the rules.' Another bang, and Carole went a bit cross-eyed, and I saw one of the three's blue jeans go a shade darker as he pissed his pants. A strong smell of cannabis-flavoured urine filled the air.

Robber smiled. 'You three never, I repeat never, darken the doorstep of any of Mr Coffey's stores again. I will be watching as I do my regular shop.' He looked at John who nodded. Nothing needed to be said, but I knew Jack had a free pass. 'The occasional lobster tail or steak and chips for my supper.' Another look, another nod from John. 'And you know where the bloke you threatened lives. Make sure you're never seen close. You or your mates. In fact, if I ever hear that him or his family as much as have a hair out of place, no matter what the cause, I will find you whether you had anything to do with it or not, and make your lives more miserable than they already are. Understand?'

Carole nodded.

'Say it.'

'I understand.'

'Carole. That's a girl's name isn't it?' He didn't wait for an answer. 'And don't think I won't be looking you up in criminal records. I know you're in there and I'll find you. So Carole from now on, you and your little girlfriends are my bitches. Understood? Remember my name. Jack Robber. I want all three of you to think of my name when you go to beddy bye at night, and when you wake up in the morning. And another thing, I know you boys love to cry police brutality. Forget it. This meeting never took place. I'll swear to that, my friend Nick will swear to it, that nice lady will swear to it, Mr Coffey's security man will swear to it. And most importantly, Mr Coffey, a huge influence in your community, and well known to be as honest as the day is long, will swear to it.' Yet another nod from John, which I think is what finally sealed the deal and even got through to this dope-addled trio. 'Get the picture?'

Carole and his pals had the picture. Any more might have been too much, and Robber knew it. He was a master of interrogation, always knowing when less was more. 'So, my little friends, that's us,' Robber said. 'Now fuck off and thank your lucky stars and Mr Coffey that this goes no further, unless you make the mistake of pushing it.'

He stood back, and Carole and his mates slunk off, never to be heard off again, at least in that neck of the woods.

His last words were, 'Carole, put some TCP and a plaster on your head. It'll heal quicker.'

Then he turned and grinned at us and lit a cigarette. Case closed.

I got to keep John's cheque and I took Madge out for lunch as promised. Not the Ritz, but the Savoy where her husband used to take her for a treat. It was my pleasure.

35

I'm Going To Get Me A Gun
– Cat Stevens

Back to the present.

It was getting late, but Madge seemed to get by on little sleep, so I didn't feel guilty giving her a bell. She had, after all, asked to be part of my life, and me hers, all that time ago, and like I said, she'd helped me out more than once when I needed an ally.

'It's me, Nick,' I said, when she picked up. 'Hello,' she said back. 'I thought you might call.'

'Knew I would, you mean.'

'Maybe.'

'I need a place to stay again. Mine's a bit warm.'

'The spare bed is made up as always.'

'And I need some of my stuff.'

'It's all here, cleaned and loaded.'

'Brilliant.'

'When?'

'Tonight?'

'Anytime. You know that.'

'I'll be with you shortly.'

'I'll leave the door on the latch.'

I packed a few necessities in a leather holdall and left. Luckily, the black guy had let me keep all my keys, so I went to my car, started it, and drove off. I parked it on a quiet back street, locked it up, then walked to Madge's. When my guy had fitted new security, he'd put in a motion-sensitive light by her front door, but she'd switched it off, and the whole house was in darkness. The door was on the latch as she'd promised, and opened quietly. I closed it behind me, and said into the darkness, lit only by two tiny green eyes belonging to Schmoo the cat, 'OK, Madge, you can turn the light on now,' I whispered, though it wasn't necessary.

She did as I said.

'Hello, Nick,' she said, 'you've been busy.'

'You don't know the half of it.'

'Come through and tell me. It's still so bloody hot and humid. Reminds me of the tropics. We can sit on the veranda. I've made you some sandwiches and coffee. And there's a glass of brandy.'

'Madge, you're a lifesaver,' I said. 'I can't remember when I last ate. Hope you weren't doing anything important.'

'Just watching TV.'

'Nothing good, I hope.'

'Something about buying property. Awful. Jesus, TV presenters and estate agents in one show. Great examples of two kinds of people who are convinced you can polish a turd.'

'Madge!'

'Sorry. Naval language. I forgot you were never in.'

'You've taught me well, though, over the years.'

I picked up the cat and she purred hard, and we went out and sat at the same table where we'd had tea all that time before. She let the light from the big room leak out, and moths and midges made a halo above us. She'd made ham and mustard and cheese and pickle sandwiches. The coffee was hot and strong, the brandy was cold and even stronger. Between sips and mouthfuls, I gave her the full SP. She didn't interrupt. That's one of the things I most liked about her. When I'd finished, she said. 'Well, it's even more exciting than I thought. You know I've met men and women like your man Smyth, or whatever he calls himself.'

'My friend Robber called him a "fucking spook".'

'He's probably right. Sounds about par for the course.'

'I lost the phone he brought me. And the cash.'

'I've got cash if you need it. '

'I'd probably lose it too.'

'And I've got your stuff.'

She got up and went back into the house, and returned with the canvas bag I'd left with her after a previous adventure.

Inside, all carefully wrapped in clean white cotton, was a Mossberg seven shot repeating riot shotgun with a pistol grip, a Colt .38 hammerless revolver, and a Browning nine, with spare ammunition for all of them, and a soft leather shoulder holster for the automatic, all carefully cleaned, oiled and loaded. I figured if any wild animals came out of the undergrowth at the bottom of her garden, we'd be able to fight them off with no trouble.

All the time I sat there, the cat kept lookout for intruders.

36

Blood On The Tracks
– Bob Dylan

When I'd finished my meal, I lit a cigarette, and said, 'I guess you're harbouring a fugitive again.'

'I'll say you held me up at gunpoint.'

'Makes sense.'

'Let's go inside, and I'll make fresh coffee, then you can get some sleep.'

'Sounds good,' I said, stubbed out my cigarette in the ashtray she'd brought out for me, and we both went into the sitting room.

'You're bleeding,' she said, and nodded towards my legs.

There were bloodstains on the denim from the wounds on my legs leaking. 'I've got plasters,' I said. 'But I might ruin your sheets.'

'There's always bleach and the washing machine.'

'No need. I'll buy you a new pair. Egyptian cotton.'

'The first day I met you, Nick, I knew you were a man with good taste.'

'And how right you were.'

She was as good as her word, and produced more coffee in

short order. Between us we finished the pot, and, leaving the crocks, both headed to our separate rooms.

Mine was at the top of the house. The old servants' quarters Madge told me. Walls had been knocked through and turned into a proper guest's suite. Dormer windows had been fitted into the roof, and at one end was a double bed, and at the other, a sofa, two easy chairs and a large screen TV. Next door was an en-suite bathroom and lavatory.

Madge had opened all the windows, but the air was still heavy with the remains of the day's heat. It hung around me like a thick blanket, and caught in my throat as I tried to breathe.

I carefully undressed, pulled off the plasters and looked at my wounds. Not too bad.

I took a cool shower, dried myself off, and put on some of the plasters I'd brought with me.

Then, just in my underwear, I lay on the bed and fell asleep.

37

Bed And Breakfast Man
– Madness

Next morning, at eight twenty by the digital clock by the bed, there was a knock on the suite door. 'Are you decent?' Madge called.

'As I'll ever be,' I replied.

She came in carrying a mug. 'I brought you a cuppa,' she said.

'If I asked you to marry me, what would you say?'

'I'd say, don't be a silly goose.'

'You've got me there. Is that some new street slang?'

She just shook her head and laid the tray down next to my bed. 'How are the scars of war?'

'Stinging a bit, but I'll live. And no bloodstains on the bedding.'

'Good. Breakfast in half an hour. Don't be late.'

'Yes, ma'am.'

I was as good as my word and reported for my breakfast half an hour later. She served it up in the breakfast room next to the kitchen in the basement. At least it was cooler down there, the morning having dawned hot and heavy again. Madge had done me a full English, but this time the mushrooms and tomatoes were fresh, not tinned. I commented on that.

'Did you know,' she asked, 'that when I was in the navy, if we had mushrooms for breakfast, the officers had the cups, and the ratings made do with the stalks?'

'Life's like that. A right bugger.'

'I agree.'

I finished the plate and went out for a cigarette.

She followed me. 'So what are you doing today?' she asked.

'Keeping a low profile, round here if you don't mind. But first, I need a new phone. Old Bill nicked mine. And my other one ended up a burnt offering.'

'That's not even slightly funny. Anyway, I thought you had no cash.'

'Luckily, both the cops and those two last night let me keep my wallet. Still got credit on my card. Great breakfast, by the way.'

'I like cooking for a man.'

'And I like eating what you cook.'

'Joking aside. You should get yourself a wife.'

'Been there, done that. What's the weather forecast, by the way?'

'More of the same. Hot, hot, hot.'

'Oh well, I suppose we'd be complaining if it was raining.'

'Not me, or my bedding plants.'

I had a sudden thought. 'Here, Madge,' I said.

'Yes.'

'Smyth. Fan of crime writing. He said something.' Her eyebrows rose in an unasked question.

'The Squeaker,' I said. 'Ring any bells?'

'Easy. Edgar Wallace. A prolific crime writer. Written nineteen thirty or thereabouts. Made into a film several years later. It's good, but dated. The Squeaker was what you'd call a grass these days.'

'Makes sense. Do you have a copy?'

'Of course, under W in the library.'

'Mind if I take a look?'

'Course not.'

'Is it valuable?'

'The dust jacket is worth more than the book.'

'And you have one?

'Of course.'

'I promise to handle it with kid gloves.'

'Cotton ones are better. You'll find fresh ones in a drawer in the room.'

And I did, and found the book. A first edition in a colourful jacket. And in the heat of the morning, I was taken back to smoggy old London Town in the years between the wars. Dated it was, but I enjoyed it. The story was simple. A bloke who architects robberies grasses up the wrongdoers if they piss him off. And he did have a black heart. Could be Smyth thought Stowe-Hartley did the same. Or wanted him to. Fair enough.

38

Johnny Angel
– Shelly Fabares

After breakfast and a cigarette out in the garden, I pulled on a baseball cap, turned up my collar, and went shopping. There was a small branch of my mobile provider on Norwood Road, and after just a few minutes, I left with a brand new, latest model telephone with a brand new number.

It was too early for the *Standard* to check out the coverage of last evening's adventure, so I headed back to Madge's. On the way, I heard someone shout, 'Mr Sharman'. So much for my disguise. I turned slowly, fearing the worst, and was relieved to see it was only a bloke called Gabriel, the main man in our local neighbourhood watch.

He was a right pain in the arse. Short, with a typical Napoleon complex, and I always thought he probably wore lifts in his shoes. He was about seventy, retired from some corporate job in the city. White hair, bristly white moustache, and a red face that hinted at more than a passing acquaintance with the whiskey bottle. He always wore a collar and tie during the week, and slacks, a sports jacket, and a cravat at the weekend. A cravat, I ask you. He'd had a stroke a couple of years previously, and it would have been better, as far as most of us in the street were concerned, if he'd just turned up his toes and gone to meet St Peter and maybe met his namesake at the pearly gates.

'Mr Gabriel,' I said. 'Enjoying the weather?'

'Not particularly' he replied, and I believed him. His face was even redder than usual, and it looked like his old school tie was strangling him. 'Were you at home last night?' he asked.

'No,' I replied, although it was none of his business. 'I stayed at a friend's.'

'Thought as much. No car, and there was a bloody commotion last night at your front door about two. Woke me and the wife up. I didn't go out, because, frankly, some of your friends leave a lot to be desired.'

Charming, I thought.

'Called the police, but as usual, no one came for an hour, and by then all was quiet.'

'I'm sorry,' I said. 'I have no idea who it could have been.' Although I was pretty sure. 'Are you sure it was my place?'

He gave me what my old gran would've called an old-fashioned look. 'I may be getting on, Mr Sharman, but I'm not senile. It was your house, and I know the couple in the other flat are away. You see, they have the politeness to let me know their movements, so that in my capacity in the community I can keep my eye on things.'

Pompous little twerp. In another life, I would've grabbed him by both ears and head butted his ugly little face. But not this one. Instead, I apologised again and promised to be a better boy in future.

When I got back to Madge's, I filled her in on developments. I put my new number in her mobile, and texted Robber with the same.

'What are you going to do now?' she asked.

'I should check the place. See what surprises they left me.'

'No. You're too obvious. Why don't I take a wander?'

'No, Madge. I'll wait 'til it gets dark and see for myself.'

'If you say so. How about some lunch? There's a ham salad in the fridge. Then I'm going to get an afternoon paper, see the reports of your exploits last night.'

'Sounds fine. I could get used to staying in this hotel.'

She just snorted, and went to get the lunch ready.

I sat out in the garden, smoking a cigarette, petting the cat, and watching the grass turn brown in the sun.

39

New Boots And Panties
– Ian Dury And The Blockheads

Luncheon was served, and eaten, and the long day dragged on. I was sitting in the garden again when my new phone chirruped. It was Robber. 'Listen, Nick,' he said, 'I'm not having much luck with your men. There's no Martineau working for the Revenue. The Spencer, I told you about, and Smyth with a y don't exist as far as the Met and Special Branch would let on. Who knows what the truth is? You never know with these fuckers. So I've come up a blank, and don't bother asking for your money back, it's already spent.'

'On a new suit?' I asked.

There was a long pause. 'Funny,' was all he said.

I didn't tell him about my adventure the previous evening after we'd met. Too much information for even a slightly dodgy cop to ignore. 'Fair enough, Jack' I said. 'If anything comes up, let me know.'

'You'll be the first,' he said, and rang off.

Then Madge said she was going to the shops for more supplies. My latest big mistake was letting her. When she hadn't come back after an hour, the penny dropped. I tried her mobile and a man answered. 'This must be Sharman,' the man said. 'I was just going to call you. We've got your girlfriend. Bit old for you, I would've thought.'

'Stowe-Hartley, of course.'

'If you've hurt…'

'Save the histrionics for someone who might appreciate them. She's as good as gold. It's you we want to talk to. You've cost us dear already.'

'And more, if I have anything…'

The voice cut me off again. 'I said save it. You got satnav?'

'Sure.'

'Then get in your car and get here.' He gave me instructions. 'It's not far. And I don't have to tell you to say nothing to anyone. If you do, we'll know and she'll pay. It'll be on your head. Come now. And alone. You've got an hour. Be here or she'll get hurt.' With that, he cut me off.

Shit. Not Madge. Not another innocent hurt because of me.

I looked at the bag of guns. I was walking into a trap. There was more than one of them. A whole fucking army if Smyth was right. Fat chance I'd have to sneak up on them. They had the high ground. The advantage of their territory and numbers.

Regretfully, I left the ordnance and headed for my motor.

40

Driving Sideways
– Freddie King

I went to where I'd left my car. It was still there, just a bit dustier. I fed the information I'd been given into the satnav, and it led me down through south London towards Croydon. It was still baking hot, the tarmac shimmering in the heat, and although I had the air con on high I was still sweating like a dog. More from worry about Madge than the weather.

Stowe-Hartley had been spot on with the timing. Just under an hour after I'd got the call, I arrived at an industrial estate on the south side of Croydon. It had seen better days, but then so had I.

I drove through a set of open gates, and saw a tattooed skinhead sitting in a deck chair under a striped umbrella, drinking from a can of special brew.

He was expecting me, and he pointed to a warehouse with huge doors wide open. Another big bloke, this time with hair, heard me coming, and beckoned me inside. The place was empty apart from several tarpaulin-covered cars at the far end, plus a beautiful pearl white Bentley GT, which probably cost about the same as my flat, with a personalised number plate

V12 LNS, which told me who had answered Madge's phone. As if I hadn't known. There was a third bloke giving the motor a wash and brush up, who stopped as I drove in. I stopped the car, as the warehouse doors closed behind it, filling the place with shadows.

The first bloke opened the car door. 'Out,' he said.

I did as I was told, and yet another bloke appeared from the darkness. He slammed me against the side of the car and gave me a thorough frisking, including a good punch in the kidneys for good luck, and, just to add injury to insult, whilst the first bloke watched, after showing me the butt of a pistol stuck in his belt.

'Did you really think I'd be stupid enough to come here carrying?' I asked.

'Who knows how stupid you are?' the handy bloke said.

'Not that stupid,' I said. 'I'm come only armed with my sunny disposition.' That got me another painful jab. One day I'll learn to keep my big mouth shut. 'I hope we get to meet again,' I said, through clenched teeth.

'It'll be my pleasure,' he said. That time I said nothing.

When they were both sure I was unarmed, bloke number one drove my car down to where the others were parked, got out and locked with a chirrup from the horn, and a flash from the indicators.

'Valet parking,' I said. 'Give it a wash whilst it's here,' I said to the geezer still holding a chamois leather who was polishing the Bentley.

Nothing back.

'Just in case you had any surprises waiting for us under your seat,' said bloke number two. Then he gestured towards a set of metal stairs leading up to a mezzanine floor. 'Up you go,' he said. 'The boss is waiting for you in the office.'

41

Radar Love
– Golden Earring

I did as I was told again, climbed the stairs, then went along a wide platform towards a half glass door at the end. Inside, in air conditioned cool, sitting behind a metal desk, toying with a small revolver, and listening to some forgotten song from the sixties playing on a portable radio, was Stowe-Hartley. Still looking like a shark waiting for his lunch.

Unfortunately for me, it looked like I was the main course.

'We meet again, Mr Sharman,' he said. 'Sit.'

'Where is she?' I demanded.

'Don't worry. She's in good hands. At the moment she's receiving the hospitality of my home for the elderly. I must say she's a feisty old girl. But then, my staff are used to difficult customers.'

The old folks' home. Where this whole mess had started.

'I'm warning you,' I said.

'Stop it,' he said back. 'No one's interested in your empty threats. Let's have no more of them. Just sit down, you're giving me a crick in my neck.'

I had no choice but to do as I was told again, and I was

getting sick and tired of it. 'I have no idea where you sprung from,' he said when I was sitting. 'Or why you wanted to interfere in my affairs, but you managed to kill two of my best men yesterday, and walk away without a scratch.'

Not quite true, I thought, but I wasn't going to show him the scabs on my body from the broken glass in the SUV.

'But possibly even more intriguing,' he went on, 'is where you got the cash from the bank robbery that got you arrested. That money has not been touched since it was carefully hidden away until such time as it seemed safe to allow it back into circulation.'

'I got it from someone who wanted to piss on your parade. And if those were your best men, I feel sorry for you. I killed them both with a fucking biro. And as for those four downstairs, one is working on his tan drinking Special Brew, another one's giving your car a wash and brush up, the third one, when he's not giving my kidneys a seeing-to, is probably hiding away with a dirty magazine having a J Arthur. And as for the other, all he seems to be interested in is the size of his weapon. Pathetic!'

'Very clever. But you're here on my orders. Help me out, who is this mysterious person who has it in for me?'

'If I knew, I'd tell you. He's a right royal pain in my arse. He's something in law enforcement. Something secret.'

'Name?'

'He has several. Martineau when he was part of the Inland Revenue when he hired me to deliver those papers, Spencer, a Met detective inspector, and Smyth with a y, Special Branch.'

He looked genuinely surprised. 'Describe him.'

'Average height, average build, dark hair, dresses like a dummy in a Moss Bros window, and talks like an extra in an Agatha Christie film.'

He shook his head. 'That doesn't ring any bells with me. Martineau was the grandson of the old lady who died. But he's in the south of France, and nothing to do with the Revenue as far as I know. And he's in a wheelchair.'

'This bloke was definitely able-bodied. But he did have a stick. But more for show than to help him walk, I think. A sword stick probably.'

It felt as if the pair of us were just like old buddies catching up.

'He told me that you were some kind of criminal mastermind, and he wanted to put a spanner in your works. In other words, me.'

'It seems to have worked, up to a point,' he said. 'You've given me a lot of problems. The driver you killed last night was my best wheel man. He was about to do a very special job for me. According to the web,' he nodded in the direction of a computer on another desk, 'you were a police driver. If you want to see your friend again, you'll fill in.'

Fucking computers, fucking web. Does nobody have any secrets anymore? 'Are you having a laugh?' I asked, but I didn't think he was. 'I'm not even smiling,' he said.

'What about those four downstairs?' I said. 'And if this bloke who got me involved is anything to go by, plenty more?'

'They have their specialities, driving is not one of them. And with the hold I have over you, you're best fitted for the job. You have a lot to lose.'

He cocked the gun, and pointed it at my head. 'Make up your mind now, or I will kill you, then your friend also. Then I will find your other friends, your family, and kill them too. You have five seconds.'

It looked like I didn't have much choice. Not for now, but things would change. Or I would die in the attempt.

On the radio, a weatherman said that the heatwave was going to break tomorrow.

42

I Didn't Know The Gun Was Loaded
– The Cannons

'OK, OK, you win,' I said. 'Point that thing another way.'
He did as I asked.

'But I have to speak to her. Make sure she's alright.'

He pondered for a second, then reached for the phone on his desk and punched in numbers. 'Put her on,' he said, when the phone was answered. He paused, then put the receiver on the desk and nodded at me. I leant forward and the gun swung in my direction again. I picked the phone up and said, 'Madge...'

'Nick, are you alright?' said the familiar voice of my friend.

'More importantly, are you?' I said.

'I'll survive. I've been stationed in Taiwan.'

'I'm going to get you out.'

'I know, dear. Don't worry.'

'I didn't feed the cat.'

'She'll survive too. She's a huntress.'

Stowe-Hartley gestured impatiently, and I handed the phone back. He dropped it onto the receiver. 'Happy now?' he said.

'For now,' I replied. 'So what's the plan?' It was masterful in its simplicity.

In Waterloo, close to the station, was an anonymous building that housed a firm of jewellers. At approximately noon the next day, there was to be a delivery of uncut gems valued at somewhere between one and two million pounds sterling.

Deliveries of greater and lesser amounts had been made since time immemorial with no problems, and security was lax. Stowe-Hartley had been watching for months, gathering intel and now he was ready to strike.

One car, three men, two to do the job, one to remain with the motor, then a quick spin through London's lunch hour traffic to a second car waiting in a supermarket car park opposite the London Hospital, then on again to Mile End, dump the second motor, tube to Waterloo, then overland train to West Croydon where we'd be met by another gang member, and back by car to the warehouse with the swag.

Bob's your uncle, Lily's your aunt.

43

Jaguar And Thunderbird
– Chuck Berry

I spent an uncomfortable night on a cot in a locked room in the warehouse, with only mice for company. I could've done with Schmoo the cat to keep them at bay. I got woken up by the tattooed skinhead at seven am with cold McDonald's and warm coffee. 'They'll be here in a minute,' he said. I assumed he was speaking about my fellow armed bandits.

I stretched my legs outside in the car park. It looked like the weathermen on the radio the day before had been right. Black clouds loomed over the South Downs, there was the faintest rumble of thunder if you listened closely, the atmosphere was thick with moisture, and electricity fizzled in the air.

But it was still boiling hot, and most unpleasant, especially as I was still wearing yesterday's sweaty clothes.

I sluiced myself down in the dirty warehouse toilet and went to meet my partners in crime.

There were two of them. I never got names, just christened them Itchy and Twitchy. Itchy because he looked like he couldn't wait to use the sawn-off double barrelled shotgun he was carrying, virtually making love to it, and Twitchy because he did. Twitch, that is.

They were both wearing long macs, and we were each issued with balaclavas, that, rolled up, worked as watch caps.

Two cars were waiting, a big Jaguar, and an equally big Mercedes. Both automatic, both gassed up, both presumably stolen, presumably with false number plates. I didn't ask. The skinhead showed me how to pop the boot lid of the Jag from the driver's seat. 'Use it,' he said.

Before we left, with the skinhead driving the Mercedes, Itchy tapped me on the shoulder with his gun. 'Don't fuck up,' he said.

And that was almost all he said to me the entire morning. Twitchy on the other hand never shut up. Itchy must've been used to him. We mounted up and headed north like the wild bunch, all ready to kick arse, but actually more like the gang who couldn't shoot straight.

44

Crosstown Traffic
– The Jimmy Hendrix Experience

We went as a convoy through the rush hour traffic. Even though it was Saturday, and early, the traffic was still heavy and it took an age. How commuters did the journey daily I couldn't comprehend. It would have sent me postal. Itch and Twitch sat in the back. Twitch kept up a running commentary. I put on Capital Radio. It was as crappy as always, but it drowned out Twitch a bit. I hate DJs.

The skinhead had told me we'd do a dry run.

I followed the Merc round the back streets of Waterloo. Itchy leaned forward and whispered in my ear. 'Don't look now, but that's the place.'

Of course, I looked. It was a scruffy office building, dating I guessed from around WWI. It certainly didn't look like the sort of place to house millions in easily converted jewels. Maybe that was the idea.

We cruised down the street, left into the Cut, left at the lights again by the Ring public house, over Blackfriars Bridge, into the city and on towards the London Hospital.

Part of the journey covered what had been my beat when

I was a young police constable stationed at Kennington nick, the rest where I'd spent part of my misspent youth. I knew it like the back of my hand.

The area might've changed cosmetically, skyscrapers springing up everywhere, but the streets remained the same.

We stopped in the Sainsbury's car park opposite the hospital. It was pay and display, and we bought four hours for the Mercedes.

The skinhead handed me the keys to the Merc and went off without a word in the direction of the tube.

We went back to the Jag, and I did a reverse of the trip from Waterloo. Itch and Twitch sat in the back as usual. Itch was still playing with his gun like it might have an orgasm soon. Or him.

We spotted a cafe that was open, parked the Jag on a meter and went inside.

It was the usual deal. Full English all day breakfast, and roasts for lunch. We couldn't eat. Just ordered teas. Itch and Twitch sat at one table, I sat on my own, looking through the steamy window at an ever darkening sky. The tea was stewed, and I figured you could track my recent life through greasy spoons and dodgy boozers. One thing was that there was a vintage Rock-Ola jukebox buzzing in the corner. I checked it out, and for fifty pence got 'Crosstown Traffic' by Hendrix and 'Hard Work' by John Handy?

A few minutes after the music stopped, Itchy's phone rang. I guessed it was the inside man, and I was right. 'It's on the move,' he said to me. 'Let's go.'

So we went.

We went back to the car, and I drove slowly into the street housing the target building. There was a vacant parking meter maybe fifty yards opposite the front door. 'God's smiling,' said Twitch, as I drove in.

We sat for fifteen minutes, then a Ford Granada passed us

and pulled over to the far side, bang outside the door. Both front doors opened, and two blokes in dark suits exited. They walked to the back of the car on opposite sides, and the driver keyed the boot open.

Itchy and Twitchy were out of the Jag fast, just closing the near side door without catching the latch. 'Open the door for us when we're done,' said Twitchy, as he followed his mate outside. They walked fast across the road as the two from the Granada hitched two cases from its boot. Cases larger than a briefcase but smaller than suitcases. One of the blokes blimped the pair heading their way, but too late. Itchy cracked him one on his head and he went hard against the body of the car. Twitchy tugged his shooter from under his coat, said something I didn't catch, and the other bloke put his case on the ground.

Started the engine, popped the boot, leant back and pushed the near side door open as Itch and Twitch headed my way, each carrying a case. I pulled over beside them.

One case went into the boot, lid slammed shut, the other chucked in the back and they jammed themselves in beside it as I took off with a yelp from the tyres and the door closed hard.

'Gently,' Twitchy shouted, and I slowed, then turned into the Cut again and away. In my mirror, I saw the bloke who hadn't been smacked pull a mobile from his pocket and start tapping the keyboard.

45

Shotgun – Junior Walker And The Allstars

We had green lights all the way to Blackfriars Bridge. Twitchy was in seventh heaven, thanking God, Jesus, Allah and probably Buddha and Hari Krishna as well. I wasn't listening, just concentrating on getting the hell out of Dodge as the saying goes.

As usual Itchy said nothing.

As we hit the bridge, green turned to blue as a squad car peeled out from Upper Ground with a squeal of tyres and a blare from its klaxon. Blues and twos, just what we didn't want or need. But there it was, and catching up fast.

'Hold on tight,' I said out loud. 'This could get nasty,' and tromped the kick down on the Jag hard. The car reared back then took off like the trouper I knew its makers had made it.

The motor screamed, and the river was just a silver streak as we came off the bridge, over the centre barrier with an expensive sounding bang from the undercarriage, my heart in my mouth as I poured on more acceleration and shot through the traffic opposite heading for the bridge going south. Chaos ensued, with horns blaring at us, cars bucking and sliding to avoid a collision, and pedestrians flying in all directions as we entered Queen Victoria Street more by luck than judgement, and straight up towards Mansion House, with the cops still on our tail. Then, like a bloody leviathan, a two storey block of flats on a dozen fat tyres, a bloody tourist bus, pulled out of its parking bay straight ahead. I dragged the wheel to the right and swung the Jag into the oncoming traffic. More horns, more drivers panicking at the sight of the Jag's big chrome grille and headlights in full beam heading towards them. Inside the car Twitchy was bleating like a nanny goat and even Itchy's face was pale when I clocked him in the inside mirror.

And still the cop car kept coming.

I slammed hard left and back into our lane leaving the bus stuck at an angle, and did a left at Mansion House tube, the police car coming up on my back bumper, so there was only one thing to do. So I did it. A handbrake turn in an automatic is harder than with a stick shift, but I'd been taught by experts. Crash the gear lever down to ONE, spin the steering wheel hard clockwise, whack on the handbrake, back into DRIVE, foot like a club on the accelerator for the kick down again and let the laws of physics do the rest. Or hope they will. And they did. The big old beauty spun round like a top, black smoke pouring off the back tyres and the last I saw of that particular squad car was two open mouthed old Bill bouncing their vehicle up on the pavement to avoid a head on, hitting the wall of an old warehouse in a shower of sparks and pieces of cop car flying left, right and centre. Next left, left again into a narrow alley with only a green garbage bin blocking the way. I kept going hard. If it was plastic – OK. If it was metal, then Christ knows what. Luckily it was the former which exploded like a bomb, and plastic and trash that covered the Jag as I hit it hard. The windscreen was covered in greasy shit and I was glad I'd learned which switch was which back at the warehouse. Then I turned left again, and right into another alleyway, and braked to a halt between a couple of delivery vans.

The Jag was a disgrace, with all kinds of crap sticking to the bodywork, and the motor was running rough after the treatment I'd given it, and the temperature gauge was creeping up towards the red. That had been really no way to treat the beautiful lady who had got us out of the hands of the local guardians of law and order.

'What've you stopped for?' Demanded Itchy. No 'well done' for the superb getaway, but then, what did I expect? He stuck the muzzle of his shotgun into the back of my neck as he spoke. Fat chance he was going to blow my head off under the circumstances, so I just let it go. We were all feeling the stress. No point in making things worse. With a bit of luck this would all be over soon, and we could all get on with our lives.

'Just laying low for a minute. Don't fret,' I said. Up ahead I'd seen another flash of blue light, but it moved off and all seemed serene. I gently took off again, clocked the next street right and left, and once again by luck, there we were in Old Street, bang up close to Aldgate and Whitechapel Road, exactly where we needed to be, and with not a copper in sight.

'Trust me, boys, 'I said. 'All is well.'

Just a slow run past the London Hospital on the right and the street market on the left, then there was Sainsbury's on the corner of Cambridge Heath Road. The sky was blacker than ever as we want into the supermarket car park. We all got out, I left the keys in the car as ordered, and we headed towards the Mercedes and freedom, Itch and Twitch carrying a case of tom each. Trouble is, something was wrong. It was like the earth had stopped spinning. It was quiet, too quiet. Just like they used to say in old western movies. No pedestrians on what would normally be a busy Saturday shopping hour, or a lunchtime rush for drinks and sandwiches. Itchy noticed too, and pulled his shooter from under his coat as armed coppers appeared as if by magic from behind parked cars and vans, and from the entrance to the store, machine guns at the ready, and red dots appeared on all three of us big bad robbers' clothes.

'Armed police,' came the cry from several mouths. 'Drop you weapons.'

Itchy lifted his shotgun, I yelled, 'no', and dropping the car keys from my hand hit the ground face down, arms spread. I knew the drill. I shut my eyes, expecting to hear the sound of shots fired, but instead both Itchy and Twitchy dropped their weapons and the cases they were carrying, and joined me on the floor.

And then the heavens opened.

46

Rain
– The Beatles

First of all, it was huge warm drops that made the off-white concrete where we stood dark, then sheets of water that turned cold, then freezing. We were all soaked in seconds. Police and thieves all equal under God's sky.

Drains filled and overflowed fast, until the car park was like a lake, and I had to turn my face sideways to avoid being drowned. Twitchy wasn't so lucky. He was yapping so much, the copper next to him put his boot on his neck and forced his face into the flood. He came up coughing and retching, but at least he shut up. Officers appeared behind us, we were dragged to our feet, cuffed and read the old, old story of what we could and couldn't do, and what we had been arrested for, then each of us was put in the back of different unmarked cars, which sped off in different directions, with the jewel cases stuck in the back of a van. I never saw either of them again. Someone had grassed us up. I wondered who.

I ended up in Mile End nick.

I started to say something to the officer next to me en route but was told to shut up and wait to be questioned.

The temperature had dropped like a rock down a coal mine, and I was shaking like a shitting dog in my wet clothes by the time we arrived at the station. The desk sergeant at the nick was in a bit of a flap when we arrived. 'He'll have to share,' he told my copper. 'Bloody place is flooded downstairs. Sodding weather. Always a famine or a feast.'

At least I was given some dry clothes, a sweat shirt and pants from the homeless and nutters' box. Musty, but warm. When I was changing, the sergeant noticed the plasters on my legs. 'Cut yourself shaving?' he asked.

'Something like that,' I replied.

Then, after I'd surrendered all my belongings for the umpteenth time recently, I was escorted to a cell which already had one customer.

He was in his sixties, with long grey dreadlocks surrounding a saucer-sized bald spot. In my opinion, dreads on white folks don't work. Some say it's stealing black culture. I couldn't care less about that, considering white culture in this country seems to me to be six penn'oth of chips and Gerry and the fucking Pacemakers. He was wearing a cowboy shirt, a leather waistcoat, blue jeans faded to white and leopard skin cowboy boots held together by gaffer tape. On the bed next to him was a straw cowboy hat. Fucking Tom Mix, I thought. 'Hey, man,' he said, when the door was closed behind me. 'Got any straights?'

'Sorry, mate,' I said. 'They cleaned me out.'

'Me too. Nothing else I suppose?'

'Not a sausage.' I took a seat next to him on the thin mattress, covered in blue plastic to let the piss roll off, on the hard bed attached to one wall. I took a look round. I might have to get used to places like that. Miserable as shit, with one grubby commode in the corner.

'Bastards,' he went on, as if I hadn't spoken. 'They took all my rings, my turquoise, and my axe.' I think he meant his guitar.

'It's a bad deal,' I said.

'And the weather. Rain. Had to happen. It's Glastonbury next week. You going?'

'Mate, I don't think I'll be going anywhere for a long time.'

He looked interested. 'What did you do?'

'Nothing. But they've got me for armed robbery and I'm out on bail for a bank job.'

His eyes widened. 'Heavy duty.'

'You can say that again. You?'

'Begging, vagrancy. Just because I don't have a regular crash.'

'That's tough.'

'Yeah, man. When I think of the places I've lived. Trouble is I've always been one for the ladies. Cost me fortunes. I used to be famous... for a while, anyway.'

'Famous?'

'Yeah. I was lead guitar in the Skittles. Three top tens in 1966. *Top of the Pops. Ready, Steady, Go.* The works.'

'Christ,' I said. 'I remember them. I saw you on *Top of the Pops* one week.'

'You must've been in short trousers.'

'Not really. I'm older than I look.'

'Me, too.' And he laughed. 'We recorded it at Abbey Road. The Beatles were in studio two recording *Revolver*. We were in some pokey little studio down the corridor. One night the door opens and there's George Harrison. He says that he's broken an e string, and his man Mal has gone off with the others. Have I got one he could borrow? He's a fucking Beatle, man. Says he'd buy one off me, but he doesn't carry cash. I give him the string, and he says he'll get me one back, but never does. That's life, eh? When you don't need anything, people queue up to give you stuff. If you're broke, you can go get stuffed. Life, man.'

'It's a bitch,' I agreed.

'You know, it used to be easy. Grow your hair, buy a tight black suit, a skinny tie, a pair of Anello Cuban heeled boots, and a red Fender. Take some speed, drink a lot of booze, get the ladies. Then, grow your hair longer, wear a flowery shirt and flared pants and furry moccasins. Take different drugs, drink loads of booze and get the ladies. Someone once said that if you write a hit song it'll earn you money for years, and it don't talk back. I wrote hits. Lots. And boy did I get ripped off. And what hurts most it was by people I counted as my friends. Crap. The more they said they loved me, the more money they stole. Not just money, mind. My talent. That's what really hurts. I just rolled another joint and signed any bit of paper they put in front of me. When I asked for my dough, all I got was a solicitor's letter. It was easier to let the fuckers win. See, whatever money they got off me, whatever lies they told, deep down inside they knew they were traitors, robbers, failures. They knew, I knew, and I knew they knew.'

'Did that make you feel better?'

He shrugged. 'Not really. But I don't sign anything any more.'

'I thought it was all peace and love in those days,' I said.

He snorted. 'Peace and love. What a bunch of crap. Same old, same old. Free love still got you the clap. Thank Christ for penicillin.'

'And you're telling me this, why?' I asked.

'Sorry if I talk too much. But this is like karma. You and me. Normally, we'd never meet. Me a beggar, you a bank robber…'

'Actually no,' I interrupted, but what was the point? 'Go on then,' I said.

'We changed the band's name to the Purple Frenzies. More hits. More shit. *Top of the Pops. Late Night Line-Up.* The works. All over again.'

'I remember them too.'

'A fan.' I thought this geezer had definitely taken too many drugs. He was talking to me like we'd known each other for years. But then, in another karmic lifetime, maybe we had. And it was better than dwelling on my own predicament.

'And do you know how much I made out of all the hits? Hits I wrote, or part wrote?'

I shook my head.

'Fuck all, mate. Alright, I had clothes and posh grub. Flats and cars. None of them my own, and we paid top dollar for everything. We got ripped left, right and centre. All we made was playing live, and even then the managers took half. Except when we played the Kray Twins' club. Afterwards, we got asked to the office and the pair of them are sitting there with four stacks of cash on the desk. Our manager expects to get the dough, but one of the Twins says, no, they played, they get the money, and he lobs us two hundred and fifty notes each. Christ, we were rich. The manager asked for it back, but we told him to sod off. And he did. Happy days.

He shut up then, but just for a minute. Eventually, he asked, 'Do you remember Woodstock?'

'I saw the film on TV.'

He huffed like I'd sworn in church. 'We went there. The band and me. We were touring. We hired a fucking Cadillac. Traffic jams so long it overheated. We dumped it and started hitching. We didn't play. Just went for the crack. Wasn't even in Woodstock. Did you know that?'

I shook my head.

'We didn't. We got run out of town. The festival was forty miles down the road. Bad road. Ended up sitting in shit for two days in last week's underwear.'

'I remember the song,' I ventured.

'Fucking crap. Stardust, golden. The only golden thing I saw was liquid shit. And bad acid. Bastards thought it was funny to spike you. Didn't dare eat or drink anything that wasn't sealed up tight. You ever taken acid?'

'A few times. Didn't like it. Couldn't control it.'

'A control freak.'

'If you like.'

'Wish I was. Wouldn't've been married three times. You married?'

'Only once. Was. Not any more.'

'Take my advice. Leave it at that. My first wife, lovely girl. We were only kids. She wouldn't sleep with me without a ring. So we got wed. Lasted eighteen months until I found someone who would only sleep with me without a ring.' I nodded.

'Then wife number two. What a smasher. Bought her the world. Nothing was too good for her. She took the lot. Left with the kid and my Roller. Sold the house, all my records, most of my clothes, my jukebox, all I had was what I had on my back and a tax demand.'

'Any more?' I asked. Despite myself, I was getting interested. This poor fucker had had a worse time than me.

'Just one more,' he said. 'Picked her up in a bar room in Memphis. Took me to Graceland. We broke in, got arrested, and spent the night in jail. It was love at first arraignment, as they say over there.'

'And?'

'I lost her to transcendental meditation and Pringles. She got as big as a house. Never marry a musician.'

'Or a copper.'

'No. You?'

'Yes me.'

'Copper and gangsta. Blood run with de hare and de hounds.' He did a pretty decent patois. Normally white talking black is just annoying. 'I was in a Bob Marley and The Wailers tribute band,' he added.

Fair enough. Hence the dreads and the accent, I imagined. I didn't ask him if he blacked up. I thought I might be rude.

'Now where was I?' he asked.

'Woodstock. The song.'

'Shit. Joni fucking Mitchell. What did she know? She was in a fucking helicopter. Cosying up to Graham fucking Nash. Lucky bugger.'

'Happy days,' I said.

'For some. Fucking shit for the rest of us. As always.' I couldn't argue with that.

Just then the cell door opened with a bang and the sergeant appeared.

'Come on Sharman,' he said to me. 'You're wanted.'

'What about me?' said the old hippy.

'Wait your turn.'

'How about something to eat?'

'The canteen's closed. Flooding. I'll send out for something.'

'I'm vegan.'

'You would be. Now, come on Sharman. Shake a leg.'

Leg dutifully shaken.

47

Theme from Special Branch
– Norman Kay

I was left in another room with nothing but a metal table and four metal chairs, all bolted to the floor as furniture. There was a tiny window, less than a foot square, sunken into the pale green painted brickwork on one wall, complete with spider, a web and several flies in a worse position than me. On the table was a recorder; in one corner, high up, was a CCTV camera. Its little light, like the flies, was dead.

I sat in the chill that pervaded the room and wondered when next I would see freedom.

After ten minutes, the door opened, and, as I might have guessed, my man Smyth swept in, wearing a Burberry raincoat, and carrying a Burberry golfing umbrella.

'I might have guessed,' I said.

'Sharman. I'm delighted to see you.'

'I wish I could say the same.'

'Come, come, there's no need to be like that,' he said, taking off his mac and folding it neatly over the back of one chair opposite me, and sitting on the other, carefully setting the creases in his trousers, so as not to bag the knees. Today, his suit was navy blue with a thick pinstripe, teamed with a pink, pin-through collar shirt, and a flowery tie. Natty fucking dread.

'I think there is,' I replied, 'and I see you came dressed for the weather.' I nodded at his macintosh.

He looked at my sad outfit, and said, 'and you obviously didn't.'

'*Touché.*'

He grinned a big grin. 'I was in the area, picking up the loot you hijacked, when I heard you were here, and couldn't go without saying hello.'

'Hello,' I said.

'You never called me. I did leave you a new telephone, after all.'

'I lost it. I seem to be in the habit of doing that lately. Well, not so much losing them as having them taken away from me by various parties of one side of the law or the other.'

'I can understand you being a bit peevish, but I did warn you,' he said.

'You did, when you were Special Branch. Who are you today?'

'National Security. Covers a multitude of sins. Literally.'

'And your name?'

'It's of no matter. I won't be using it again.'

'And I can do for you, what?'

'That's the spirit, old chap. You'll find out. Now I must run.'

He stood, collected his coat and umbrella, and banged on the metal door of the room.

It was answered post haste, and he left with only a cheerful 'TTFN' and a hint of sandalwood aftershave to show he had ever been there.

48

Have A Whiff On Me
– Lead Belly

I got put back in the cell. The old hippy was still there, looking glum. In his hand, he was holding one of those triangular cardboard sandwich packs. 'He got me a cheese sandwich,' he moaned. 'I told him I was vegan. He didn't know the difference between vegan and vegetarian, want it?'

I hadn't eaten since my McDonald's breakfast. 'Sure,' I said. As usual, it took a fight to open the pack, but eventually I got it open and dived in. Cheese, pickle, white bread. What was not to love?

'So, how did it go?' he asked.

'Do you know?' I replied. 'I really don't know.'

'Could be worse then,' he said.

'Hardly.'

'You need cheering up,' he said. 'Fancy a taste?'

'Of?'

He winked and pulled off his right boot. His sock was more hole than sock, but he didn't smell bad. He pulled and twisted the high heel, and it swung round, and it was hollow inside. He pulled out a silver paper wrap, and said, 'It was this or a night's lodging. Looks like I'm in for the night anyway. So I made the right choice.'

He carefully opened the wrap to show white powder with a few lumps. He held the paper in his left hand, and his right hand's fingernails were hard and yellow, the little fingernail being at least an inch long. He dug it into the powder and stuck it up, first my right, then my left nostril. I'll admit it, I inhaled.

It hit the spot too. 'Thanks,' I said.

'A pleasure.'

'Listen,' he said, after he'd taken a nose full and returned the wrap to his boot heel, and his boot to his foot. 'I like you. Give me a call and we'll go for a drink.' He pulled a scrap of paper and a nub of pencil from his shirt pocket. 'Not very good at the searching here.' Scribbled down a number and handed it to me.

'Well, I don't think I'm going to be free for a drink for a long time,' I said. 'But thanks.' A little kindness goes a long way.

Just then, the cell door opened again, and the sergeant said, 'OK, you're free to go.'

The hippy got up from the bed. 'Not you, you,' said the copper, chucking me a plastic sack full of my still damp clothes.

'Are you sure?'

'That's what it says here,' he said, holding up a clipboard. 'You must have friends in high places. Now get dressed.'

'See, mate,' said the hippy. 'Just to show you never can tell.'

I said nothing, just did as I was told, struggled into my jeans, shirt and leather jacket, then bade my cell mate farewell, and lots of luck, and followed the sergeant through to the front office, where I signed for my belongings. When I'd arrived, I only had my watch, wallet, cigarettes and Zippo. The bag I was holding felt like there was more. It had to be Smyth, and that probably meant more trouble. But at least I wasn't banged up. Outside in the rain, I sheltered in the doorway and opened the bag I'd been given. Inside were my belongings plus a heavy envelope with SHARMAN printed on the front. Inside was a hundred pounds in tenners, a Range Rover key fob with two keys attached, an NCP parking ticket, with a parking bay number and a satnav code. I went back into the station. 'Is there an NCP close?' I asked.

'Christ,' said the sergeant. 'Second left past the tube. Now get out of here before I change my mind.'

I thanked him and got out.

49

Kevlar
– BTNG

I found the car park and the bay up close to the top floor. Neatly parked was a dark green Range Rover Vogue, this year's model with dark tints all round. Nice motor. But not as nice as me, as the saying goes. Whatever powder the hippy had given me was racing my engine. I looked at my hands and my fingers shook. Not too much, just enough to keep me sharp. I thumbed the key fob and the hazard lights blinked and all four door locks clicked open. I got behind the wheel, and found another envelope taped to the dash. Once again SHARMAN was printed on the front. I opened it and there was a piece of paper inside handwritten – 'under driver's seat'.

I felt under and found a shopping bag. Inside was a Browning nine millimetre pistol, just like the one I'd left at Madge's. I dropped out the clip. It was fully loaded with brass. I slapped it back, popped a round into the pipe, set the safety, and stuck it in the passenger side glove compartment. In the passenger well was a vest. Kevlar. With LAPD stencilled on the back. Smyth sure did get around. I stripped down to skin and pulled it on, fastened it, and put on my top again. Not comfortable, but comforting.

I threw my jacket into the truck, slid into the driver's seat, switched on the engine which started with an expensive growl, put the code into the satnav and headed down to the street. I paid the extortionate fee out of the ton Smyth had left me and headed south. I was still cold, and my clothes sticky, so I banged the heat on high to dry them. My head was buzzing, and I just had to laugh at the situation I'd let myself be put in. I caught my reflection in the mirror. I looked like hell with eyes that almost sparked red. I looked away. The screen in the dash led me to leafy Wimbledon. That's how the TV news always describes such a place when some horror has ruined the neighbourhood. Who knew what horror today would bring?

Just opposite the common, set well back from the road, was a double-fronted Victorian pile that would easily fetch a seven figure sum at auction. In front was a gravel-covered driveway, complete with three or four upmarket automobiles, including the white Bentley that had been parked at the Croydon warehouse, so I guessed Stowe-Hartley was *in situ*. Over the main gate was a sign that read, 'Marchbank Nursing Home'. This must be the place.

I dumped the Range Rover on the pavement, stuck the Browning in my waistband, and marched up to the front door like I owned the place.

The front door was up three steps and between two columns. It was open. I pushed through and into a huge hall facing a wide, carpeted staircase. On the right was a desk containing a phone and computer. Behind it was an attractive blonde woman dressed in nurse's whites.

I walked up to her. She smiled. I smiled back. 'Is Mister Stowe-Hartley available?' I asked.

'Do you have an appointment?'

'No.'

'I'm sorry, he only sees visitors by appointment. He's a very busy man.'

'Me, too. I'm sure he'll see me if you tell him I'm here. Sharman is the name.'

'I'll remember that. Maybe if you tell me what it's concerning, I'll tell him, and if you leave a number, I'll make an appointment.' I was getting fed up now, it had been a rough week, and my damp denims were chafing.

I pulled back the skirt of my leather jacket and showed her the butt of my pistol. 'This is what it's concerning,' I said.

Her eyes widened and she pulled back away from me and screamed 'Neville' at the top of her voice.

From the back of the house, appeared the tattooed skinhead who had been at the warehouse. I pulled out the Browning and pointed it at his head. 'Down now,' I ordered. 'Neville.'

He skidded to a halt and dropped to his knees as nursey dived across her desk, fingernails ready to rip my face off. I sidestepped and clouted her with the gun. Down she went like a chopped tree, and Neville pulled himself upright only to get an upswung firearm in the face. He joined the nurse on the Persian carpet.

They were both out, but not for long, so I ripped the phone out of the wall and tied them together with the cord. It wouldn't hold them for long, but I didn't need long to do what I was going to do.

I frisked Neville quickly. He was unarmed except for a heavy duty, pearl handled flicknife which I stuck in my pocket. You never know when you'll need one. During all this nothing stirred in the house. They built these places with thick walls, the Victorians. I left the sleeping beauties and headed up the staircase, two at a time.

50

I Figli Morti from the original soundtrack of
*A Fistful of Dynamite/Duck You Sucker/
Once Upon A Time In The Revolution/Gui' La Testa*
– Ennio Morricone

At the top of the stairs, two hallways dog-legged towards the back of the property. I peered round one corner. Nothing but carpet and closed doors. I peered round the other. Bingo! A dozen yards away was a sofa next to another closed door. Perched on the seat was heavy number three from the warehouse, the one who'd given me the rabbit punches, reading the *New Statesman*. Wonders would never cease.

I tiptoed round the corner, the carpet deadening my approach. Then he looked up and saw me. I put my finger to my lips and whispered, 'Not too many long words for you,' then whacked him a good one on his nut, and he joined the pair downstairs in the land of nod.

I frisked him too, and came up with another Browning niner. I was getting quite a collection. I stuck it in my waistband at the back.

I left him lying on the seat and tried the handle of the door next to him. Locked. I stepped back, and with all the frustrations of the past week, I slammed my boot heel into the door just by the lock.

The Victorians may have built doors thick too, but nothing was going to stop me.

The door burst open and hit the wall beside it with a bang like the world ending and I found Stowe-Hartley on his knees in front of an open safe. Empty.

'Get up off your fucking knees, man,' I ordered.

'What are you doing here? ' he said. 'You're supposed to be in jail.'

'The original bad penny. You see, someone up there likes me.' I looked in the safe. 'What happened there? Looks like you've been cleared out.'

He smiled. 'Bad things happen.'

'Get up,' I said again. This time he did as he was told. 'You armed?' I asked him.

He shook his head.

I screwed the barrel of my gun into his forehead, and quickly frisked him. All I found was his phone. 'I'll have this,' I said, putting it into my pocket with the flick knife. Never know when it would come in handy too. Besides, I kept losing mine. 'Now where is she?' I demanded.

'Upstairs.'

'If you've hurt her…' I didn't finish the sentence.

'She's not been hurt,' he said. 'She's just a little sleepy.'

I lost it then for a second, and smacked him round the head with the gun in my hand. He staggered a bit, then recovered. Tough guy. 'You'll be a little bit sleepy if I smack you again,' I said. 'Now lead the way, and don't mess me about. It's been a very trying week, and I can feel a headache coming on.' We went out of his office and past the sofa. I gave heavy number three another clout just to keep him out of the game. I was past caring if he already had a concussion.

We went down the hall then up more stairs to a hallway without carpet. This was where the lucky inmates were kept. It smelled like a hospital.

Stowe-Hartley led me to a large room kitted out like a hospital with a pair of windows looking out over the common. Inside was Madge in a bed, a bag hooked up to a cannula in the back of her hand. A nurse was sitting in a chair next to her bed. More of a jailer I guessed. Madge was awake but drowsy.

'Hey, Madge,' I said. 'Sleeping on the job?'

'Nick. I knew you'd come.'

'Count on it.' I shut the door, then to the nurse. 'Get that bloody thing out of her arm.'

She looked at Stowe-Hartley, then to the gun in my hand, and did as she was told.

'So where's the cash?' I said to my host.

'I don't have it.'

'Then who does?'

'The boss.'

'You're the boss.' He shook his head.

'Then who is?' I demanded.

He looked through the window. 'There,' he said.

I looked down. Standing at the back of a late model Volvo estate, grey in colour, the sort of car that looks docile until you whack down the accelerator, was, yeah, you guessed it, Smyth. He felt my eyes on him as he slammed the tailgate and looked up, then smiled and waved. No Bertie Wooster now, instead he was wearing a hoodie and jeans, and he was in the driver's seat and away with a spray of stones from the rear wheels so fast I didn't even have time to get his plate number.

'What the fuck?' I said to Stowe-Hartley. I described him.

'You didn't say he was American.'

'American! What the fuck are you talking about?'

'He had an American accent. Latin-American to be precise. Said he came from Baltimore.'

'Where the lady comes from. And I could say I came from Timbuktu. What was his name?'

'Sonajero. That's all I know.'

'Sonajero is squeaker in Spanish,' said Madge, from her bed.

'Christ,' I said. 'He's taken us all for mugs. Again.'

And that was when it went all to hell. The door suddenly burst open from a kick, and the last of the mob I'd met in Croydon came barrelling through with a pistol in each hand, and his fingers tight on the triggers. As I remember, the first bullet went through the window next to me and off onto the common. Hope it landed safely with no loss of life. The next one parted my hair, the third took a chunk out of my left arm, and after a second it hurt like hell. I grabbed Stowe-Hartley round the neck and dragged him in front of me. Two bullets hit his chest and slammed through into my vest. One broke a rib. Both nearly knocked me sparko. That's when I remembered to shoot back. My first bullet went straight through the open door and smashed a framed photo of Stowe-Hartley shaking hands with Jimmy Savile at some function; the second went through the shooter's neck in a cloud of blood spray. The third must have hit him in the heart, because he collapsed like a marionette with its strings cut. He hit the floor hard, the two guns flying across the floor.

I leant back against the wall, still winded.

Then Madge shouts 'No' and I see this other nurse has hauled a little pocket pistol from her uniform, and I'm looking straight down its black barrel, and at her finger whitening on the trigger. I couldn't hold Stowe-Hartley's body in front of me, as he was no lightweight and he gradually slid down and onto the carpet. Then Madge, doped or not, dives across to the nurse, bites hard on her gun arm, pushes her hand down just as she fires, so the bullet goes into the air mattress that deflates with a loud hiss. Not that I could hear much after all the explosions in a confined space, and the air was full of smoke and the stink of body fluids and gunpowder.

I look down and there's blood all over my front and my left sleeve. I look like I've just come out of the day shift at a slaughter house. 'It's not as bad as it looks,' I said to Madge, who by then had the nurse in a half nelson, and was spitting blood herself. Then I glanced out of the window. On the pavement was a small crowd looking up at me, a couple of them on phones, and in the distance I could hear sirens. More than one. The gunfire must have made the natives restless enough to call the cops. Personally, with all the lead flying about, I'd've taken cover somewhere out of range.

I slumped back, suddenly tired, and I pulled Stowe-Hartley's phone from my pocket and dialled Robber's number from memory. He answered straightaway, and I said, 'Jack, I need immediate assistance here.'

51

I'm Going To Be A Country Girl Again
– Buffy St Marie

Time passed, and soon that short hot summer was just a memory. I spent some time in hospital as my arm wasn't in any mood to heal quickly. Getting old, see. John Coffey fixed me up with a private room in a private hospital. Soft sheets and fine dining, all on his tab. You see I had done some other work for him, since that first job, and we'd become pretty matey. I even got served jerk chicken at his place made by his own fair hands.

But when I did come out, Madge and Judith organised a belated birthday party. Autumn was in the air, but still they did a barbecue in Madge's back garden. Judith came in full Western kit. She bought me a load of DVDs of old British Swinging London films. Why? I have no idea. But it passed the time as the year dragged itself to its end. Madge bought me a hamper from that deli I told you about. Fridge fillers for the one-armed man. Well appreciated.

I still had a sling on, and favoured double denim that day. A difficult look to get right. Madge and Judith assured me I had it down. Maybe just for my ego, though.

John and his missus bought me a vintage Levi checked cowboy shirt. Judith found it on eBay, and he coughed up. He also bought a birthday cake in a cooler. Chocolate. My favourite.

Owlsley gave me a flower. Now I forgot to tell you about Owlsley. In hospital, I thought a lot about the old musician who shared his poke with me in the pokey. I found the scrappy piece of paper that he'd given me, and I called from my bed.

'Owlsley,' he said when he answered, because it was he. He later told me it was his name when he was in a folk-rock band around 1965. 'Like Donovan,' he told me later. 'Only not so airy-fairy.'

'Hello,' I said. 'We met in Mile End nick.'

'Christ,' he bellowed. 'Nick Sharman. I've been reading about you. Quite the hero. Where are you?'

I told him what hospital, and the next day he turned up, guitar in hand, and gave an impromptu concert in the day room. Went down well.

When he'd had to get past the copper sitting in the corridor, he said, 'Is he to keep you in, or someone out?'

'You tell me.'

Of course, he met Madge, and they hit it off big time. I don't mean romantically, though who knows? I wouldn't dream of asking. But within a couple of weeks, he'd moved into her guest suite.

'It's not as if my kids come visiting,' she said. 'And there's plenty of room even if they do.'

He does the garden, sous chefs for Madge, cleans the windows and grooms the cat too, for all I know. I don't know how permanent an arrangement it's going to be, but he visited one of his ex-wives and rescued what was left of his wardrobe. So he can turn up as a mod, a hippy, a soul boy, a glam rocker, a punk rocker, a new romantic, a rude boy, or a Rasta. Or any mixture of the above.

What I do know is that it all seems to be copacetic. Home sweet home. Li turned up with a tureen of hot and sour as his contribution. Vegan too just for Owlsley.

Even Robber showed his face. He brought nothing, of course, but his precious Purple Frenzy LP on vinyl. Turns out he was a huge progressive rock fan, and when he'd found out about Owlsley in his psychedelic pomp, he was like a big kid wanting his record signed. Who knew about his hobby? Mind you, he does live with his sister, which might explain things. He even pretended not to notice the two thriving marijuana plants Owlsley was growing in one of those miniature greenhouses out behind the garden shed.

The barbie was a success; steaks and corn on the cob, mashed potato, onion rings, and hot bananas burnt black on the outside. Plenty of booze, and music from Madge's old radiogram. Elvis and Cliff. Ricky Nelson and Buddy Holly. Ray Charles' Modern Sounds in Country and Western.

As I was changing a record, Madge cornered me. 'How's it going, Nick?'

'Could be better.'

'Your arm hurting?'

'Not that. Just what happened.'

'It wasn't your fault, Nick.'

'People died.'

'Not your fault. You should be glad we survived. You saved me. Think about it. And God knows how many old folk you saved from that man. Forgive yourself, Nick.'

'Maybe.'

'Have you forgiven Smyth or whoever he really was?'

'Nothing to forgive,' I said. 'I could have blown the whistle on him any time, but I was quite enjoying it. I liked the bloke. A real chancer. Anyway, who was going to believe me, a rogue ex-copper who walks on the dirty side of the street? Anyway, it was too damn hot.'

'Yes it was, and think about what I said.' So I did, and I still am.

Later, a murmuration of starlings started throwing shapes over the garden.

'They're early,' said Madge.

'Probably means a hard winter,' said Owlsley. And it was but that's altogether a different story.

When the light went, and a chilly breeze sprang up, we moved inside, lit a fire, and Owlsley fetched his acoustic and sang a few old songs. He dedicated one of my favourite Buffy St Marie tunes especially to Judith. He just changed the 'I' to a 'She'.

The cat kept guard and we all partied like it was 1959 until the wee small hours.

EPILOGUE

The Letter
– The Box Tops

So that, my friends, is all she wrote. Or he, or us, or me.

Smyth, or whatever his real name was, got away scot free. I didn't care. No matter what shit he'd got me into. No matter that he'd wound me up like a clockwork kipper, and let me go, I'd actually become quite fond of him.

As a footnote, the police van carrying the gems we'd hijacked was hijacked itself, and the lone driver was handcuffed to the steering wheel with his own bracelets. Nothing was ever recovered.

Smyth had said he was going to collect the loot.

Whoever, or whatever he was, he was something important in the Establishment. National Security, MI5, MI6, Special Branch, the Met. None of them liked one of their top men going rogue. Off the reservation. So they gathered their skirts together and looked for the easiest way out with no scandal.

Stowe-Hartley died as a result of his wounds. What remained of his henchmen and women were rounded up and are now serving various sentences for various crimes. Madge, of course, stepped up for me. She still had friends in high places from her time in Naval Intelligence, and used them.

Me? I was given a Section 71, complete immunity on all charges, and for the second time in my life signed the Official Secrets Act. Then everything was neatly brushed under the carpet.

I got my car, my phone and my reputation back, for what the latter was worth. End of story.

Well, not quite.

Three months after that short, hot summer, I received a letter at home.

The envelope and sheet of paper inside were thick vellum, the postmark was London, but somehow it seemed to have a more international feel. I think it had been posted by a third party. It smelt of sun and suntan oil on the chilly autumn morning it was delivered. Something Spanish maybe. Or Latin American. The envelope even had a grain of sand or two at the bottom. Of course, knowing Smyth, it might have been a double bluff, and he was living it large in the Elephant and Castle.

It read:

My dear Nicholas,

I hope I may call you that. Firstly, let me apologise for the inconvenience I caused you last summer. It was simply when I looked for a loose cannon, your name just kept appearing. I'm afraid you only have yourself to blame.

Thankfully, from what little I have been able to glean from the media, you seem to have managed to have been exonerated, and remain free as a bird. Well done! I hope your wounds have healed. I take full responsibility for them.

As for my reasons for the whole debacle:

Firstly, I needed to free myself from Stowe-Hartley and co. Although I painted him as a criminal genius, in fact he was an idiot who surrounded himself with other idiots, and, incidentally, I have rather expensive tastes (you would be amazed how much a first edition Agatha Christie complete with dust jacket costs. But enough of that.) and was growing tired of sharing.

And secondly, my lords and masters in my day job were beginning to smell a rat. Nuff said.

So there you have it. I wanted to let you know there was nothing personal. My love to Blighty,

Your friend, Guess who?

And that really was the end.

I folded the letter neatly and put it inside a mint copy of Edgar Wallace's novel *The Squeaker* that I'd bought on Charing Cross Road, complete with dust jacket. It cost me a few bob, I'll tell you. But worth every penny. And yes, with Madge's help, I knew exactly how much a first edition Christie was worth.

BECAUSE THE NIGHT

In my business sometimes you need an oppo. An op-pro if you like. A professional. A wingman. Roy Caton was my go-to of choice. Me, his. He was ex-job like me. Disgraced ex-job like me as it happens. Scratching a living as a private investigator. Just like me. But that wasn't all. Roy had one specific talent. Although he was six foot four, sixteen stone, and dressed like a dandy, he could quite literally vanish at will. Dress him in nothing but one of his garish kaleidoscope patterned ties, and stand him in the middle of Oxford Street at rush hour and no one would notice. I asked him once how he did it. Turned out before joining the police he had been in the army. A sniper. He'd sometimes have to lie for days on end, wearing a nappy under his camouflage, being nibbled on by insects and small animals without moving a muscle. Surviving on dried food and an occasional sip of stale water. 'You become one with the background,' he explained. 'Simple really.'

So that was it. We'd met when I was watching a bloke who cheated older women out of money and jewels. I'd been hired by this rich old lady's grown-up children who didn't fancy seeing their inheritances going down the pan. The geezer was living on and off with the woman, who believed in the off times he was busy earning a living as a salesman for an unnamed publishing company. The suspicion was that he was in fact servicing one or more equally rich, equally aged women for all he could grab. Hence surveillance. Hence I needed another pair of eyes. My old mate Jack Robber tossed me Roy's name, we met, hit it off over a Ruby and several bottles of Cobra beer, and Bob's your uncle, Lily's your aunt. He helped me trace the bloke in question's three other living accommodations with three other elderly, rich ladies who probably lunched. He'd been quietly helping himself to their legacies, but none were prepared to press charges. It was love every time. He got clean away with Christ knows how much, but at least the original woman's kids paid the bill although mum wouldn't hear a word against the bloke who'd relieved her of close to a hundred thousand pounds. Ain't love grand?

After that Roy and I got to be really close over the years. Thing is, if you're webbed up in a motor for long periods you either get to be the best of friends or the worst of enemies. We were the former. Another of Roy's talents were puzzles. He was fiend for them. I thought I was good at the *Telegraph* crossword, but he beat me hands down. Many a happy hour we spent across and down.

The last time I saw him was in that summer. This time at our favourite Chinese in Soho. He was on his own then. He and his wife had long ago split up. I'd never met her. He'd never met mine. Him and me haunted pubs, drinking clubs, cocktail bars, restaurants. That was where we met when not at work. No cosy evenings in front of *Coronation Street* with pipes and slippers.

Me. I was having an on off on off with a young woman named Jill. A beautiful blonde. Natural as I can testify. I met her on a Monday and my heart stood still etc etc. But that never lasts. She had her own place and a key to mine. She was too young for me. A wild child I knew would soon be on her way. I don't even know if I cared that much. But more of her later. Roy had never met her either. Roy and I parted friends at Piccadilly tube that last evening. Me south, him east. We spoke on the phone a few times later that summer and he hinted there might be a shilling for me soon. But no details. When I asked, I could almost see him touch the side of his nose, smile and say 'You'll find out in time son.'

Then, one autumn evening Roy went missing. Nothing strange there, he often vanished on jobs for days, even weeks on end. Then, sometime later a headless, handless corpse was discovered in a burnt out car in a pub car park in Newham, east London. It took another few days before the body was identified as Roy's. It had been a warm season, and just like when he'd been a soldier, insects had fed on him. In fact, it was the flies swarming the car's boot that signified it was not just another stolen car, joy ridden, then torched to hide prints and DNA, that even the dumbest crook knew about from TV cop shows. I saw a bit about it in the *Standard*, but never put two and two together until I got a call from his ex to tell me. Apparently there was no one else to do the necessary. I asked if I could help as she said I was his best friend, though I never realised that, and was sorry I hadn't, but she said she had it under control and would see me at the funeral.

There was quite a fuss in the media about the mystery of the headless, handless corpse that turned out to be ex-Met slung out for what the papers, radio and TV called over zealous interrogation techniques. He told me he beat the shit out of a little cunt who turned out to have relatives in high places, and had to pay the price.

After the identification the police rounded up the usual suspects, and because I was who I was, I was scooped up too. Nick Sharman, always a ready made suspect even in the murder of a friend. As it goes, it wasn't the most thorough investigation by the look of it. No interview room with a tape on. No good cop, bad cop. More dumb cop and dumber cop. Two DCs, Bond and Blackburn in an office with two desks covered in paperwork. Bond hitched his fat bottom on one, Blackburn took a seat behind the other. This was going to be a rare occasion when I would tell the minions of the law the truth, the whole truth and nothing but the truth. For once I had absolutely nothing to hide. I swear guv'nor.

Bond kicked off. 'Mr Sharman, can you tell me when you last saw Roy Caton.

'July seventeenth,' I said. 'It's in my diary.'

'Business or pleasure?'

'We had dinner up west at our favourite Chinese. So pleasure. But he hinted there might be some work for me when we spoke on the dog a few times later.'

'What kind of work?' Asked Blackburn.

'Dunno,' I replied. 'Surveillance probably. We used to double up. It gets pretty boring on your own in a car pissing in a bottle and eating Burger King. But you'd know all about that.'

They both nodded. 'And he paid you for this?'

'Sometimes. Sometimes I paid him. Depends on which one of us had been hired. Sometimes if we were quiet, just as mates.'

'And are you quiet at the moment Mr Sharman?'

'I'm sort of between jobs at the minute.'

'Why do you think he was murdered, and left in that kind of state?' Bond asked.

'God knows. A message I suppose?'

'Who to?'

To whom, I thought, but I didn't say it. Instead I shrugged. 'I have no idea,' I said. And I didn't, but I would love to know.

'To you?'

'No. Why? Listen, we were friendly. Close. But I didn't live in his pocket or him in mine. We weren't partners. I have no idea what he was doing job wise, and he didn't know my business. Sorry. Can't help.'

'Did you kill him?' Blackburn interrupted, and the mood changed.

'He was my friend,' I said. 'I've told you that. Best friend according to his ex. I'm proud of that.'

'So you say.'

'So I do,' I replied. 'And this is starting to worry me. Do I need my solicitor?'

'No,' he said. 'If you've got nothing to hide.'

'I haven't,' I said.

'Then that's fine. Where do you think the rest of him is?'

'I have no idea. All I know is, no one deserves that.'

They both nodded. They were fishing. Putting in time, but neither really cared.

Because of the usual coroner's and police bullshit Roy's body wasn't released for weeks, so the funeral wasn't until the cusp of October and November, and London got the first chilly kiss of winter on its brow. I got an invitation from Roy's solicitor by phone. He asked me to make myself known to him at the service. I agreed.

JB came with me to keep me company. I liked her better for that. She certainly dressed the part. Black boots, long black coat, black scarf and gloves and a black beret on her blonde hair. The service was at Newham crematorium. A seventies brutal build that smelled damp and there was a constant drip from a leak in the roof. It was close to the pub where Roy's body had been found. Outside the crematorium was an attractive brunette shaking hands with those going in, but no tears. I supposed it was Roy's ex though I'd never even seen a photo. 'Hello,' I said. 'You must be Carol.'

She nodded.

'Nick Sharman. We spoke on the phone. This is my friend JB.'

'Nick, JB' she replied 'So glad you could come. Roy would have appreciated that.'

'I'm sorry it's not on happier times that we met.' I thought it best not to mention any missing body parts, because as of that day nothing had been found.

'But not surprising,' she said. 'Roy liked to keep things in boxes. The army, the police, the investigations. Me, you, all in little separate boxes. And another little box is his solicitor, Mr

Spector. See, I don't even know his Christian name. He's not arrived yet, but I'll point you out to him.'

'Thanks,' I said.

I thought I didn't know anyone, but I looked over the car park and saw a familiar figure inspecting the gravestones lined up against the wall that I guessed had been dug up when the place was built as had so many graveyards, desecrated in the name of progress. Inspecting was what Jack Robber did, so I left JB and walked over to him. 'Jack,' I said. 'Didn't know if you'd make it.'

'Always like to know where the bodies are buried,' he replied.

'Or burnt in this case.'

He gave me a stiff smile. 'Friend of your daughter?' He asked nodding towards JB.

'Funny,' I replied. 'She's not that young.'

'Too young for you son,' he said, and pulled out a packet of Rothmans. 'Better get back to her before she leaves you for a younger bloke.'

I shrugged under my smother and left him to his smoke.

'Who's that?' Asked JB when I joined her.

'You really don't want to know,' I said. 'Not a nice man.'

She accepted my answer, and we went inside the building and sat down avoiding the dripping water. It was obvious that the vicar hadn't known Roy, and didn't have much to say about him, once again obviously avoiding the obvious. The only music was 'Coming Home Baby' by Mel Tormé. I remembered Roy telling me it was his favourite record. Thank God it wasn't 'My Way'. The service ended and the coffin disappeared into the void. Roy's remains were sent to the oven, and the only reminder of my friend was a puff of smoke from the chimney as we exited the building. I saw Robber head to his car and drive off. He gave no sign he knew me as the car passed us.

JB and I shared a cigarette outside. One of the congregation, a middle aged bloke in a smart cashmere looking overcoat was talking to Carol who pointed in our direction before he headed our way. 'Mr Sharman?' he asked.

I nodded, and he held out his mitten. 'Spector,' he introduced himself. No Christian name. Old school. 'Roy's solicitor. We spoke on the telephone.'

I nodded again, and introduced JB.

He politely acknowledged her, then went on. 'I know this is unusual, but it was the way Roy wanted it. He left everything to you.'

Now I was surprised. 'You what?' Was all I managed to say.

'All his goods and chattels. He made a will a few days before he disappeared. I think he knew something was going to happen.' He made no mention of the missing head and hands either. What could anyone say?

'Christ,' I said. 'You didn't say anything when we spoke.'

'It was what Roy wanted. Don't ask me why. I'm just following his instructions. And he wanted me to hand you this when we eventually met if anything did happen to him.' He reached into his overcoat and pulled out a long, fat envelope that jingled as he handed it to me. 'Spare keys to the kingdom,' he said with a wry smile. 'My card is inside. Please ring me for anything further.'

With that, and another handshake for me and a smile to JB he left us.

'Well that was a turn up,' I said. 'I need a drink.'

There was a pub close to the church and several stragglers headed to the bar. JB and I got a table away from everyone else. 'How did he know he was going to die?' She asked when we sat down.

'I don't know. Christ. I don't believe all this. It's not often I'm lost for words, but this is a bloody puzzle. He never hinted at anything the last time we talked. Just said he was on a job.'

'Maybe the answer is in that envelope.'

'Yeah. I don't really want to know.'

'But you will.'

'Of course I will,'

And for my sins I did.

After one drink we left the pub, nodding to the people from the service and headed back to mine. The flat was chilly and reminded me of the crematorium, so I smacked the thermostat up. 'I'm going to get out of these clothes,' said JB and went to the bedroom where she kept some of her stuff in my wardrobe. 'I'll leave you alone to look at your inheritance.'

I took the envelope from my coat pocket and looked at it. I knew that inside there was going to be something life changing, and I didn't want to see. I thought about chucking the whole thing in the garbage, but I've always been cursed with insatiable curiosity. I tapped the thick paper on my own palm, then stood it on the mantelpiece with some unpaid bills. 'Fancy early doors at the Greyhound?' I called to JB.

She came back into the living room looking great in a sweater and jeans. 'Sounds good to me,' she replied.

'Let me get changed and we'll be off,' I said.

'Can't wait.'

I left her in the room and went to get out of my suit before we headed to Dulwich and our local gastropub.

I called a cab as I didn't want to drive, and I didn't want JB to drive either. Not that I was driving a cherry that year, just a Ford Ranger pickup with blacked out, highly illegal black windows all round.

We lucked out on a table by the window overlooking the forest at the back of the boozer. The music was Sinatra, the food was home made. Kate and Sidney pudding with mash and carrots. The booze was good red wine and plenty of it. We followed with apple pie and custard. JB wailed at the carbs, but I told her that with her figure she could handle them. Brandy and cappuccinos with extra shots finished the meal. Good spot with the taxis I thought as I paid up and got the waiter to call us another.

Back home we went to bed together and I didn't even look at the envelope glaring balefully at me from its home on the mantel.

Next morning, bright as day I made the coffee whilst JB lay in bed. I joined her. 'It won't open itself,' she said after taking a sip.

'What won't?'

'The letter from your friend.'

'I know. I just don't want to know what's in it.'

'Do you want me to?'

'No. It's my job. What are we doing today?'

'Being as it's Saturday, and no work for me, I think I should go home and do my laundry.'

'Do some for me will you.'

'I'm not your skivvy.'

'No. But you know you love me.'

'Sometimes.'

'As long as it's the time you're doing your smalls.'

'Behave yourself.'

But she was right, and I got up, pulled on jeans and a hoodie, left her to lie in and went to the living room, whacked up the thermostat again, and took the letter off its perch. Inside was another envelope, sealed with my name on the front in Roy's handwriting. Inside was a letter:

Dear Nick,

If you're reading this I'm dead, and you're not. Not funny I know. I've got into a bit of a pickle and I should call you up for a hand. But you know me, always going where angels fear to tread, and I'm no angel. I've got a client, details enclosed. Her boy has gone missing. Done a runner after turning into the teenager from hell. If you decide to do anything about it she'll fill you in. She knows about you. If you don't, no hard feelings. It's not pretty where he went.

I made a will that's with my brief. Once again, If you're reading this you'll have met him, and know the full SP. I've left you the lot. Only thing worth anything is the flat. Mortgage protection paid up. All that Carol left me after the divorce was just enough for the deposit on a rabbit hutch, but these days even a rabbit hutch in the East End is worth a bit. The office is rented on a short lease. Anything you can use, be my guest.

Hope you enjoyed the service if there was one.

Roy

Now that was a turn-up.

I emptied the rest of the envelope onto the sofa next to me. There were three sets of keys, all three had labels attached. One was for his office, one for his flat, one for his Range Rover.

There was also a notebook with names and addresses. The client he mentioned was on page one. Finally there was a legal pad covered in his handwriting again, telling a nasty little story, of which until then I had no idea. It didn't make easy reading.

I fancied a drink after that, but it was only half nine in the am. Fuck it, I thought and went into the kitchen and poured a stiff vodka over ice and knocked it back in one.

Well Roy, I thought as I toasted him with a second. How about that, then?

So then I go back to the bedroom where JB is standing in front of the wardrobe mirror in her underwear combing her hair. My, but she does look good. 'New pants?' I say.

She nods. I swear that girl has got more knickers than John Lewis. 'Like them?'

'Oh yes.'

'Just for you.'

'Appreciate it.'

'Did you open the letter?'

I nodded at her back, and she caught my eye in the reflection. 'And?'

'And Roy was caught in something very nasty.'

'Like?'

'Kids being used to ferry drugs round the country. One kid in particular. Ronnie Bennett went missing. Mum hired him. Looks like it went pear shaped from there.'

'And.'

'And he was going to row me in. There was too much for a solo act.'

'Why didn't he?'

'Looks like that was when someone or someones decided to do something about it.'

'What about the police?'

I almost laughed out loud. 'Sweetheart,' I said. 'The police couldn't care less about one of their own gone to the dark side. A swift sweep under the carpet and that's all she wrote.'

'Someone like you,' she said.

I'd never made any secret about my past. 'Give the lady a cigar.'

'And this is leading where?' She finally turned to look at me directly.

'He's left me his property,' I said. 'The least I can do is have a shufti.'

'A house.' She said wide eyed.

'Well, a flat. I can't take it though.'

'Why not?'

'There's his ex. I don't know how she's fixed.'

'She looked OK to me. That coat she was wearing yesterday. A thousand quid if it was a penny.' JB knows about these things. She works behind the scenes in retail. Trust me.

'I'm going to have a word. And speak to his brief. Spector.'

'So I'm with a man of property,' said JB who came over and gave me a hug which led to the pair of us spending a Saturday morning in bed. Oh, I forgot to tell you I took the vodka and two glasses with me.

After our tryst if that's what you call it we went out for a late Italian pasta and wine lunch locally. Then back to mine and some serious business. Even though it was Saturday afternoon I called Spector on his mobile. 'Sorry to bother you on a weekend,' I said.

'No bother" came the reply. 'We never sleep.'

'Glad to hear it. I need Carol's number.'

'I'll text it.'

'Great. You know I can't take all this.'

'Roy's estate?'

'Yes. I mean we were friends, but bosom buddies, no.'

'He said there was no one else.'

'Carol?'

'There was no love lost there. But it's up to you.'

'Fine. Get me her number and I'll speak to you in the week.'

'As you wish,' and with that we both hung up.

Half a minute later my phone pinged with a text and hey presto Carol's number was mine. I phoned her straight away. she answered on the third ring. 'Carol?' I said.

'Yes.'

'Nick Sharman. We met yesterday.'

'Hello Nick. What can I do for you.?'

'It's Roy's will. He left everything to me.'

'I know.'

'Well, I don't want it, Don't deserve it.'

'Obviously he thought you did.'

'But you were married to him.'

'Were is the word. And believe me the parting wasn't amicable. Nor was the divorce. I got nearly everything. The house, the cars, the money. I don't even know how he managed to scrape enough together to make deposit on that flat. Truth is Nick, I'm with someone else now. Someone well fixed. He doesn't want anything to do with Roy. Neither do I. I only helped Spector with the funeral for old times' sake. Old times I want to forget. Keep the stuff, sell it, give the money to the local cats' home. I don't care. End of story. Sorry to be blunt but that's it.'

'Fair enough,' I said. 'Thanks for being so frank.'

'So now I can get on with my life?'

'Of course. I won't bother you again.'

So ended that phone call. I hung up and answered JB's look.

'Seems like I am indeed a man of property,' I said.

The next morning I decided to take a look see at my new flat, and check Roy's office on the way. 'Can I come?' Asked JB.

'Do you want to?'

'Wouldn't have asked if I didn't.'

'Fair enough.'

'Anyway, you'll need someone to drive your new car home.'

She was right. 'OK,' I said. 'Then lunch.'

We took off in my car. Roy's office was over a hairdresser's in Blackwall. The back door was locked, and I used one of the keys Spector gave me and we went up a flight to a door covered in police tape. I pulled it off and in we went. The place was freezing and looked like a bomb site, fingerprint powder covered every flat space and papers were scattered hither and thither. 'Tidy, the Met,' I said. 'Glad I'm not looking for office space.'

We stood around for a minute, then I said. 'No. Everything he wanted me to know was in that note book. The cops must have his computer. There's nothing here for us.'

We locked up and left and headed for my new flat by the

City airport. It was new build, and on the top floor. 'Penthouse suite,' said JB after we got through the main door, past the concierge, who said Roy had been a most generous resident, moaned about the cops making a mess in his block, and into the lift. Suite wasn't in it. It was just a studio hardly big enough to swing the proverbial puss cat. One room with a plug in oven in the corner kitchen, and a tiny bathroom with toilet, shower and hand basin. Even the bed folded into the wall. There was one armchair facing a flat screen TV hanging on the wall. Depressing or what? No wonder Roy had never invited me round for dinner. Also the SOCO had left their fingerprints everywhere. 'Christ,' I said. 'What a dump.'

'Still worth a hundred grand paid for,' said JB, ever the pragmatist. I told you she knew about these kind of things.

We found Roy's car parked out back in a resident's bay so that meant he'd been jacked from home or else he'd used another, more anonymous motor on business. It was an old, but not ancient black Range Rover. It looked immaculate from outside. Roy loved cars and looked after them. I gave JB the keys. 'You take it home,' I said.

She grinned, opened it up on the fob and climbed inside. It started on the first try, and rumbled sweetly. 'Don't bend it,' I said, and watched as she reversed out of the bay, then took off with just a small screech from its wide tyres.

I went back to the Ford and followed her, but she lost me at the first set of lights.

The Rover was neatly parked up outside my flat when I got home, and JB was inside with an open bottle of red wine and a skinny spliff. 'Where you been slowcoach?' she said when I got inside.

'Obeying the speed limit. How was it?'

'Lovely car. Runs like an angel.'

'Great. I'll get the paperwork and insurance sorted tomorrow.'

'Blimey. Is that the real Nick Sharman speaking, or has

some alien inhabited his body? Obeying the rules. Being a good citizen.'

'Someone's gotta be,' I said. 'Now don't bogart that joint.'

'You do say the loveliest things,' she said, and poured me a glass of wine.

Monday morning dawned dank and drizzly. I sat in bed watching JB get her business face and suit on before heading to retail heaven, with a cup of coffee and a slice of toast prepared by her own fair hands. She rattled her car keys at the door and said, 'When will I see you?'

'I should look into Roy's things, and do what I do best.'

'Which is?'

'Detect. Why don't I call you tonight and we'll make a date?'

'Sounds fair. Don't work too hard.'

'Back at you.' And with that she left, and I knew I had to do something positive.

I got up, did my usual ablutions, made more coffee, watched the breakfast news and hauled out Roy's notebook and the photo of the young lad Ronnie Bennett. At ten I phoned the number he'd left me for his mother. The phone rang four times, then a female voice answered, 'Hello.'

'Can I speak to Mrs Estell Bennett?' I asked.

'Speaking.'

'We haven't met,' I said. 'My name is Sharman. Nick Sharman. I was a colleague of Roy Catons'

'That poor man. I read about it in the paper. I'm so sorry.'

'Yes. He was working for you.'

'You don't think...'

'I don't know. The thing is, he left me notes on the case. Has your son been found?'

Her tone changed. Saddened. 'No.'

'The police?'

'Useless.'

'Well I'd like to help.'

'Really?' Change of tone again. Suspicious. 'I paid him, I suppose you want more money.'

'No,' I said. 'No money. This is for Roy. And you. Pro bono. No charge.' For the Queen, as we used to say on the job. 'Can I come and see you?'

'If you want to.'

I read out the address in the notebook.

'That's right,' she said.

'Tomorrow morning. Say about eleven.'

'I'll be here. I'm always here.' This time her voice was distant and sad.

We made our farewells and hung up.

The rest of the day I put on my good citizen face. I put the Range Rover on my insurance. You never can have enough cars, and I added JB as a named driver. Then I found a housecleaning firm in east London and booked a clean up for Roy's flat for Thursday morning. I told them I'd leave the keys with the concierge. After that I phoned Chestertons and told them I'd need a valuation on the place on Friday, same story with the keys. I figured to get them left after I saw Mrs Bennett.

That all done I phoned JB, told her what was happening and arranged to meet at the Chinese in Soho Tuesday after she finished work. She asked if I was sure, as it was the last place I'd seen Roy, and I said we'd eat and drink to his memory. I knew he'd have done the same if it had been me deceased.

Finally I microwaved a Waitrose dinner for one, opened a decent red, watched TV and hit the sack.

The next morning I put on a smart suit and tie, took the Range Rover for an outing and headed to Hackney. Once it had been a rough old corner, but now scaffolding was everywhere and skips lined the side streets like beached whales. It seemed everywhere in London was being gentrified. I found the address Roy had left me, parked the motor, grabbed my overcoat against the chill, and rang the doorbell. It was a handsome semi, but looked like it could use some TLC. So did Mrs Bennett when she answered the door. She was too skinny, her cardigan was wrongly buttoned, and the bags under her eyes were dark with fatigue.

I introduced myself and she invited me in. The house was chilly, and she apologised for the mess. As it happens it wasn't too bad, and who was I to complain? She took my smother, sat me down on a plump sofa, and asked 'Cup of tea?'

'Love one.'

She left me alone and I heard her bustling about in the kitchen. While she was gone I stood and looked around the room. It must once have been cosy. Flat screen in the corner hooked up to DVD player, Sky and some kind of games console. Plenty of books in cases. Hard and soft cover novels, biographies of the famous and infamous, pictures on the walls, an open fireplace with cold ashes. But all a bit dusty, a bit neglected, a bit sad. Like the life had left it, and it obviously had.

She came back with two mugs, sugar, and biscuits in a tray. I felt a stab of pity, but regained my ear and smiled. 'Thanks. It's cold outside.'

'In here too,' she said. 'I should have lit the fire.'

'No. This'll warm me up.' I took a sip of the tea and put the mug on the coffee table in front of me.

'I know this is going to be hard, but can you tell me what you told Roy. From the beginning.'

So she told me. Ronald, Ronnie Bennett, named after Ronnie Wood, because her husband had been a mad Rolling Stones fan, had been a lovely boy until he changed schools at eleven. I knew how tough that could be, from my own experience and my daughter's. Then her husband had died. Didn't smoke, didn't drink, didn't do drugs, didn't play away. A loving husband and father, had a massive heart attack in Sainsbury's doing the Saturday shop in front of mum and son. Dead before he hit the ground according to the doctors. Insurance paid the mortgage and left Estelle and Ronnie enough to live, if not happily, at least comfortably off. Then it all went pear shaped. Ronnie's grades went south, he started playing up. Ended up staying out to all hours. First of all with expensive new kit. Then dirty and starved. When mum wanted to know what was going on he turned nasty. Hitting, spitting. The full nine yards. Then a few months before she went to Roy, he did a proper David Nixon and went right off the radar. Cops were informed, but didn't do much.

End of song, beginning of story. By the time the tale was told Mrs B was crying into a tissue. I felt for her. Felt like crying myself if truth was told. My daughter had done a runner once. I knew the feeling.

Finally, she said, 'Then last summer Roy rang me and said he might have some news for me. Good news. When I heard nothing I tried phoning, but only got his voice mail. Then I saw what happened to him on the news. I couldn't believe it. It wasn't my fault was it?'

I told her no, but I didn't know. Not then. And anyway I wasn't in the business of making her feel worse.

'Did the police not ask you any questions.'

'No. No police.'

Just like I'd thought. They didn't give a monkeys for Roy or his ilk. In other words, the likes of me.

'Well, I said. 'If you want me to look further?'

'Would you?'

'Yes. I owe Roy. And like I said on the phone. No charge. I'm taking a sabbatical at the moment. It'll give me something to do.'

'But you mustn't put yourself in danger.'

I didn't say that danger was my middle name.

'No. I'm very careful.'

After more tea and biscuits I left her. I took Roy's flat keys over to his block, told the concierge who was coming and crossed his palm with silver. Actually a crisp new fifty pound note. We parted the best of friends.

Then I did what I should have done weeks before. I went to the pub where Roy's body had been found. The car park was afternoon empty, and the only trace an oblong of melted tarmac the shape of a car. I stood for a few moments then split. Did I feel a tear in my eye? Actually, yes.

I went back home, changed into jeans and leather jacket and treated myself to a cab to Soho. I was sitting in the restaurant drinking a long mojito when JB arrived looking as stunning as ever and making young men jealous and old men wish they were young again. Me included. She really was the kind of woman to make a bishop take a flying kick at his mitre.

I stood, she air kissed me and sat. I followed suit and she asked me what was cooking.

I told her all.

'I worry about you,' she said.' I don't want to have to identify a burnt body sans hands and head.'

'I'll never happen.' Famous last words.

We wined and dined on the finest Chinese in London in my opinion, drunk too much expensive wine and brandy, fell out of the place at last knocking, then headed to Ronnies for some late jazz. Ironic, two Ronnies in one day. But life's sometimes like that.

We left the club at three, and I splurged again on fifty nicker to an obliging cabbie who deigned to take us south of the drink, although, first he made me swear we didn't live on a council estate. Bloody cheek.

Next day, both heads banging we parted lovers and I decided to get down to business.

First job, I phoned DI Jack Robber. 'I wondered when you'd be back on my case,' he said.

'Good morning to you too, Jack,' I said back. 'Well that's more than your colleagues have been on Roy.'

'Meaning.'

'Meaning they pulled me in, but haven't even been to visit the lady he was working his last job for.'

'What did you expect? No special treatment for bent ex-coppers. NHI.'

That fucking stung, NHI. No humans involved. 'Christ, Jack. He was a fucking human. He was a pal of yours.'

'But it's not on my beat. And between you and him, being friends gets me a bad name.'

'And a few quid in your bin.' Like I may have said before, Jack Robber's take on being bent was extremely elastic. He did favours for mates for a few shills, no questions asked.

No answer, came the reply.

'Let's meet,' I said.

'Usual time, usual place tonight,' and the phone died in my hand.

Usual time, seven pm, usual place the Dog boozer in Loughborough junction.

Seven o'clock rolled round and the Dog was its usual warm and friendly self. Sticky carpets, dull brasses, mucky glasses, the same dead Wurlitzer juke box that hadn't been switched on since Kojak was number one on the TV charts, and that feeling that tumbleweed was about to roll across the floor. I ordered a half of lager from our glamorous toothless barmaid and headed for a table. I didn't wipe the chair off with my hanky, but I wanted to. Robber rolled up his usual ten minutes late and bought his usual mild and bitter in a dimpled jug. Old school through and through.

I handed him his usual two ton in old notes which he secreted away in his usual nicotine brown whistle. 'I hear you've come into money,' he said through a mouthful of foamy suds.

'Blimey, the old jungle drums have been beating.'

'Seems like you owe me a finder's fee, seeing as I introduced the pair of you.'

'Leave off, Jack, he's hardly cold in his box.'

'More like hot considering he was cremated.'

'Funny.'

'Not so's you'd notice. Chestertons isn't it. Good firm. A hundred and fifty grand I reckon. Ten per cent should do.'

'My girlfriend reckons a hundred.'

'She's behind the times my son. Property in Docklands is shooting up. You've probably earned a grand since you inherited. Just let me know, I don't want to go looking.'

I held up my hands. 'So what DO you know?' I asked.

'Not much, and that's a fact. He had a base, but I reckon he kept his office in his hat as they used to say. Computer threw nothing up, except he played a lot of Solitaire and PAC-Man whatever that is.'

For once I knew but I didn't let on.

'So that's all I get for my money,' I said.

'Some you win, some you lose. Why don't you just take the money and run. Take that lovely girlfriend of yours on a cruise. Somewhere warm.'

'Because it looks like nobody cares. Not for Roy, and not for the boy he was looking for, and his mum.'

'Your choice. Don't say I didn't warn you.'

Those words would come back and haunt me.

We separated then and I headed home to another go round at the microwave. I sat up late, the TV on, turned down low and watched tough guys beat seven kinds of shit out of each other.

The weekend came and went again, as it is wont to do. Roy's flat got cleaned and the estate agent called and valued the place at close to two hundred grand, and reckoned he'd get a sale pronto. So both JB and Robber had been short in their prophecies. I told the bloke to take an offer. He said he would.

Meanwhile I'd taken a shufti around Ronnie Bennett's school. Now, remember folks don't like grown men eyeing up young boys and girls in the playground. It can lead to all sorts of trouble. Cops, or worse, vigilante justice and broken bones. The whole village turning out with flaming torches and pitchforks, so I kept a very low profile, but did notice that the naughty boys and girls gathered together outside a local chip shop at lunchtime to smoke and eat. And I also noticed a certain older lad who seemed to be their supplier of weed and pills.

So, that Monday, that dawned black cold and wet I ramped up to the chippie as the first cod was being battered, and our young vagabond dope dealer arrived for a coffee and bath bun. I joined him at his table with a smile.

'What?' He said with a sneer.

'What you got?'

'Nothing for you, old man.'

Christ, I wasn't that old.

'Sorted for e's and whizz? Or is that before your time?'

'A bloody old hipster,' he laughed.

'Used to be.'

'So what can I get you?' He took a bite of bun and a sip of tea. The place was warming up nicely as the first batch of chips went in.

'Information.'

'That's in short supply round here. 'Specially to strangers. 'Specially to strangers who look like old Bill.'

'Many of them been around lately?'

'How lately?'

'Summertime. Looking for a lad named Ronnie. Goes to the local comp.'

He grinned like a wolf. 'Old bloke like you. Big, clever bastard. You never saw him coming.'

'Sounds about right.'

'Yeah. He was here a lot. Then not. Left owing.'

'Owing what?'

'A ton would cover it.'

My turn to grin. 'You wouldn't be mugging me off would you?'

'What me guv?'

What the hell I thought. What was a ton when I'd just come into easy money?

I took out my wallet and pulled out a wad of twenties, counted off five and held them out to him. He reached, I pulled back. 'So tell me.'

'He's gone in country,' said the lad whose name I didn't even know.

What the fuck, I thought. Vietnam? 'What do you mean?' I asked.

'Gone where you wouldn't want to go. With bad people you wouldn't want to meet.'

'I need more before you get this,' I said.

'Go to Euston or Paddington. Any main line railway station or coach station late at night. You'll see the country boys and girls if you look hard enough. Is that enough?'

I nodded and he took the money, abandoned the rest of his snack and left.

'You ordering?' asked the chip man.

I shook my head. 'Maybe later,' I said, and left too. Outside the street was streaked with frost, and I turned my collar to the cold and damp and went home to think.

I thought about the web, but it wasn't a help. Type 'In country' and all you get is a film, a book and the usual military jargon explained. Nothing about kids and drugs.

JB arrived early evening with an Indian take out and I filled her in with the story so far. She chased her chicken jalfrezi round the plate, sipped at a beer and asked. 'So!'

'So I guess I'll take a run around the main London termini and see what I can find.'

'Can I come?'

'Really?'

'Really. If you were worried about a grown man hanging round the school gates, think about a grown man following runaways at London termini as you so beautifully put it.'

'Never thought of that.'

'Then you should have.'

'You're right. When?'

'When I haven't got work the next day.'

'Friday?'

'Sounds good to me.'

So that was that for a few days.

Meanwhile, on the property front things were looking up. My bloke from Chestertons phoned to say there'd been an offer of one hundred and eighty grand, but he said we could do better if we waited. 'Take it,' I said.

He sounded disappointed, and tried to make me change my mind. 'Take it,' I said again. 'I'll clear the place tomorrow.'

Which I did. I'd like to say I found some hidden documents to help me solve the case, but the only things hidden were ancient copies of *Playboy* magazine. Roy, old school to the end.

I thanked the concierge on my last trip to the car, told him I'd sold up, and to pass on the spare keys to the new owner, but if he expected another tip he was disappointed too.

At last Friday evening came round as it always does, and we set off on a search for any news of Ronnie. We scoured the train stations with not much luck and eventually ended up at Victoria coach station around midnight. That's when we met Sheila. At least that's what she called herself. She was sitting on a bench by the entrance wrapped up against the weather.

She was small, dark haired and didn't take to us much at first.

'I don't believe in God, and I don't do threesomes,' she said when we approached her.

'Fair enough,' said JB taking the lead. 'We just want a word.'

'About?'

'About him,' I said, bringing out the photo of Ronnie. 'His mum misses him.'

'Are you cops?'

'No,' said JB.

'He looks like cop.' She nodded at me.

'No,' said JB. 'He's just ugly.'

The girl cracked a smile at that.

'Listen,' I said. 'You hungry?'

She nodded.

'There's an all night burger bar round the back. Fancy a bite?'

'OK, but I don't get in no cars.'

'You're safe,' I said. 'Come on.'

The restaurant, if you could use that word about it was warm and dry. I ordered three cheeseburgers, two coffees, and a coke, and took the tray to a table at the back away from the few other punters. 'What's your name?' I said when the food was in front of us.

'Sheila,' she said.

'How old are you?'

'No,' she came back. 'None of that is any of your business.'

'Fair enough.'

By that time her cheeseburger had vanished and I pushed mine towards her.

'Cheers' she said and dived in.

'So Ronnie. The lad in the photo. Do you know him?'

'Might do.'

'We mean him no harm,' said JB. 'His mum is really worried.'

Sheila shrugged. I imagine a lot of my mums and dads were worried that night. Sheila's included.

'I heard he was in country,' I said.

Sheila nodded. 'Makes sense.'

I shrugged too, and she went on, 'I did see him.'

'Really.' Me again.

'I'm not lying,' said Sheila.

'Never thought you were,' I said. 'Where?'

'Euston, last week.'

'What was he doing there?'

'Catching a train.'

'Where to?'

'Dunno. Didn't ask. He looked rough though.'

'But he had a ticket?'

'Sure. They've always got tickets.'

'Who? The carriers?'

'How do you mean?' she asked. Though I knew.

The second burger and most of her coke had gone by then, and JB passed her untouched food over. Sheila grabbed a handful of paper napkins and wrapped it neatly and stowed it away in her rucksack. 'Breakfast,' she said.

'You were saying,' I said. 'About the carriers. What do they carry?'

'What do you think?'

'You tell me.'

'Drugs, stupid.'

'And you don't know where Ronnie was going.?'

She shook her head. 'It was the last train though. The station was nearly empty.'

'Good,' I said. 'Thanks. You've been a big help. Where are you staying tonight?'

She shrugged again, and I took out my wallet, pulled out five twenties and slid them across the table. 'Get somewhere warm,' I said. Then put my card on top of the cash. 'Call me if you see Ronnie again, or hear anything, or just to talk.'

'About?'

It was my turn to shrug again. 'Anything,' I said. 'I'm a good listener.'

The money and my card followed the cheeseburger into her rucksack, and she got up to leave. 'Cheers,' she said. 'Don't believe everything you hear.' And with that, she left.

'Do you reckon she was lying?' I asked JB as I took a sip of my cold coffee.

She shrugged too. 'Who knows?'

We were to before too long.

We got home around two, and chatted about what we'd heard and seen, then hit the sack.

It was about ten the next morning and we were both still asleep when the house was shaken by hammering on the front door, and continuous ringing on my flat bell. My downstairs neighbours were away again, and besides, they weren't the types to get that sort of disturbance to their beauty sleep.

I dragged on jeans and a t-shirt and left JB rubbing her eyes as I headed downstairs. Two characters were standing outside the front door, and I didn't need to see ID to know they were plain clothes cops.

'Nick Sharman?' Demanded one, a man mountain in leather jacket and jeans.

'That's me.'

'We need to talk.'

'About?'

'About her.' he showed me a photo on his phone. It was tiny, but I recognised Sheila, even though one eye was black, her nose was sideways, and there was a stitch in her top lip.' Christ,' I said. 'What happened?'

'We thought you might know.'

'Leave off. She was alright when she left.'

'Left where?'

'You'd better come in,' I said.

We all trooped upstairs and JB was waiting looking the business, which kind of stunned the cops. 'What's up?' she asked.

'Someone smacked Sheila around after we left her last night.'

'Her name's Pam.' Interjected the second cop. 'Leastways that's the ID she had on her. Pam Dixon.'

'Jesus,' said JB. 'You don't think we…'

'She had your card in her hand.' Said cop number one.

'Which I left after doing that to her I suppose,' I said. 'I don't beat up little girls.'

'Did you give her money.'

'I gave her a ton to find somewhere safe for the night.'

'That worked out well.' Cop two.

'Funny.'

'Not so's you notice.'

'Listen,' said JB. 'Whatever you think he's capable of, that's not me. We bought the girl some food, sorted her for a couple of nights lodging because she told us about a boy we're looking for. That's it. Nothing else. Then we came home.'

The cops looked frustrated. 'Right,' said the first one. 'We'll be talking to the girl as soon as she's able. We know about you Sharman. And it's not good.'

I thought he was going to tell me not to leave town.

'And don't leave town.' He said as he left.

'Christ,' I said to JB. 'Looks like someone didn't like us asking questions.'

'That poor girl. She thought she was so tough…'

'It's rough out there on the streets,' I said. 'Even for the toughest.'

'We should do something for her.'

'Don't you think we've done enough?' But of course she was right.

Then, I'm afraid things went from bad to worse.

Sunday afternoon my phone rang. It was Robber. 'Just to let you know,' he said. 'We've found the body of a young lad.'

I said nothing. Couldn't.

'Looks like your boy. His mum has been notified. It wasn't pretty. It's him though.'

'Christ,' I said.

'Christ is right. He's malnourished, and badly beaten.'

Just like Shiela I thought.

'OK Jack,' I said. 'Thanks for letting me know. I'm sorry.'

'Not your fault.' And he hung up.

But I couldn't stop thinking that it was. I still do, after all this time.

I told JB the bad news.

'Don't blame yourself,' she said.

'But I do, and I intend to do something about it.'

'Nothing too drastic,' she said.

'Of course not,' I said.

Then there was Ronnie's mum.

The next morning after JB had left for work, I drove back to Hackney. The woman who answered the door was just a shadow of the woman I had met before, and she'd been no more than a shadow then. 'You heard,' she said.

'I still have a friend on the force. I'm so sorry. I thought I was getting somewhere.'

'It doesn't matter now.'

'It matters more.'

'Not to me. My life is over.'

'Don't say that.'

'It's true. I should pay you for your time.'

'I told you before. No charge. In fact I wish I hadn't started. I feel responsible.'

'Only the people who did this to Ronnie are to blame.'

'If you say so.'

'I do.'

And with that I left the grieving mother to her grief.

Then I headed back to the chip shop where I'd met the junior drug dealer. He sat alone at the same table. The cafe was warm with moisture running down the windows inside. I sat opposite him again. 'Help you?' He asked with the same aggravating smirk.

'They found Ronnie,' I said.

'Is he well?'

'No.'

'Sorry to hear it.'

'I'm sure you are. Just short of another customer.'

'Plenty of those. Here comes a couple now.'

Two young girls came through the door, waved at our table, then went to the counter and ordered chips.

'You know I don't even know your name,' I said.

'People call me Sonny.'

'People call me Nick,' I said. 'So tell me who's the brains behind this country operation?'

'As if I would.'

'You will.'

'No chance.'

'Believe me.' And with that I left my seat, grabbed him by the collar of his leather jacket and dragged him across the floor, through the gap beside the counter, and round to the fryers.

'You can't,' said the woman doing the frying.

'Just watch me,' I said and thrust Sonny's hand down close to where the chips were bubbling at Christ knows what temperature. He screamed, the woman screamed, and the two girls putting ketchup on their chips screamed. I almost screamed myself.

'OK, OK,' he shouted. 'I'll tell you.'

The woman had fled to the back of the shop yelling for the guv'nor, and I shoved Sonny back through the shop out into the cold morning and over to my car.

I slung him in the front passenger seat, and cuffed him with plastic ties. 'You can't do this,' he whined.

'I'm doing it.' There was no argument with that, and I went to the driver's seat and took off, just in case the chippies had called the police. I drove to a quiet street, parked up, turned off the engine and looked at him. On the drive he'd protested even more, and had only shut up when I threatened to gag him.

'So,' I said, 'you were saying.'

He schtummed up then, so I had to show him I meant business, as if a deep fried hand wasn't enough. 'Listen Sonny,' I said. 'I'm taking Ronnie's murder extremely personally. Plus a young girl I met ended up in hospital because she talked to me. I want to find out who was behind the attacks. Tell me, and you can go. Don't tell me and I'll break your pretty face. Now I know you wouldn't like that.'

I didn't put a hand on him, just sat patiently looking at him, and after five minutes, he broke. Just like I knew he would.

'If I tell you,' he stuttered. 'You'll let me go?'

'Scouts' honour.' He looked like he'd never heard of the scouts, or indeed, honour.

'It's a bloke. Campbell they call him. Just Campbell. He's a wholesaler. Supplies me, and captures these silly kids. Promises them the world. Buys them shit. Computer games, trainers, clothes, booze, fags, drugs. And when they're hooked he sends them all over the country delivering gear. If they do the business, all's good. But God protect them if they screw up.'

I liked the God part.

'So where's Campbell?' I asked.

'If he ever knew...'

'He's not here, I am. And I have all sorts of nasty things in this motor. Painful things.'

As it happens I didn't, but he didn't know. 'You carrying now?' I said.

'A bit.'

'Tell me.'

'Inside pocket. Left hand side.'

'Nothing sharp?'

He shook his head.

'You'd better be telling the truth.'

And he was. I reached into his sweaty jacket and pulled out a nice little parcel of goodies. Weed in see through plastic baggies, coke, I presumed in several silver paper wraps. Pills by the dozen. Speed, downers, ecstasy. I didn't much care. I stuffed them back. 'Campbell,' I said.

He gave me an address in North London maybe half an hour away, and I switched on the engine again. 'So what will I find?'

He sneered again. 'Not something you'll like. I guarantee that.'

'Exactly.'

He shook his head. 'You'll find out if you're stupid enough to go in there. Check the basement. But I promise you'll never be the same again.'

I chucked the motor into gear and took off.

'Ain't you going to let me go?' he asked.

'Don't be silly. I want to see the gaff first.'

I headed off in a north westerly direction, and when we got close I made him direct me. Though it was winter, the street he took me to seemed darker than the ones that led there. Darker and colder and the air seemed thicker and more acrid smelling through my open window. The house he pointed to was a crooked house on a crooked street next to a crooked railway bridge that carried trains from London to the north, and seemed to lean close to the house, as if they were partners in crime.

The house itself was dirty grey brick, with a dirty grey tiled roof, and dirty grey curtains covered every window as if to keep whatever secrets were inside, inside.

The front door was dirty grey too, and the few pedestrians that passed by on that dirty grey afternoon, seemed to make a wide berth as they passed. If ever I'd seen an evil place, this was it.

I called Robber then and told him what was cooking. 'I'll meet you there,' he said.

He arrived about thirty minutes later and parked his car close behind mine. 'Who's your friend?' He asked when he climbed into the back seat.

I explained.

'Any sign of life at the house?

'Nothing,' I replied.

'Well let's take a shufti,' he said.

We trussed Sonny up where he sat and crossed the road that smelled slightly of brimstone. Even Robber wrinkled his nose. 'Nasty,' he said.

We climbed the three steps to the front door, that, although the paint was peeling and the wood warped looked pretty secure. I pushed it and it felt like it pushed back, annoyed at being interfered with. 'Shit,' I said. 'This one won't be easy.'

'You're out of touch Sharman, Robber whispered back and pulled what looked like a short screwdriver from one of his pockets. He stuck the bit into the Yale lock, it purred happily, and the door slumped open, almost I felt against its will. 'Simple when you know how,' said Robber. 'After you.'

I went inside and wished I hadn't. The place stunk like spoiled meat and old shit. Robber followed me and pulled the door shut behind him. Immediately all noise from the street ceased. When he spoke the words seemed out of sync to his mouth's movements. Like one of those dubbed spaghetti westerns I watch on late night TV. 'I've got a very bad feeling about this,' he said. At least it sounded like him. A bit.

'Downstairs, he said,' I said. I pointed at another door, darkness behind it. Robber showed me the palm of his hand and said, 'After you.'

I pushed the door and felt round inside for a switch, and there was one, and when I pushed it down a dim light showed steps leading downwards. I went ahead and the smell was worse. I counted a dozen steps and then there was a rough concrete floor, in front of another door that I pushed open, found another switch and hit it. The single bulb that came on illuminated a single wooden armchair, a chest freezer plugged into the wall with a dim red light shining malignantly on its handle and in the corner a small chain saw next to what looked like a can of petrol. The chain on the saw was discoloured with some brown dried liquid. If it wasn't blood then I was a monkey's uncle.

Then when I looked closely at the arms on the chair there were more brown stains that ran down to the floor and had once pooled on the concrete.

'Nice,' said Robber. 'I think I could put this all together and make a decent case for murder.'

I walked over to the freezer, tugged the top open against the vacuum and staring at me through a clear plastic bag were the eyes of my old friend Roy. Next to his head were his hands. I'd recognise them anywhere, especially as on his left hand ring finger was his wedding ring that he'd never been without, divorced or not.

'Fuck,' I said. 'Let's find this Campbell cunt.'

'I'm right here,' said a voice from behind us, and in the doorway was sight for sore eyes, or at least a sight to make your eyes sore. He was neither tall nor short, fat nor thin. And I imagine he was a he, though he could have been either sex. Or neither, or for that matter neuter. Whatever he, she or it was, was in a long black overcoat that badly needed darning. It's face was rat like but cat like, but dog like, but human like, but none of the above. The only thing that was easy to describe was the sexy, matte black, Italian looking pump action shot gun with an underslung stock, and a bore that looked as wide as the Blackwell tunnel as it moved between me and Robber.

'I'm not armed,' I said.

'That's not like you Mr Sharman,' he said. 'Yes, I know you. Know of you. Now take off your coat and throw it over there.' He gestured with the gun.

I did as I was told.

'Now your jacket. The same.'

I obeyed.

'Lift your sweater and turn around.'

I did it.

'Pull up your trouser legs.'

Checking for an ankle holster. I did it, and eventually he seemed satisfied.

'Now sit. Place your hands on the arms, and if you as much as lift them an inch I will blow your head off.'

I sat on the hard wooden seat and placed my hands where I guessed Roy had placed his before they were chopped off.

'And now you,' Campbell said to Robber, and the barrel of the shotgun moved to his stomach. 'What's your story?'

'I'm just a broken down old copper driving a desk,' said Robber in a voice that was not his own. Wheedling, frightened. Not like Jack at all. And he gently pushed the gun's barrel away in my direction again. 'Don't hurt me. I only come to help that mug there.'

Meaning me, of course.

And then his voice changed again. Deepened. More like growl. 'And I wanted to bring you something.'

Campbell's expression changed and his eyes widened, and

Jack snapped the fingers of his right hand and something flew out of his sleeve into his palm, a click, and a silver blade shimmied in the light as he slammed it upwards under Campbell's jaw, up into his brain, and the shotgun fell to the floor with a clatter and Campbell followed, stone dead.

'Well, that's bloody inconvenient,' said Jack as he wiped the flick knife's blade on Campbell's coat.

'Christ,' I said. 'He was pointing that thing at me. He could've pulled the trigger on reflex and blown me in half. Then when he dropped it, it could've blown my feet off.' Let me tell you I was shaking in my shoes.

'Neither option happened. I think he wanted us next to your mate in the freezer. Thank your lucky stars.'

There was that of course.

'Now what?' I said.

Robber walked over, picked up the can next to the chainsaw, shook it, and liquid sloshed inside. He opened the top, sniffed, grimaced, said 'petrol' and started to chuck it round the room over Campbell's body and the freezer.

He took out his Zippo, and I said, 'hold on, there might be people upstairs.'

'Or he might have a pussy cat,' said Robber. 'Christ, you're going soft in your old age.'

'Still worth checking,' I said, picked up the shotgun, racked the action and left the basement.

The place was full of rooms. It seemed like dozens. More than should've been there from outside. Some were empty, some held sticks of furniture, some mattresses with a few blankets. One room was like a tart's parlour. A round bed, red silk covers and a mirror in the ceiling. Another was a bathroom appointed like I imagined the Ritz would be, and yet another, a state of the art kitchen. And finally in the eaves was a small office. There was a desk, two chairs, one facing, one in front and a huge old fashioned safe, door standing open. Inside were stacks of cash all neatly banded with the amount inside written in thick black ink. But all in all, no sign of life either human or feline.

Robber literally rubbed his hands together. 'Well,' he said. 'I've broken enough laws already today. What's one more.' And he started emptying the safe, packing money into his pockets until he resembled the Michelin man. When his pockets could take no more, he said. 'Come on Nick. There's plenty more. Fill your boots.'

He moved out of my way and I picked up a couple of bundles both marked £5000. I flicked the cash and it felt dirty, greasy and I threw it back. Didn't seem right. I'd found the remains of my friend, and we'd finish the job the crematorium had started. Job done.

Robber shrugged, then doused the room with more petrol and continued down the stairs. At the front door I propped the shotgun up, opened the door and Robber flicked his lighter and threw it inside. I closed the door on what was already a conflagration and we walked away.

We got back to the cars sharpish. Sonny was still sitting trussed up in the front of mine. 'Lend us your knife,' I said to Robber. He pulled it out and handed it to me. It felt slick and ugly in my hand. I slashed the ties round Sony's wrists. 'Scarper,' I said.

'Ain't you going to give me a lift?'

'The tube's round the corner,' I said.

'I'm skint.'

'Ain't you got your Oyster card?'

'It's empty.

'Christ,' I said. 'Here.' I pulled out my wallet and found two twenties. 'Treat yourself. Take a cab. Now go.'

I could see black smoke coming out of the house and I shoved him on his way, shut the flick knife and gave it back to Robber.

'Time for us to go too,' I said. 'Thanks for everything.'

Robber grinned. 'No. Thank you,' he said.

'There's cameras,' I said.

'Leave them to me. Everything will be fine. Just go.'

So I did. And so did he. The fire was on the evening news. Big story in the end when they found the remains of the freezer and Roy. But true to his word no one came knocking on my door.

So that was that. Robber just kept being a Robber, and I just kept being me. JB? Well we lasted a bit longer and had another adventure, but that's another story altogether. Eventually we went our separate ways. Last I heard she was married to someone her own age and expecting her first baby. I think of her often. Fondly. I hope she does the same for me.

MURDER AT THE VICARAGE

So, here's how it started: Early one winter's morning before it was properly light JB was preparing for her daily executive battle at retail heaven. Black suit: bolero jacket, pencil skirt. White blouse, black tights, black patent leather pumps, and putting the finishing touches to the make-up she really didn't need. The radio was tuned to LBC, and Steve Allen was blathering away in his usual style, the volume just about audible for the news and time checks.

I was in bed, in t-shirt and Calvins, chewing on a slice of Warburtons farmhouse bread toasted by her own fair hand, smothered with Waitrose Brittany Butter avec sea salt crystals, and some very expensive French raspberry jam whose name I couldn't pronounce, but cost a bomb and tasted heavenly. How come the French make the best jam, Or framboise I believe they call it? Rhetorical question. They just do. I was washing it down with strong Italian blend coffee delivered in my favourite cup, also brewed by JB. I should've known something was in the air. Everything was just too perfect.

'I've got some holiday owing,' she said. 'We should take a break.'

My mind went to infinity pools, sun loungers, long, cold, sweet cocktails, and warm evenings eating dinner, watching the sun sink into the Mediterranean, but before I could say a word, she said, 'I got an email. There's a cottage to let in Suffolk. An old stable conversion behind a church…'

'Suffolk,' I interrupted. 'Christ love, it's March. If you want a holiday let's head for the sun.'

'It's nearly Easter.'

'I'll buy you an egg at the airport.'

'It's a bargain. Aga. Wood burning open fire. All the wood

we can burn thrown in. Big screen TV. DVDs. A beautiful part of the country. A fourteenth century church. There's a Michelin starred restaurant just by the A12. We could have lunch on the way. I'll drive so you can have a drink. What's not to like?'

So my plan for sun, sea, sex and sangria was vanishing in the haze.

'What?' she said.

'I was just wishing and hoping as Mr Bacharach said to Mr David.'

'Who?'

I knew I'd lost an argument when there wasn't even one. 'Never mind. You're too young.' She ignored that comment. 'And you're flush, and not doing anything.' She said.

She was right. I'd copped a few quid from the sale of a flat I'd inherited, and even though I'd had to straighten out my old friend DI Jack Robber, and no doubt the revenue would be calling soon for some capital gains tax, I was richer than I'd been for a long time. If ever.

'It'd be great,' she said as she shrugged into her overcoat. 'You could take your Range Rover off road.'

'And get mud on the paintwork,' I said. 'I don't think so.'

'I'll book it then,' she said as she left the room. 'I'll call you later and get your card number.'

Game, set and match to the lady in the black coat.

So the following Thursday found us setting out for Bungay St Edmundsbury, yeah, I know, for a week in the country. I'd looked it up in my AA book, and it was about as far in the boondocks it could be, before coming out the other side. Hardly even a dot on the map. Get a rubber and it would be erased in the blink of an eye. Anyway, I'd invested some of my cash in one of these state-of-the-art, brand new sat-nav inventions, with a nice lady talking through the directions.

Blimey, but there ain't half some clever bastards.

We were both in jeans, boots and leather jackets all ready for anything the country could throw at us, or so we thought. I took the first turn at the wheel and we dawdled through the usual post rush hour traffic up through east London towards the A12 and Suffolk beyond. On that leg of the journey it was JB's choice of music on the stereo. Today it was Madonna's greatest hits. I could put up with that if she could put up with 'Ruby Baby' by Dion DiMucci. Live, and let live is my motto.

True to JB's word, there was a Michelin starred restaurant in an old mill just off the highway, and she'd booked us in for lunch as promised. And what a lunch it was. I won't bore you with details, but it was first class. Don't ask me how much it cost, but I bet it was a purse breaker. The menu I was given had no prices on it. It was that sort of place.

JB stuck to water, except for a very weak spritzer. Me, I finished the bottle, and was in a fine mood when we left the restaurant and I sunk into the leather luxury of the Range Rover's heated front seats as JB obeyed the lady in the sat-nav, and took us into the wild and woolly Suffolk countryside.

Eventually we came off the A12 and joined a succession of B and probably C roads. By then it was the Adderley brothers doing 'Mercy, Mercy, Mercy'. Real mellow, as the leafless trees loomed over us, and the ground was covered in daffodils. A lot. A fucking host as the poet didn't say, but maybe should've. It was dark before we hit the village. Lunch had taken longer than we thought. But then we were on holiday, so what the hell.

'Just look for the spire. That's what it said in the mail,' said JB, and lo and behold, even in the gloom there it was. Not that it would be hard to miss as the village itself was just a couple of streets, a pub, a green, a short row of shops and a duck pond sans ducks. They were probably sheltering from the cold. 'And the stable's at the back,' she added.

Everything in its place, I thought.

JB swung the motor through a gap in a waist high stone wall, then past the church which looked every year of its fourteenth century age, then, what turned out to be the vicarage. Exactly the same birthday by the state of it. Then a crunch of pebble-covered drive, and a low, single-storied building that looked more recent, with a dim light in its windows, and a single bulb over the front door to welcome the weary travellers. Then, suddenly, a figure showed up in the head lights. Big. JB slammed on the anchors and the car skidded to a halt, and the figure took off dragging one leg behind him.

'Bloody hell,' I said. 'Who the fuck is that? Quasimodo?'

'Don't be cruel.'

'OK. Just a local inbred.'

'Nick...'

'Sorry. Made me jump.'

'Not like you.'

'I was dozing. Too much wine with lunch.'

We got out of the car. By then the drive was empty. I opened the back and unloaded our bags, plus a couple of bags of supplies JB had insisted we bring. 'Key's under the flowerpot by the front door,' she said.

'Trusting souls.'

'This isn't Tulse Hill.'

'Well that's a plus,' I said.

The key was where she said it would be, and I opened the door and in we went. It was warm and smelled of cooking. Good cooking. The downstairs was open plan. By the door was a tall cupboard holding a telephone and telephone books. The room itself was dominated by a long dining table. On top was a vase of daffodils, a bowl full of fruit and a bottle of red wine holding down a note. We dropped the bags and JB rescued the paper. 'Welcome,' she read out. 'Hope you like red wine. There's a lamb hotpot in the Aga. Should be perfect by seven. Apologies if you're vegetarian. Forgot to ask. Milk and butter in the fridge. Bread in the bread bin. We'll leave you in peace this afternoon, but please pop round for coffee tomorrow morning around eleven. Signed by the vicar's wife, Mrs Whitechurch.'

'Good name for a vicar. She seems to have thought of everything,' I said. 'Nice digs.'

'I said you'd love it given time.'

'Maybe it's you I love.'

'Just maybe?'

'Just about.'

'Which is just about enough for me. I'm going to unpack,' said JB. 'Give us a hand with these bags.'

I did as I was asked, then left her in the master bedroom, complete with king size bed, soft mattress, softer duvet, and a en suite with a huge bath, and went back downstairs. We'd bought a dozen bottles of white which I dumped in the fridge. The fireplace was big enough to roast a pig, with cords of wood stacked waist high. The grate was laid with paper and fire lighters, so I struck a foot long match from the box on the mantelpiece and started a blaze and checked out the TV. A brand new looking thin big screen attached to the wall. Underneath was a PlayStation and a pile of games and DVDs. All mod cons, and reminded myself to replace my old set at home now I had some spare cash. I switched on, selected Sky news and slumped on the sofa. Happy days.

The evening went well. The hotpot was just right at seven as the note had said. Even after my large lunch I did it justice. The chops were small, tender, and greasy, the gravy not too thick, not too thin, and potatoes crisp and brown on top, soft and white underneath. The vicar's wife obviously knew her rhythm and blues.

Afterwards we collapsed on the sofa in front of the fire and the TV with the remains of the bottle of red, which we'd started with our meal, and smoked one of the ready rolled joints I'd brought with us. 'Is it blasphemous to smoke drugs on hallowed ground?' Asked JB.

'This was the stables,' I said.

'Jesus was born in a stable.'

'Not in Suffolk he wasn't.'

'Fair comment. Do you think the vicar and his wife will smell it?'

'We'll tell them it's herbal.'

'We really shouldn't smoke in here at all.'

'There's an open fire. That smokes. I don't think it matters.'

'You're right.'

We watched one of the stack of DVDs that were on a shelf by the TV. *Pulp Fiction* as it happens. Not a very religious choice, but then we're in an increasingly secular world.

About eleven we locked all the doors, turned everything off downstairs, raked the fireplace and headed upstairs to the king size bed, and whatever fate would bring. Wishing and hoping as Mr Bacharach once said to Mr David.

I woke up early and left JB snoring gently in bed. I slipped into jeans, a sweat shirt and thick socks and headed downstairs. There was a chill in the air so I set the fire going and pumped up the Aga. I went outside for a cigarette where the chill was chillier. I took a little walk and discovered an empty grave in, you guessed it, the graveyard. Not every holiday home has one of those I thought.

JB had put our supplies away and I decided on a full English for breakfast. Eggs over easy, crispy smoked streaky bacon, mini sausages, baked beans, fried cherry tomatoes, fat mushrooms, fried bread and loads of coffee. The place was getting a bit smokey when she glided down the stairs to join me. 'Blimey,' she said. 'You've been busy. I thought I smelt something good, but I reckoned I was dreaming.'

'No dreams here babe,' I replied. 'Just me. Your dreamboat come home.'

She sniggered at that, but I forgave her as I recited the menu and laid out warm plates.

'You'll have me fat,' she complained. 'You know I'm watching my figure.'

'Leave that to me darlin',' I said, twiddling a fake moustache. 'That's my job.'

We made good inroads to the food, hardly leaving a crumb and took our coffees to the sofa. 'What's the plan?' she said.

'I cooked, so you can clean up.'

She snorted.

'Dishwasher,' I said. 'Save your lovely hands. I saw a newsagent as we drove in last night. I think I'll go and get a paper. Then we've been invited for coffee with our hosts, don't forget.' I looked at my watch. It wasn't yet nine-thirty. 'Stacks of time,' I said.

I got fully dressed and hit the road, lighting a cigarette as I went past the vicarage and the church, through the opening in the wall we'd driven through the night before, and headed into the centre of the village, if you could call it that. That was when I got my first surprise in a day full of them. The first person I passed, a chubby woman of maybe forty, wished me 'good morning'; I nearly dropped my Silk Cut but managed to stammer back 'morning'. This was definitely not south London. On those mean streets you learned to keep your mouth shut early.

The next villager, this time male, also wished me the same. Me back. The third I beat to it and got 'And a very good morning to you, young man'. Now I knew was in a strange land.

I got to the newsagents/mini mart in the short row of shops I'd seen as we'd arrived. A hairdressers/barbers, a real butcher, a bakery and an iron mongers that seemed to stock everything but irons. I pushed open the door, and a bell attached to it announced out my appearance.

Next surprise was that the proprietor of the newsagent was a middle aged white man. Like I said. Definitely not south London.

There was an old dear at the counter picking up her copy of the *Mail*, a jam Swiss roll and a bunch of sweeties. Haribo, a Milk Tray Easter egg, and assorted bars of chocolate. I looked round the place as I waited. Everything but the kitchen sink, food, booze, greeting cards, paperbacks, all crammed together in a couple of aisles, and at the back a pay phone mounted on the wall. The woman paid up, saw me looking and said, 'For my grandchildren.'

'I hope they're worth it,' I said back.

'Every penny.'

She collected her purchases and headed for the door which burst open and a tall figure in a black overcoat charged in nearly knocking her over. I caught her on the rebound as the figure pushed past me. No 'good morning' from him.

'You alright?' I said to the lady.

'Fine,' she said. 'Some people have no manners.'

She left and the figure picked up a copy of the *Times* and demanded, 'The *Spectator*, and my usual cigars.'

The proprietor supplied what was asked for, the magazine and a pack of Wintermans, and the figure said, 'on my account,' picked up his stuff and pushed past me again without a word. That was much more like what I was used to, I almost felt homesick.

I went to the counter where the shopkeeper greeted me warmly. 'Charming fellow,' I said, nodding back at the door.

'The young Fitzwilliam,' he said.

'I would've thought he'd be smoking Monte Cristo,' I said.

'He might have to pay for them.'

'Ah, the account. Not a regular payer.'

'Not a payer at all if he can help it, but that's my problem. Now what can I get you?'

I bought the *Telegraph*, the *Sun* and twenty Silkies. 'Just passing through?' He asked as I paid.

'Staying at the cottage behind the church,' I said. 'A winter break.'

'Lovely place,' he said. 'The village put a lot of work into it. That church takes some financing. Just heating it nearly breaks the bank.'

'I can imagine.'

'And as for a winter's break,' he added. 'You might find it especially wintery soon. There's talk of snow on the wireless.'

Wireless. Blimey. I was so amazed at the anachronism that I didn't listen to his warning.

Silly me.

It was noticeably colder on the way back to the cottage, but I put that down to March winds that do blow.

I got inside, and JB was watching a cartoon on the TV and eating a banana from the bowl. 'Improving your mind?' I said.

'Just thinking of you.' It was Wylie Coyote.

'Sweet.'

We both grabbed a paper. I got the short straw *Sun*. I didn't mind.

Around eleven we jacketed up and headed next door to meet the reverend and his missus. She answered our knock. A grey haired, slightly harassed looking woman in old jeans and an older looking sweater. 'Hello,' she said, 'Mr and Mrs Sharman.'

Neither of us corrected her, as she ushered us down a short hall and into a large, comfortable looking kitchen, which smelt of coffee, and where a white haired gent in a sports jacket and flannels with a white reversed collar was sitting at the table doing the *Guardian* crossword. As we went in he dumped the paper and rose to greet us. 'Mr and Mrs Sharman,' He said too. 'Welcome.'

'Nick and JB,' I said. 'Reverend.'

'Douglas, please, and my wife Edna.'

Now there's a name you don't hear much these days. There was a big, hairy dog sitting in a basket by the back door. He yawned as he settled himself, then faintly growled. 'That's Jake,' Douglas said. 'All bark and no bite. He's harmless.'

'Sit down,' he added. 'You had no trouble finding us last night.' Not a question. The answer was obvious otherwise we wouldn't be there.

'Satellite navigation,' I said.

'The wonders of the age,' he said. Then to his missus. 'Dearest, didn't we promise our visitors refreshments.'

Edna smiled and headed for the stove, on which an old fashioned silver coffee percolator with a glass top which was bubbling dark brown. Hence the smell. And the coffee tasted as good as it smelt. Especially when Douglas hauled out a bottle of Courvoisier to sweeten the brew.

'Douglas,' said Edna, holding her hand over her cup. 'Really. What will our guests think?'

'They'll think we're perfect hosts won't you?' He asked.

Both JB and I nodded as he slung a decent belt into each of our cups, then his.

'Besides, the sun is over the yardarm somewhere in the Commonwealth.'

We sat and drank coffee and chatted about the church and the vicarage, and the amount they cost to keep up. I asked about the stables and they explained that the villagers had clubbed together with money and labour to turn the old stables into a money making scheme. The Aga and the big screen TV with all the extras had been donated by 'The Fitzwilliams'. The name spoken with deference. Apparently they were the lords and ladies of the manor, and had been as long as the church had existed. They lived in the Manor House on the other side of the village from the way we'd come in. If we went past the stables, through a lych gate, and across a copse of trees we could see the house. But not to go too close. 'Dogs,' said Douglas darkly.

'I think I met one at the shop,' I said. 'Youngish, tallish. Takes the *Times* and the *Spectator*, and smokes cigars.' I didn't add that I thought he might be improved by a good hiding, and he didn't pay his bills.

Both of their faces darkened at the mention. 'That would be young William Fitzwilliam,' said Douglas. 'I'm afraid as a man of God I shouldn't speak ill of a fellow human, but young William or should I say young William Spenser St John(pronounced sinjun) Ignatius Prendergast Tobias Chancellor Fitzwilliam to give him his full title, and I should know as I baptised the little blighter, is not one of my favourite people.' It seemed the brandy was loosening his tongue.

'Yes,' I agreed. 'He struck me as a rather unpleasant bloke.'

Douglas just gave me what my old mum would call an old fashioned look and said no more.

'Oh Douglas,' said Edna. 'He was a lovely boy. You remember when he was at infants school, at the fetes and the Christmas parties.'

'Yes. Then he went to prep school and Eton and Oxford, and came back a little monster. Or not so little. Frightening actually.'

So much for public school I thought, then said. 'Talking of frightening, I think we frightened someone when we arrived last night. Someone with a limp. I hope it wasn't an intruder.'

'No,' said Edna. 'That's Bertram. He's a strange lad. Not entirely with us if you see what I mean. He lives with his mother down the lane. Helps to keep the grounds of the church tidy. Makes sure the graves are kept clean. Chopped your wood for you. We pay him a bit. Not much. Just pocket money really. I hope he didn't scare you.'

'No,' I replied. 'Just glad you know him'

'It's not difficult to know everyone in a place this small,' said Douglas as he refreshed our cups. 'As you're here will we see you at church on Sunday?'

'Douglas,' said Edna. 'They're on holiday.'

'God never takes a holiday,' he said.

I looked at JB, and she looked at me. 'Of course,' I said. 'It'll be a pleasure to see the inside of your beautiful church as it's meant to be.'

'The eleven o'clock service is our most popular. Most attended. Most parishioners. If indeed you could count half a dozen halt and lame most.'

When we asked about a venue for lunch, they said the pub did a decent shepherd's if we didn't want to get the car out. I didn't. Nor did JB. But Edna told us about a decent gastro pub about three miles away for future reference. Anyway, after we had signed the visitors' book as requested and finished our coffee, we left and took a stroll through the village. It was getting colder, and I told JB about the impending snow, but she just shrugged.

Silly her.

The pub looked to be the same age as the church and vicarage. The Whale and Coffin. 'Peculiar name,' said JB.

'Hope it's not like the Slaughtered Lamb.'

'The what?'

American Werewolf In London.

She shook her head. I was believing that maybe I needed an older girlfriend. 'Never mind,' I said.

It wasn't exactly the same, but close. I had to duck to get through the door, and all conversation stopped when we entered. Not that there had been much before, as the place was almost empty.

I ducked another beam and grabbed a stool by the bar. JB joined me, and a happy faced woman popped up from behind the jump. 'Help you?' she asked.

'Pint of bitter,' I said. 'JB?'

'White wine.'

'Two ticks.' And the happy face bustled off.

I looked round. Usual stuff. Horse brasses, open fire. All surfaces gleaming. I liked a well looked after boozer.

When the drinks arrived I asked about the pub's name. Happy face just shrugged. 'No one knows,' she said. 'Been the name since God was a boy. Someone just made it up for a joke probably.'

That seemed fair enough, and I said the vicar's wife had recommended the shepherd's pie.

'Good for her,' she said, which led to us explaining that we were staying in the cottage and Happy Face introduced herself as Doris, call me Dorrie. Which we did.

After all that, Dorrie went out back again, then, two plates of shepherd's pie and peas arrived pronto. Dorrie accepted my payment, said, 'enjoy,' and vanished out back. By then the conversations in the bar had started again.

The food was as good as promised. Just like mother used to make. We dawdled over the grub, had another drink each and left promising to call again.

We went back to the cottage, opened a bottle of white and toasted each other.

'What now?' asked JB.

'Now we just relax. Wine and maybe a spliff. Me and you. Lock the doors and windows, draw the blinds. Us time. Holiday time.'

'Sounds grand,' she said.

And it was until around seven, after dark, sandwiches for supper, and me reading an Agatha Christie I'd found in the bookcase, as JB watched a quiz show I couldn't fathom out when our peaceful world was interrupted by the sound of engines, shouting and music from outside.

'What the hell...?' I said, and got up from the sofa, went

to the window just in time to see Douglas come out of the vicarage and add his voice to the racket.

'Leave it,' said JB.

'No. Something's up and Douglas will be out of his depth.' I slung on my jacket, unlocked the door and headed out. 'Keep it shut,' I said as I went.

Outside, away from the buildings I could see what looked like a party going on. A trio of big motorbikes were parked, headlamps on, and a bunch of leather clad young men and women were gathered round a ghetto blaster the size of a prefab, rocking out some heavy metal, and one semi goth girl was draped over a headstone, and the stench of weed filled the air. More like south London again.

Douglas was remonstrating with the party, and they were answering back in a threatening way. Jake was with him, but not making much of a job of guard jobbing. Two old grey heads well out of their depth. I felt sorry for the pair of them.

I walked up and said, 'I think the reverend would like you to leave.'

The geezer doing most of the talking was tall, long haired, and thought a lot of himself. You could just tell. 'The reverend,' he said mockingly.

'That's right.' I moved between him and Douglas, and I said softly. 'And me. Time to go. You've had your fun and you're spoiling a quiet night in for us.'

'Oh dear,' he said, and I saw his eyes shift and he threw a short right hander, that if it had connected could have seen me out of the game. I whipped my head back and he missed, coming off balance, and the follow up left missed too. When the third shot came I caught his fist in my right hand and spun him, and then it was him over a gravestone, his arm up his back, and under my control.

'Sexy,' said one of the girls which I could tell didn't go down well with the other geezers who moved forward.

'Any closer and I'll break his arm,' I said calmly. That didn't go down well either.

'Now clear off home, I think it's past your bedtime. And don't come back or someone will really get hurt bad,' I ordered.

'Leave it, Nigel,' said the goth girl. 'It's not worth it.'

'Nigel,' I said. 'Christ. Not many Nigels in the Hell's Angels.'

They got themselves together turned off the music, and those riding rode, and those walking walked. The last one to go was the bloke I'd held down.

As he left, he shouted out, 'Be careful. This ain't over.'

I didn't bother to reply. No point. The whole thing was so old fashioned. Like something out of some terrible British B-film from the fifties. Or something from the Christie novel I'd been reading. Bikers and their molls. Fucking pathetic.

'Thank you,' said Douglas when they'd left. 'I think I'm getting too old for fisticuffs.'

Fisticuffs, I ask you. 'Not a problem. Does that happen often?'

'Occasionally. I'd rather it hadn't when we had guests. I hope it hasn't upset you.'

'Not at all.'

'Yes. I noticed you handled yourself well. Military?'

'Police.'

He nodded, then said. 'Well, thanks again. See you on Sunday if not before.' I tipped an imaginary hat to him and headed indoors.

'My hero,' said JB. 'Do you think that's it?'

'I hope so,' I said.

But it wasn't, as I was afraid. About eleven when we were watching *Newsnight* and thinking about turning in, from outside I head a shout. 'Come on out you cockney fucker.'

'Shit,' I said. 'Some people never listen.'

I was still booted up and went to the door. Outside in the moonlight I saw Nigel and one of his mates, and the little goth girl who I guessed was at the bottom of everything those two twerps got up to. Probably including her. I stepped out onto the gravel. 'I thought I…' But Nigel didn't let me finish, just came at me with a blade in his hand. Simple really. I just remembered what my unarmed combat teacher at Hendon had drummed into me all those years ago. Minimum de blah blah, maximum de ya ya. Also, a wiseman once said: There is no good knife defence, only a defence that is better than nothing. Can't remember who, but it's true. Nigel probably thought I'd move backwards at the sight of the knife, instead, I let him come towards me, grabbed his knife hand with my right, pulled him forward, let his own momentum carry him past me, and more by luck than judgement tripped him so he went face down on the ground, knife flying.

Meanwhile the second geezer was coming fast towards me, twirling a motor bike chain as he came. I ask you. Just like I said a bad British B movie. But that bloody thing could take my head off my shoulders if it connected.

'Get him Charlie,' said the bird. 'Go on, kill him.'

Just then the door to the cottage flew open and JB appeared with a wine bottle in her hand, she hit the girl something shocking and she went down like a building collapsing. At this, the second bloke forgot about me and turned towards JB, the chain wrapping itself around his arm. 'Oi,' I said, and as he turned back I kicked him hard in his bollocks, and when he doubled up in pain I caught his head and slammed it down on my raised knee. I heard and felt his nose break and I knew there'd be claret and tears, and that he was out of the game. I dropped him then and went back to Nigel who was on his hands and knees so I kicked him as hard as I could in his ribs. He rolled over and I stomped him again and just once more for luck. In literally seconds the fight was over.

JB and I stood over the three bodies lying on the ground, and I said, 'I hope she's alive.'

'She's fine, 'said JB and pushed her with her foot. The girl moaned so I knew she'd live. Nigel was moaning too, and Charlie was holding his hand to his nose. He'd never look as pretty again.

'Come on,' I said. 'Let's get these fuckers off the premises.'

JB dragged the girl to her feet, and I helped Nigel and Charlie up. I took the knife and the chain and tossed them into the front door of the cottage. 'Come on, move,' I said to the trio. And they limped to the front entrance where two bikes were parked. 'Listen,' I said to Nigel. 'And listen good. This ends now. If I see any of you lot again I'll kill you, then them,' pointing to the others. 'Then everyone you love, and everyone they love. Scorched earth policy it's called. Do you get me Nige?' He nodded, 'Then get on your bike and think yourself lucky you still can.'

With that I walked away to where JB was waiting. I took a chance, turning my back, but I reckoned the fight had gone out of them. I was right. And if I hadn't been, there was always that empty grave.

'Do you think they'll come back?' said JB.

'Not if they know what's good for them.' I said.

'Well it certainly got my juices running,' she said, and it wasn't long before she showed me how juicy she meant.

Next morning I got up early again and went outside to check the motor. Cellulose shining in the cold with a light dusting of frost, and all tyres intact. So they hadn't come back to do a little damage. There were some blood stains on the gravel which I kicked about so you'd never known they'd been there. I hoped the same went for Nigel and his mates. Inside, JB was making busy with the pots and pans and rustling up omelettes and toast for breakfast. 'Everything OK?' she asked.

'Copacetic,' I replied. 'But bloody freezing. Where's the ketchup?'

After breakfast I took another stroll to pick up the papers.

Lots of 'good mornings' again as I went, but I was used to it by now. The same bell rang when I entered the shop and the same bloke was behind the jump and welcomed me like an old friend. I bought the usual pair of papers and headed back for coffee with JB.

We decided to take the Rover out for a spin and check out the gastro pub Edna had told us about.

Which we did. And very good it was too, so replete, we headed back to yet another bottle of cold white. Not as cold as it was outside. 'The old boy at the paper shop says it's definitely snow tonight.'

'Too cold for snow,' said JB. 'That's what my mum would say.'

Wrong.

'So what now?' she asked after a glass.

'Why don't we explore. I fancy taking a look at the old Manor House.' Says me.

'Do we have to?'

'We don't have to do anything. We're on holiday. Just interested.'

A sigh, then a smile. 'Come on then.' She said.

We booted up again and as directed went past my truck to the end of the drive, then a short walk to an old fashioned lych gate, through the copse of trees and ended up in front of a high fence thick with evergreen. All we could see of the house was a black tiled roof and what seemed like a dozen chimney pots. No sign of dogs.

'Satisfied?' asked JB.

'Sorry.'

She just shook her head. 'There's half a bottle of white wine waiting back there. And another full bottle in the fridge. Last one back is it.'

'Lead on,' I said.

We went back the way we'd come and just as the cottage

was in sight complete with bottle and a half of wine and who knew what delights to follow, we saw the character we'd scared when we arrived. He was standing by an open grave with a shovel in his hand, and at the sight of us he took off sharpish. 'Looks like Bertram doesn't want to make friends,' said JB.

'And us so sweet and gentle.'

'Well, me anyway.'

I didn't argue, just grabbed her hand and made for our temporary home, when suddenly it all kicked off, and was never the same again.

Just before we got to our door, the door to the vicarage crashed open and Edna appeared shouting. 'Thank God you're here. I think he's dead.' Jake was with her on his lead looking nonplussed as only dogs can.

I bolted for the door. 'Where?' I yelled.

'In the library.'

'Where?' I yelled again. I hardly knew the layout of the place.

'Through that door.' She pointed.

I guessed where she meant and in a room piled with books I saw Douglas on his back by the fireplace, blood everywhere and a poker, covered in claret next to him. 'Have you called an ambulance?' I shouted.

'No.'

'Do it Edna, and the police.'

She vanished, I felt for a pulse, and it was there, but weak.

'He's alive,' I yelled again. I was getting hoarse. 'Be quick.'

Next thing the churchyard was full of blue flashing lights as cops and ambulance arrived together. But it was too late. They knew, and the paramedics both looked grim as they carried him out, and one just shook his head at me.

I took Edna back to the cottage, where she had the obligatory strong, sweet tea. By then CID had turned up, and a SOCO van was parked next to my truck. We left Edna to the ministrations of the Suffolk murder squad as it turned out to be. JB and I took a bottle to the bedroom. What else was there to do?

When the cops had finished with Edna who fast resembling a wrung out rag, they turned to me.

'Your name Sharman?' said the lead. A lean beanpole who needed a haircut.

I nodded.

'Nicholas Sharman?' The other one. A bit of a smoothy, who I bet went down well with the local housewives.

'Correct.'

'*The* Nicholas Sharman?' Haircut.

'Could be.'

'You used to be Job?' Him again.

'Long ago and far away, or is that a song?'

I don't think he got it.

'A little bell went ping when we put your name and address from the visitors' book,' said Haircut.

'Little bells do have a habit of going ping when they're rung,' I said, thinking of the shop.

'So. What are you doing here?'

'I'm on holiday. Good food, good wine and a good time with my imorata who's sitting over there.'

He looked puzzled at that and JB interrupted. 'He means his girlfriend, his bird. Or at least that was the idea until circumstances interrupted.'

They asked me if we'd seen anything, and I told them about the bikers from the night before, and seeing Bertram by the grave before the alarm was raised, but nothing else suspicious. No fleeing murderers for example. They took notes. 'Thank you Mr Sharman,' said Smoothy. Next, he was going to say don't leave town.

'OK. Just one thing, don't leave town.'

'I wouldn't dream of it.'

'Can Mrs Whitechurch stay with you tonight?' asked Haircut. 'Next door is still a crime scene.'

'Of course,' said JB. 'There's three bedrooms.'

'And the dog?'

'We're animal lovers,' I added.

'Good.'

After the cops had left allowing Edna to fetch night things, fresh clothes, and everything she needed for the morning, plus dog food and bowls for Jake, they locked up the vicarage, smothering it in police tape, leaving one poor soul outside the door in the cold all wrapped up like an Eskimo to make sure nobody nicked the building in the night.

JB got busy with the teabags again, and I parked Edna and Jake on the sofa and asked her exactly what had happened.

'I'd taken Jake out for a walk to the shop after lunch. Well, a bit later in fact. I came back and called for Douglas. When there was no answer, I went through to the library where he writes his sermons, and there he was. You know the rest.'

'Did you see anybody leaving?'

'No.'

I told her that we'd seen Bertram.

'You don't think... No. He's a gentle soul. Wouldn't hurt a fly.'

The tea arrived and Edna told us that she and Douglas had planned on retirement to Cromer where her sister lived.

'I must tell her. And the bishop. And friends.'

She cried again, but not so hard. I guessed a vicar's wife would have to have a backbone of steel to contend with all that life would throw at her, and I think I was right. When we'd drunk our tea, we left Edna by the front door with the landline to make all the calls she had to make, and we went upstairs to give her some privacy.

When she'd finished, she came and got us and JB made a late supper though no one felt much like eating. 'I phoned the bishop,' said Edna. 'He's coming tomorrow to take a service. Then my sister. Looks like I'll be taking early retirement. The diocese will want the vicarage for the new incumbent. Life goes on I'm afraid. Even in death.' At that she broke down into tears again, and JB gave her a hug. I sat on the sofa like a spare part.

'You know,' said Edna, 'You've had such a time of it, what with those yobs yesterday, and now this, I should give you your money back. It's been no holiday. But the cheque book is back in the house, and I can't get in for all that tape.'

'Police tape, like promises are easy to break,' I said back. 'But I wouldn't dream of taking back a penny.' I didn't add that I hadn't had as much fun for ages, as I didn't think it would go down well with the recently bereaved.

'Do you think it's going to snow tonight?' I asked her, to change the subject.

'It might. There have been warnings on the news.'

'And in the shop.'

'Tom likes to be a bringer of tidings, both good and bad. If it does, there's a cupboard under the stairs with Wellington boots, all sizes. You're welcome to use them.'

'I hope it won't come to that.'

Around nine-thirty we got Edna and Jake settled in the second bedroom with cocoa for her and fresh water for him, then went downstairs, and JB took a cup of tea out to the poor copper freezing by the vicarage door, and opened one of our last bottles of wine. 'So much for a quiet holiday,' I said.

'My fault,' said JB. 'We should have gone for the infinity pool alternative.'

'Yes, I remember mentioning that at some point for what it was worth. Well we're stuck here now. Might as well make the best of it.'

We knocked back the bottle and headed upstairs to bed. JB

peered out if the window and said. 'It's started to snow.'

'At last.'

'Just a shower I expect.'

Wrong again.

Next morning I woke to a strange light in the bedroom. JB was standing by the window looking through the curtains. 'What's up?' I said.

She turned. 'You're not going to believe this,' she said.

I climbed out from under the duvet and joined her. She pulled the curtain aside to expose a sea of white. I could hardly believe my eyes. Snow covered everything to a depth of at least two feet. The car was just a white hump on the drive. Completely covered. 'Blimey,' I said. 'So much for too cold for snow.'

'Maybe mum was wrong,' said JB.

'Mums often are.'

We did our ablutions, got dressed and headed downstairs. The Aga had kept the temperature up, but I cleaned out the fireplace and started a fire while JB got the coffee on. There was so far no sign of Edna or Jake.

I opened the cupboard Edna had pointed out and amongst half a dozen pairs of wellies I found a pair that fitted perfectly. When I tried the front door I had to fight a snow drift, pushing and shoving until I could get outside. The air was glacial, but the snow was pretty soft. I trudged round to the vicarage door where the police tape was looking a bit sad under the snow. Of the young copper who'd been guarding the site there was no sign.

I went back indoors, pulled off the boots and headed for a steaming mug of coffee on the table. 'Something tells me the bish won't be making any services today,' I said.

'That bad?'

'Worse.'

'Worse still,' she said. 'No signal for the phones. No web on my laptop, and the land line's dead.'

'Blimey,' I said again. 'Apocalypse now.'

JB nodded glumly.

'There's a phone at the shop,' I said. 'I'll go see if it's open, and if it works. It would be nice to find if the rest of the world is still there.'

About then Edna came downstairs in her dressing gown. 'This is awful,' she said.

'Tom was right. On top of everything else.'

I told her about the lack of communication and my idea of going to the shop. 'Well if anything's open it'll be Tom's,' she said. 'It would take a bomb to get him to close. And would you take Jake. He'll need to do his business.'

'Fine by me.'

'I hate to ask, but if he does anything solid please put it in a bag.'

I looked at JB and she looked back. 'Of course,' I said.

'It's just what we do to keep the village nice,' said Edna. No one would have guessed she'd just been widowed.

I booted up again, and put Jake's lead on his collar and headed out. As I left JB solemnly gave me a plastic carrier bag. I looked at Jake and he looked at me. I made no joke about being gone for a while.

Outside it was almost total whiteout, the snow almost reaching the top of my boots. I trudged along and Jake lolloped after me. I think he was enjoying the snow. He stopped once for a wee, but nothing stronger. On the way I passed no one. Once we hit the main street there were a few tracks in the snow, and as Edna had prophesied there were lights on in the store.

I parked Jake outside, his lead tied to a railing. The door opened and the bell rang as before, and as before Tom stood behind his counter, king of all he surveyed.

'You're brave,' said with a smile when I was inside and the door closed behind me.

'Dog needed a walk,' I said.

Suddenly he was serious. 'Oh, you've got Jake. Terrible thing yesterday. Poor Douglas. Any news?'

'Just what I was going to ask you.'

'Well, no papers as you can see. Nothing's moving according to Radio Suffolk. I've only opened in case anyone needs emergency rations.'

'Do you know what happened to the copper who was guarding the vicarage?'

'There I can help you. I stayed open late last night, being Saturday. He came in about eleven. There'd been a crash, or crashes on the bypass. He was called out. Said someone would come and replace him.'

'No sign,' I said.

'Like I said, roads blocked.'

'Oh well. Is your phone working?' I nodded at the instrument on the wall.

'Sorry. Dead as a dodo.'

'Well, I tried.'

'You did. Anything else?'

I bought cigarettes and half a dozen bottles of wine. Emergency rations indeed. As I was leaving he left his spot and grabbed a chewy bone off one of the shelves. 'Give this to Jake for me. He loves them.'

Outside I did the deed, and the old dog trotted along behind me all the way home with the bone sticking out of his mouth.

I went back to the cottage, and we passed the day warmly. I cooked lunch out of what was left of our supplies, and we all gathered together in front of the fire in the afternoon, and tried to act as normally as possible under the circumstances.

Round about nine there was a sharp rap on the front door. 'Are we expecting anyone,' I asked as a rhetorical question, not expecting an answer, but got one anyway.

'Could be the bishop,' said Edna

'Or the police,' JB chipped in.

'I doubt that,' I said.

Jake just growled, but not so's you'd think he was picking a fight. Just adding to the conversation.

'Only one way to find out,' I said. Once again, just a comment.

With it I got up and headed to the door. I switched on the porch light and opened the door, thankfully now free of snowdrifts. Stood outside was the bloke who'd almost knocked me over at the newsagents. Fitzwilliam.

He looked at me and I looked back, then from inside his coat he produced a long double barrelled shotgun, its stock and barrels beautifully engraved with whirls and swirls that gleamed in the porch light. Probably a Purdey I thought. Probably one of a pair. He stuck the barrels in my face and demanded. 'Where is it?'

'What?' I said.

'You know very well. The icon you've come to value.'

'Sorry,' I said, quite reasonably under the circumstances. 'I don't know what the hell you're talking about. And do you mind getting that thing out of my face.'

'Get inside,' he ordered, and I did. He followed and slammed the door behind himself. He stamped the snow off his boots, right posh green ones. Hunters I think they're called. Funny what you think about when you're in the probability of being chopped in half with buckshot. 'So you're not from Sotheby's,' he said, chewing the insides of his mouth, there was white foam around his lips, and it wasn't just cheap cigars that were his drug of choice I guessed. In fact I knew, as I'd been in that state myself often.

'No,' I said as I backed into the room.

'Who are you then?'

'We're here on holiday,' I explained. 'Destressing was the idea, but as you can see it hasn't worked.'

'What do you do?'

I thought enquiry agent might set him off further, so I lied. 'Something in the city,' I said.

'And her?

He moved the gun onto JB.

'I sell lingerie for...' She mentioned her employer.

'Christ,' he said. 'That bastard Whitechurch.'

'You really shouldn't speak ill of the dead,' I said. 'Especially when you killed him.'

He ignored that. Just turned on Edna. 'Have you hidden it?'

'What?' The poor woman was close to having a fit of hysterics.

Through gritted teeth Fitzwilliam said, 'A wedding bowl. Fifteenth century. Russian. Decorated with painted icons.'

'Why would I hide it?'

'Because I had a buyer. Russian. A fucking billionaire. He offered me two million cash. But your bloody husband insisted on having it valued and auctioned and giving the proceeds to the church. This bloody church. I told him I'd give him a percentage to do with as he wanted, but he wouldn't listen.'

'And you killed him,' I interrupted.

'Bloody fool. I just lost it. I need that money. I owe too many bad people. Without it I'm finished. My family are finished. They couldn't bear the shame.'

Shame. Now there's a word you don't hear often these days. And that really is a shame. 'And the icon?' I asked.

'Shut up,' he spat. Literally. He was really foaming at the mouth now.

Then a thought crossed my mind. I looked at the table as we'd come in on Thursday evening. Wine, flowers, a note, And the fruit in a decorated bowl. The same bowl JB had filled with salad for our supper. 'That bowl,' I said. 'The fruit bowl. The salad bowl.'

'Yes,' she said.

'The bowl with the pretty designs.'

I think her jaw dropped. I know Fitzwilliam's did. 'Where is it?' he demanded.

'I put it in the dishwasher. The cycle's just finished. I thought it would be dishwasher friendly,' she said.

I thought he was going to cry. 'Get it,' he screamed.

JB did as he ordered. She pulled the bowl from the steaming machine, and I must say it looked pretty good to me. Anyway, it had managed to exist for five hundred years give or take without any damage, so what was some hot water and detergent going to hurt?

He told her to put it on the draining board and looked closely. 'All serene,' I said.

He nodded, forgetting we were there almost, but not quite. 'Dry it,' he said to JB. 'And be careful.'

Jesus, this wasn't the time to be butterfingers. She did as she was told, dabbing at it with a dish cloth. 'Give it the me. And something to carry it in,' he said.

She obeyed again, passing him a Waitrose carrier in which he put the icon. Just like I would have carried Jake's shit.

'You won't get away with it,' I said. Maybe rashly, but I didn't think he had the balls to murder us all in cold blood. Of course I could have been wrong. Luckily I wasn't.

'Don't worry. I have a vehicle every inch capable of getting through the snow. I'll be in France by breakfast time, and then this will be sold.'

He walked out of the front door and I followed closely, followed by JB. We watched as he walked across the drive, and then vanished without a sound leaving only the bag containing the icon and the shotgun visible in the snow. 'What the...? said JB, and I twigged. The open grave that Bertram had dug.

I pulled on my wellingtons and ran through the snow, and sure enough, snug as a bug in a rug there lay the young Fitzwilliam, out cold.

So that was that. We dragged him up and locked him in the cellar of the vicarage until we could get in touch with the outside world. He was arrested for murder, the icon, thankfully unharmed, although we never mentioned the dishwasher incident, was valued by Sotheby's and sold at auction for close on four million quid. The church and the vicarage was saved. Douglas was buried in the very grave Fitzwilliam ended up in, and Edna and Jake finished up in Cromer.

JB and I went home once the ice melted and lived happily ever after, at least for a while.

So that was how it ended.

BAGS' GROOVE

That Monday lunchtime in June it was on page three of the early edition of the *Standard*. Front page was a rail strike that was or wasn't about to happen, and the fact that Madonna had decided to dress like she'd been brought up in the Shires, and was going to open an olde English pub in London with her dozy husband. I read the paper with a BLT that I'd managed to wrestle out of it's usual cardboard and plastic coffin, and a cup of decent coffee from the office machine. On page three, half way down was a headline that read: MYSTERY OF SHOOTING VICTIM AT LUXURY HOTEL. Underneath was the report of an unnamed man found with bullet wounds in the car park of the five star Dulwich Blenheim hotel. He had been taken to a local hospital for treatment, where his condition was reported to be critical but stable. Nothing more. I bit off a bit more of the sandwich that I could chew and washed it down with a swallow of coffee, then moved on to page four, and some problem with rubbish collection in Hammersmith. The paper and my lunch finished, I dumped the detritus into my waste paper bin and went back to the Stephen Hunter paperback I'd been reading, put on the stereo and forgot all about the story.

As you might have guessed, business was slow that June.

I walked home about six, ordered a pizza to be delivered and put on the news to pass the time while I waited. Then came the local news just as the door went. I collected the pizza and began to eat it straight out of the box. The main story was the rail strike, now postponed, then the shooting in the Blenheim, the victim now identified as William Bridges, who was under guard in King's College Hospital, still critical but stable. Still of no interest to me as I munched my extra Pepperoni. Then more local stories, followed by the sport and weather, which boded well, and I thought no more about it, finished my supper, watched a couple of films on video and went to my solitary bed.

The cops came to my office the next morning. Two of them. Female and male, female leading. A DI, her oppo, a DC. Her name was Riley, his Ward. I was drinking coffee again, but things weren't all bad as I was still reading the Stephen Hunter paperback and listening to Miles Davis playing 'Bags' Groove' with a whole bunch of the finest American jazzmen of the century. Life could have been worse, then, as was often the case, it deteriorated when Lily Law came calling.

I asked them to sit. They did. I offered them coffee. They refused. So I made myself another cup, sat behind my desk and lit a Silk Cut.

Ward coughed. Good. Riley looked like she could murder a fag, but I didn't offer.

From a voluminous bag Riley produced a plastic evidence bag. Inside was a business card. One of mine. I'd've recognised it anywhere. Don't forget I'm a detective. Luckily it wasn't one with crossed machine guns.

I made a 'yes, it's mine, but so what?' gesture. At least that's what I meant.

'Recognise it?' asked Riley.

I felt like saying 'I'd be blind if I didn't' but realised that levity was not the best direction to take under the circumstances, although I was not yet sure what the circumstances were. Not good, that was for sure. 'Yes. It's mine, or was. I hand them out like confetti. You never know when someone will get in touch.' Like now, I thought. Like the old Bill.

'Do you know Charlie Barnett?' asked Ward.

Charlie Barnett. Now that was a name from the past. If it was the same Charlie Barnett, and I had to assume it was, he'd been a snout for me, and Christ knew how many others, back when I'd been a DS at Kennington nick. But that hadn't been all, and I felt just a little tingle in my sphincter at the mention of his name.

'I remember him,' I said. 'Why?'

Silence. As if maybe I should know.

'From the look of you, I imagine all is not well with Charlie,' I added.

Ward snorted, and Riley gave him a dirty look. His face reddened.

She told me what had happened to Charlie. He was the shooting victim, left for dead in the car park of the Blenheim, next to his Mercedes Benz. The make of car had not been on the news.

'It wasn't his name given out on the news last night. Bridges wasn't it?' I asked.

'You keep up with events,' said Riley.

'I try. Especially when people are being shot in leafy Dulwich. That's something that doesn't happen everyday.'

Another silence. Longer this time. Maybe they were expecting me to confess. I didn't comply.

'Now Mr Sharman,' said Riley, when the silence dragged on. 'We know a lot about you. You were the law, then you broke the law. Several times. But we're in bit of a pickle with this one. We need to find out who shot Mr Barnett, and our only lead is your card.'

'It wasn't you was it?' Ward interrupted. I'd bet a pound to a peanut they'd rehearsed that in the car coming over.

I shook my head. 'No. I haven't seen Charlie, or thought about him for years.' Not true, but they didn't need to know that.

'He must have thought about you.'

'Why don't you ask him?' But critical, even though stable, probably put the kibosh on that.

'We would,' said Riley. 'But circumstances prevent that.

And now I'm going to tell you things I probably shouldn't. Things that only a few people are aware. And if any of it leaks to the media, I'm afraid we'll come calling again, but not in such a pleasant way.'

'I'm no fan of the media,' I said.

'Good. The night before last. Sunday. An employee of the Blenheim hotel went out to the car park for a cigarette and found Mr Barnett lying by the driver's door of his car. The boy thought he was dead. He almost was. In fact he died in the ambulance on the way to hospital but was brought back. He'd been shot twice. One was a through and through and got smashed against the car park wall. The other was in his chest, and the bullet bounced off a rib and ended up in his neck close to his spinal column.' She touched her own neck as if in sympathy. I liked her then, and looked at her properly for the first time. Pretty decent, if a bit strung out looking. Some other time, some other place we might have got together for a drink. Had a laugh. Not much to laugh about today though. She had a hard job for a woman in the nineteen-nineties. Hard job any time.

'He needs an operation to remove the bullet,' she went on. 'But there's a great deal of tissue damage, so it can't be done right now. If the bullet moves in the wrong direction he's a quadriplegic, in the other direction he's dead, so the hospital has put him in an induced coma. So, unfortunately we cannot ask him anything. Also the bullet might be from a gun involved in other shootings.'

'Any particular reason for that?' Silly question really.

'Well, he's an interesting fellow.'

'Always was.'

'When he was found he was wearing a very expensive tailored Hugo Boss suit, that my friend here,' she looked over at Ward, 'tells me would set you back about a thousand pounds. A handmade shirt and silk tie from Jermyn Street,

Lobb brogues. He was wearing an Omega Speedmaster watch that is list priced at seven thousand pounds. In his pocket was a wallet with his driving licence, bank and credit cards, a bundle of cash and of course your card. We're waiting for a court order to see inside his accounts. The house keys were for a nice little town house in Battersea worth a few bob. The house was also his office. And here's something interesting. He was the managing director of a record company that has never released a record, and an entertainment agency with no clients. The Mercedes and a Bentley were leased by the company. The Bentley is nowhere to be found. And finally, in the safe in his suite was ten thousand pounds in used notes, and a brand new passport in the name of William Bridges. Now you know everything we do, so over to you.'

'Nobody saw or heard the shooting?' I asked.

'No. And what's a sickener is that the hotel just fitted closed circuit TV in the underground garage and grounds. It's the latest thing, but it hadn't gone live. In fact we have no idea who fired the shots. So that's why we're here.'

I put on my serious face, frowned a bit and started. 'I really don't know what to say,' I said. 'I haven't seen Charlie for years. He was a grass.' They both pulled faces at that so I backtracked. 'A paid informant, and a good one. He used to hang out at a boozer in Herne Hill that had bands in at the weekend. He was something to do with the management. The place is flats now. But I never knew anything about a record company, or the other business. We were matey, but not mates. There used to be lots of lock ins at the pub. Then there were plenty of Rubys and Chinese as well. In those days you didn't always know who you were eating and drinking with. Cops and villains, pretty much of the same stamp.'

That didn't go down well either, but it was the truth.

'He was good at what he did, but he ruffled quite a few feathers, and maybe some of those feather have ruffled back.

Have you checked any of his successes have recently been released?'

'It's not that easy Mr Sharman,' said Riley.

'That's why they pay you the big bucks.'

'Anything else?' said Riley.

I shook my head. I'd told the truth up to a point, but some things that happened years ago were better off left years ago. That is, until there's nothing left but the truth, and the truth can sometimes set you free. But not always. Who said that? Me, as it happens.

'So, can I see him?' I asked after a moment.

'There's nothing much to see,' said Riley. 'Just a man lying in bed being fed through a tube.'

'I mean when he wakes up.'

'If he wakes up,' said Ward. And that pretty well was the end of that.

'Do I need a lawyer?' I asked

'Do you think you need one?'

'I didn't shoot him.'

'Then no. If we thought you did, we wouldn't be having this conversation here.'

I had no smart answer for that, so I kept quiet.

'Well thank you for your time,' said Riley, and she collected her bag, my card and her detective constable and left.

I waited a moment and went to pick up the phone and call my old friend DI Jack Robber, but the phone beat me to it, and there he was. What a coincidence.

'Had visitors?' he asked.

'As if you didn't know.'

'We should meet.'

'Not at the Dog.' The disgusting boozer in Loughborough Junction that seemed like his second home.

'No. Is Li's open?'

'Should be.' Li was Lionel, our Vietnamese friend who

ran a tasty bistro just up the way from my office.

'You can buy me lunch.'

'By all means.'

So, half an hour later the door to my office slams open and Jack Robber breezes in all poshed up in an electric blue whistle and matching tie and hankie. What a geezer.

'Carnaby Street?' I asked. 'Or Oxfam?'

'Piss right off. You got my usual?'

'Cash or cheque?' I asked.

'Cash is king.'

I slung him over an envelope containing two hundred sovs, the usual. He actually counted it. After all these years.

When he'd finished he tucked it away and gave me a questioning look. 'Tell me all,' I said.

'Lunch,' he said.

'Come on then.'

Lionel's Vietnamese was doing well and had recently expanded into the shop next door. It was a balmy afternoon as Robber and I arrived. Lionel, or Li as he was most often known, was standing in the front in his chef's whites. By coincidence in this day of many coincidences, his stereo was playing 'Bags' Groove', his favourite tune ever since I'd introduced him to it. This time it was the Milt Jackson's version.

'Gentlemen,' he cried as we went inside. 'How grand to see you both.'

'Li,' we said in unison.

'Today is indeed an auspicious one, and you are both here. I have something for you to try. A new recipe of my own invention.' As he was talking he led us through to the back of the building, and a table for two tucked away from the main room. His girlfriend Maureen who also waited tables was laying out silverware on the snow white tablecloth.

'Mo.' Robber and I again in unison.

'Hello,' she said back.

'Chicken and pork,' Li continued. 'A marriage made in heaven. Minced together with a special secret chilli sauce that will creep up and smack you in the neck.'

'Sounds good,' said Robber as we sat, and Maureen poured iced water for us both.

'And beer,' said Li. 'Ice cold.'

'Yes, your highness,' said Maureen.

'I'll get it ready,' said Li. 'Fragrant rice. Mustn't forget fragrant rice.'

'What is this feast called?' I asked.

Li pointed at the stereo speaker above our head. 'Why, Bags' Groove, of course,' he said.

And then they both left us alone.

'So what's all this about?' I said to Robber.

'Looks like you've upset somebody.'

'Not for the first time.'

'Or the last probably.'

'If I don't end up in jail.'

'You didn't shoot him.'

'I know that. You know that. And I think Riley and Ward are of the same opinion, Thank God. I don't need a night in the cells.'

'They're a good team. Maybe a great one. Murder squad. She's single. Married to the job. No significant other as far as anyone knows. Never has been. Lives alone in a flat in Streatham. Not even a cat. A bit like you Sharman, at the moment.'

I nodded. He was right. But then he so often was.

'Maybe you two should get together. As you're both on your lonesome.'

'How do you know that I am?' I asked.

'Not difficult. I saw the dry cleaning bag in your office. No one ironing your shirts?'

'Jack,' I said. 'The usual kind of women I go out with aren't great shirt ironers. They generally have other talents.'

'Anyway, I know when your birds are on the go.' He went on. 'Not literally. I don't have an ear at your bedroom door.'

'That's a blessing.'

'But back to Riley. When she's not working she goes to see musicals. Her only vice apparently. As for him. Twenty five, though he looks about fourteen. He's on a fast track. Might be her boss in five years. Married with a kid, and another on the way. Loves Oasis apparently. And yes, I do know who they are. Plays guitar, badly.'

'Clean I suppose.'

'As Colgate. Both of them.'

'And Charlie?'

'Alright bloke. I've paid him a shilling or two over the years. You too I imagine.'

I nodded. The music had changed to Charlie Parker with strings. Another coincidence that we were talking about one.

'Who wanted him dead?' I asked. A rhetorical question. Any south London lowlife he'd sold out for cash.

'Your guess is as good as mine,' said Robber, as our food and bottles of beer, freezing cold and coated with moisture arrived. 'It all looks like a bit of a pickle.'

I could do nothing but agree.

Li didn't embarrass himself or us by hanging around for our verdict. The food was as good as he'd promised. The chilli subtle at first, but then exploding on the tongue and lips like a tiny volcano. Robber wiped his eyes before he swallowed a mouthful of cold lager. 'By Christ,' he said. 'That's got a kick.'

'But in a good way,' I said around a mouthful of beer. 'The thing is, why would Charlie have my card on him? I'm not hard to find. I'm in the Yellow Pages for Godsakes. Like I told Riley and co. I hand those babies out like sweeties.'

'You've been framed.'

'Funny.'

'Not for you.'

Li had seen our empty plates and bounced up to the table with a big grin on his face. He didn't say a word, just raised his eyebrows.

'Ten out of ten, son,' I said.

His smile widened.

'Ditto,' said Robber. 'Nearly took the roof of my mouth off.'

Li's smile almost spilt his face in half at that, as Maureen arrived behind him. 'Coffee?' She asked.

'Irish,' said Robber.

I nodded my agreement, and she vanished again.

When we'd finished lunch Robber left, two hundred quid richer, and I stayed, two hundred and twenty quid poorer. The lunch had been on the house as we'd been Li's guinea pigs. But on the way out I put a twenty in the jar by the door for a Vietnamese donkey charity. You should see how they treat those poor beasts.

Back in the office I regarded my dry cleaning bag and took it with me over to the pub. I felt like an afternoon away from my troubles.

But troubles have a way of catching one up. That was when the pickle turned to piccalilli.

I bought a pint and sat at a corner table. I draped my cleaning over one of the chairs opposite. I sat and let the news of the day rattle round my brain like pieces of a jigsaw. Nothing fitted.

Five minutes after I arrived a bloke in a decent suit came in, went to the bar, ordered a double malt, no ice and when it arrived added just a dash of soda from the siphon on the bar. I wondered how long it had been since anyone used it, but after a sip he seemed satisfied, turned, surveyed the room and strolled over to my table. 'Mind if I join you?' he asked.

Now, it was a summer weekday, past lunch time, but too early for any commuters and the pub was almost empty. Me. Two likely looking lads in the far corner, a couple of old boys nursing pints, and that was that. Plenty of empty tables. I nodded and he put his drink on a beer mat and sat down. 'My name's Colin Palmer,' he said. 'I'm a gangster.'

'Never heard of you,' I said.

'That's because I'm good at gangstering.'

'So where's the rest of the gang?'

'Well there's two over there.' He indicated the likely lads who didn't acknowledge. 'And there's two more outside in a car. They're all armed by the way.' He looked at my dry cleaning as if he expected one of the shirts to slide out and open fire with a semi-automatic.

'I'm not,' I assured him. 'Not when there's an R in the month.'

He didn't seem amused. 'Charlie Barnett was found shot in a hotel in Dulwich with your card in his pocket. He'd stolen a great deal of money from me. I want you to get it back.'

'How do you know all this?' I asked. 'About him, I mean. And my card?'

'I have my methods.'

'Cops on the payroll.' Not a question.

He shrugged.

'Riley and Ward?' I asked.

He smiled and shook his head. 'No. They're the untouchables.'

'Jack Robber?'

That was a question, but I thought I already knew the answer.

'Now that would be telling,' he said. He didn't touch the side of his nose, but he might as well have done. Of course it was Robber playing both ends against the middle as usual. But without him I wouldn't be half the private investigator that I was.

'How much?' I asked.

'How much did he steal, or how much am I prepared to pay for getting it back?'

'The former. The latter would be a donation to a charity

of my choice.' I thought of the donkeys.

'They said you were strange Sharman, and of course that's assuming you'll get it.'

'And I assume if I don't I'll end up like Charlie.'

'We had nothing to do with that.'

'I believe you. Thousands wouldn't.'

'Why would I have him shot when he still had my money. No return in that.'

'Unless he'd already spent it.'

'Feckless, he might be, he'd have a hard job spending what he took in the short time between doing the deed and being left for dead.'

'OK, you've piqued my interest. And as you're here I'll have another pint and you can tell me all.'

'You're a cheeky bastard, but I think I'm getting to like you,' he said and raised a finger, and likely lad number one was at the tables smartish. 'Lager?' Colin asked me. I nodded. 'And my usual. Send the others outside home. There's nothing to worry about here. We'll be a while. Relax.'

The geezer got our drinks, popped out, came back and sat down again, and Colin told me his tale.

Although he'd told me he was good at gangstering, our Colin had made one big mistake: trusting Charlie Barnett. The scam was smuggling blood diamonds jetted in from South Africa. Then onwards to Antwerp via Harwich to the Hook of Holland, delivered by Charlie in a Bentley with a hidden compartment under the back seat.

Diamonds out, Dollars, Euros and Sterling in. Charlie had managed clubs and bands in a small way when I knew him, like I'd hinted at with Riley and Ward. Nothing earth shattering. No number ones, just bog standard heavy metal. Charlie's cover story was that he was scouting out venues and musicians. Colin even formed a record company which never issued any music, and an agency that never agented.

It worked too for a year or more, and Colin and his gangsters were sucked in by Charlie's *joie de vivre*. Enough so that when a particularly heavy consignment didn't arrive as expected, it took a day or so for the penny to drop.

'How much?' I asked.

'A million five,' said Colin.

'When?'

'Ten days ago.'

'The car?'

'Turned up in the long term car park at Gatwick.'

'Riley and Ward don't know that.'

'Nor should they.'

'Did he book a ticket?'

'Not according to my sources.'

'More coppers?'

'Customs.'

Maybe he was as good at gangstering as he said. Anyone can make a mistake. And Charlie had been a cunning devil. That was why he was such a good snout.

'And only ten grand was found at the hotel with a passport not in his name, nothing else?'

He shook his head. 'Just your card.'

It seemed pointless to tell him again that I'd had hundreds, maybe thousands printed over the years.

'And your mission, if you chose to accept it is to bring the cash home to me,' he said.

And the tape will self destruct in five seconds, I thought. And maybe me with it.

'OK,' I said. 'How do I get in touch?'

'Don't worry your pretty little head about that. I'll be in touch with you.'

With that, he swallowed the remains of his drink, collected his likely lads and left. It was as if he'd never been there. And I wished he hadn't.

I went back home carrying my dry cleaning with me. Once inside I called Robber. 'I met a mate of yours today,' I said.

'Who?'

'Colin the gangster.'

'Oh Coll.'

'Yes Coll.'

'Yeah, I gave him a shout after lunch. I told him you'd probably be in the pub.'

'I need to change my local. Why'd you sick him onto me?'

'He's got a bit of the hump about some cash Charlie nicked off him. I thought you could help.'

'Cheers. He thinks I know something because of that bleedin' card Charlie was carrying.'

'Shame about that.'

'Too bloody right. You've left me up shit creek.'

'Looks like you're the victim of circumstances, my son. Never mind, you've been in worse places. Coll's all right, as long as he gets what he wants.'

'Lovely. No more recommendations to your criminal mates please,' and I hung up.

Wednesday finds me back at the office. I'm no closer to working out my next move when my next move arrives with a bang as the door flies open and a young woman dressed in jeans and a Jack Daniels sweatshirt arrives, all raven hair, black sunglasses and scarlet lipstick carrying a large notebook and not much else. I'm guessing she's late teens or early twenties when she asks 'Nick Sharman?'

I nod in agreement, and she carries on, 'I need to talk to you.'

'Sit down,' I say, and she takes one of the clients' chairs, and puts the book on the edge of my desk.'

'And you are?' I ask.

'Charlotte,' she replies. 'Charlotte Swift. But I used to be Barnett. Charlotte Barnett. Charlie Barnett.'

Did my mouth gape open? Yes it did. 'Christ,' I said. 'Your father...'

'My father is in hospital. I found out yesterday. It was on TV.'

'That's how you found out?'

'Yes.'

'No one told you?'

'No one knows who I am. I hadn't seen him for years, until he found me recently.'

'He used to talk about you.'

'That was dad. All talk, little action.'

'How about your mother?'

'My mother died three years ago. I live with my Nan in Brixton. She runs an antique shop in the market. Well, a junk shop.'

'Brixton's up and coming.'

'Not if you live in a housing association flat.'

I nodded at that. 'So what do you do?'

'I'm at St Martin's. I study design.'

'That's good.'

'There's no need to patronise me, Mr Sharman.'

'I'm not, or I don't mean to, and if I am, I'm sorry.' She softened up a bit at that.

'And it's Nick. Mr Sharman was my father.'

'OK, Nick.'

'So why exactly are you here?'

'My dad gave me this.' She stood, pulled a wallet from the back pocket of her jeans, opened it and pulled out a card. You guessed it. One of mine. But this one was different to the one Charlie had when he was shot. On the back neatly printed was the name WILLIAM BRIDGES.

I'd wondered how she'd known it was her father when his real name hadn't been released. 'When did he give you this?'

'Last week. I hadn't seen him or heard from him for years.

Ever since mum died. Then, out of the blue he walks into Nan's shop and takes me up west for lunch.'

'But why my card, did he say?'

She nodded. 'He said don't trust the filth. But I could trust you. He said you were his friend. He said if anything happened to him to contact you.'

'How did you find my office?'

'You're in Yellow Pages.'

'It pays to advertise. Did he by any chance give you anything else?'

'Like what?'

'Like a million and a half quid in various currencies.'

She laughed at that. 'Sorry, no. Where would he get money like that? And if he had I think me and Nan would be in Benidorm, all inclusive by now.' She suddenly got serious. 'But where?'

'From some very bad people. Are you sure no one knows where you or granny are?'

'No. We don't use that name now. I just took Nan's surname when mum died. No deed poll or anything.'

'That is probably just as well.'

'So what do I do? I can't bear the thought of him lying in a hospital bed all alone. I am his next of kin.'

She took off her bins and I saw tears in the corners of her beautiful blue eyes.

'Believe me a lot of people care,' I said. 'Trouble is a lot are of the wrong kind. But don't worry, you're in safe hands now. Do you have a lawyer?'

'Nick. People like me and Nan go to the Citizen's Advice Bureau.'

'Fair enough. Got a pound coin?'

'Yes.'

'Gimme.'

'I don't understand'

'You will. Give us a quid.'

She stood again, reached into her jeans pocket, pulled some change, separated a pound coin and passed it over. 'Right,' I said. 'You're now my client. Anything you tell me I keep secret. Now. Do you trust me?'

She nodded.

I reached for the phone and called my lawyer, Bobby D. 'You've got a new client,' I said.

'Rich?'

'Could be.'

'I'm interested.'

'My office at two. We're just going to lunch.'

'Bon appetite.'

'Do you like spicy food?' I asked Charlie.

She nodded.

'Then you're in for a treat. We'll talk more over lunch.'

We went to Lionel's and off course he made a big fuss of Charlotte. We hit the menu hard, and it was a treat to see her enjoy the food. It made me think, no know, that I didn't see my daughter enough, and when this was all over I'd make it up to her.

'This is more than I expected,' she told me over the food as I filled her in on what I knew.

'The least I could do.'

Then, she opens her note book, pulls a pen from where it's stuck down the spine, and with a few lines she draws a picture of me. It was good too. Maybe a few more laughter lines than I would have liked. She tears the page out and gives it to me.

'That's brilliant,' I said, 'and that's not being patronising.'

'A pleasure.'

After cappuccinos, time was marching on, so I paid the bill and we went back to the office. Now Bobby D was a strange kind of lawyer. He didn't have an office, just worked from home, or more often from the back of a seven series BMW.

I called him the Beemer brief, which he seemed to like. At exactly 2pm the motor cruised round the corner and parked opposite my office. Bobby D locked it up and headed to the door. I introduced him to Charlie and between us we told our stories. Bobby sat taking notes and accepted another pound coin as his retainer.

After we'd finished he took down Charlie's address, the address of her grandmother's shop and her home phone number. She didn't have a mobile. Too expensive on what she earned as a barmaid and from helping Nan out in the shop.

'No more student grants,' she said with a shrug.

Bobby D told her needed to see her birth certificate with her Barnett name, and she winced, 'It could be in with mother's papers at home. Otherwise...'

'Otherwise we'll worry about that as and when,' said Bobby.

He noticed her portrait of me and told Charlie she was extremely talented, and then he took his notes back to his car and drove off. 'I'll be in touch,' he said as he left.

'I'd better go too,' said Charlie.

'How are you getting home?' I asked.

'Same as the way I came,' she replied. 'The 2B drops me off at my door.'

'I'll go and get my car,' I said. 'Give you a lift.'

'Don't be silly. You've done enough. I've got my travel card.' And with that, she kissed me on the cheek and left.

I missed her straight away.

The next day nothing. Nada. No visitors. No cops, no gangsters, no estranged daughters, no lawyers. Nothing to do with the case, if you could call it that, except I rang Riley to ask about Charlie's condition. No change. No operation.

So I just sat in my office drinking coffee and listening to CDs on shuffle. 'Bags' Groove' played often.

In the late afternoon I took fish and chips home and ate them out of the paper washed down with cold white wine.

That was kind of the calm before one of the many storms to come.

Back to the office the next morning. A fine London June day, with blue skies, and a warm breeze from the south.

About eleven Bobby D's Beemer turns into the street and he parks opposite. He gets out, slams the door and marches over. His face is how they say? Like thunder.

Bang goes the door, and he shakes his head and says 'Well Nick, this is one for the books.'

'What?'

'Just that Charlie Barnett, at least the female of the species does not exist.'

'What?'

'The phone number she gave us is dead. Her home address is a kebab shop with storage above that the owner was kind enough to let me see. Gran's shop is indeed second hand stuff. Old records, run by a gent who has never heard the name. St Martin's have no record. Can I say more?'

I had no answer.

'So what did you tell her?' he asked.

'Everything.' And I told him. Everything Riley had told me, and my visit from Colin the gangster. Every bloody detail.

'Well I don't know how she could use that information, but use it she will. I tell you what to do. Write GUM on your forehead so that every time you look in the mirror, what will you see?'

I got the picture.

'And another thing.' He reached into his pocket and took out a pound coin and dropped it onto the metal of my stereo. Instead of ringing true it landed with a dull thud. 'Even that nicker she gave you was snide. And I'll be billing you for my time,' he added as he walked out.

So that told me.

I spent the rest of the day hanging around my office, figuring out what I could do. Leave town was an option, but I never had been one who took the easy option. To my own regret often. The hell with it, I thought. *Bon temps roule*, as the saying goes. Let the good times roll and the dice fall as they may. I had lunch at Lionel's again.

Long and liquid. What the hell? Then it was over to the boozer. Again. No gangsters this time. I know I said I'd change my local, but I was used to the place and they were used to me.

By seven I must admit I was a bit pissed. A bit more than a bit actually. I made my farewells to staff and regulars and headed home. I wasn't staggering, but close. When I saw the street door to my flat open I sobered up quickly. The people who lived downstairs had finally got tired of my shenanigans and moved. Or maybe they'd just felt like a change. Whichever, I was in sole occupation for now. I pushed the door open and saw the door to my flat open too. I wasn't armed. Not even a Swiss Army knife or a Mont Blanc biro. And certainly no firearm. Actually I was trying to give them up. Foolishly maybe, I pushed that door open too, and quietly crept upstairs. If the open front door had partially sobered me up, what I found it in my living room did the complete job.

Sitting on my sofa, dressed as she had been when she left my office, but minus the dark glasses, was the fake Charlie Barnett very quiet and very dead. Someone had wrapped a leather belt round her neck and tightened it until her eyes bulged, and her bladder relaxed, and filled the room with the scent of urine. She was stone cold dead in the market. Even so I felt for a pulse. Nothing, although she was just slightly warm. Not quite stone cold, so I figured she'd been there for several hours. I used the landline to call an ambulance and the police. Then Bobby D.

'Not you again,' he said.

'Bobby. No messing. Get to my house quick.'

'Why should I after…'

'Fuck's sake man, she's dead.'

'Who?'

'Charlie Barnett's fake daughter.'

'Christ Sharman! You sure she's dead?'

'She is.'

'Have you called an ambulance just in case?'

'Of course. And the police.'

'Don't touch anything. I'll be there fast. Don't let the cops take you away.'

With that he cut me off. I took Riley's card out of my pocket and called her. If I was going to have cops all over me I wanted at least one to be untouchable.

Pretty soon the outside of my place looked like a scene from *The Bill*. An ambulance, a couple of squad cars, a SOCO van, all but the van with blues flashing.

It was if my downstairs neighbours knew what was going to happen. Me, I was in the back of an unmarked police car with a couple of detectives. No expense spared when Sharman was back in the frame. Bobby D and Riley and Ward arrived pretty much at the same time. Riley took over. Murder squad trumps plain old local plain clothes every time.

I got slung in the back of the Riley/Ward mobile and off we went to Streatham police station with Bobby D in the Beemer close behind. 'Not a word,' was all he said as we left.

I obeyed.

We ended up in an interview room. It looked recently decorated and was certainly more comfortable than some I'd been in. Both in and out of the Job.

The usual rigmarole of our identities for the tape, then Bobby D said. 'Can we go now?'

Riley gave him a look. 'Is it true you work out of the back of a car?'

'Sometimes.'

'Fascinating. Now Mr Sharman how about bringing us up to speed.'

I told them as much as I wanted them to know. I kept an eye on Bobby in case I was saying too much. I left out the bit about Colin the gangster and what I knew about what Charlie had been doing to earn a crust.

'And you didn't think to tell us about this young woman pretending to be Charlie Barnett's long lost daughter.'

'That's down to me,' said Bobby. 'I thought we'd never hear from her again when I asked for a birth certificate to validate her next of kinship.'

'And why do you think she ended up in your flat, deceased. Murdered.' She asked me.

I felt like saying, 'You're the Detective', but that never goes down well. Instead I said, 'Somebody wants me in jail.'

'Somebody certainly wants something. We've estimated time of death as between ten and two. You were?'

'In my office. In the Vietnamese restaurant up the road from my office, and in the pub opposite my office.'

'But you could have nipped home.'

'And left the body as I understand it lying on his sofa,' said Bobby. 'That would have been wise.'

'Sitting,' I explained.

'Sitting. And then of course he gave you a call. Frankly, if he had murdered her he might have tried to get rid of the body.'

I nodded.

Riley looked at Ward, then at me. 'Where will you stay tonight? Your flat is a crime scene.'

'You mean I can go?' I asked.

'There's no room at this inn,' she said. 'If we need you I'm sure we'll find you.'

I ended up at a local generic hotel chain. No five stars for me. Bobby D gave me a lift. I bought a toothbrush and paste at a BP garage. He promised he'd get me into my flat to pack a bag the next morning. Which he did. I loaded it into my car and drove to my office.

What next? I wondered as I opened up and stuck on the coffee pot. Through all this, don't think I didn't feel sympathy for the dead girl whatever her real name was.

Because I did. Obviously she had stuck her nose in something that had got it cut off. Curiosity certainly killed that cat.

Riley called me after lunch. 'Not gone on the run then,' she said. I was getting quite fond of her. I figured that the local cops would've locked me up for the night just for badness.

'Nowhere to run to.'

'Where are you staying?'

I told her.

'You'll get your flat back soon.'

'Don't know that I want it.'

'You could run guided tours.'

'Not funny. She may not have been Charlie Barnett's daughter, but she was someone's.'

'Yeah. Sorry. This job hardens you. But you know that. Does the name Barbara Green mean anything?'

'No. Was that her?'

'Yes. Went by the name Krystal with a K.'

'A prostitute.'

'Escort. She looked younger than she was. That was her USP apparently.'

'She had a record?'

'Nothing much. Kid's stuff, but she was in the system. Kicked out of home. Mum and dad junkies. Abused. Fostered. A nightmare apparently. Poor kid.'

'Who done it?'

'Who knows? Someone who knew you, and didn't like you.'

'Plenty of suspects then. Thanks for letting me go yesterday by the way.'

'Didn't go down well with some.'

'But fuck 'em if they can't take a joke.'

'Exactly.'

'Any news on Charlie? The real Charlie that is.'

'He's healing. Should go under the knife next week.'

'Then maybe we'll know something.'

'Everything. If he wakes up.'

I wish people wouldn't keep saying that.

'By the by, does the name McIntyre ring any bells. Harry McIntyre. Goes by Mac?'

'No. should it?'

'Just a thought. His fingerprints were found at your flat.'

'Do you know him?'

'Personally, no. But he has a record any petty crim would be proud of. Lately, living off immoral.'

'Krystal's pimp.'

'Ten out of ten. I knew you didn't do it.'

'I still owe you one.'

'Just one? You disappoint me Sharman.'

With that we finished our conversation.

The week dragged on, and the weekend. No one was murdered and I wasn't arrested. Colin gave me a couple of calls. He told me his patience was wearing thin. I told him I was doing my best. Without Charlie that wasn't much good. On the Monday, Robber told me that Charlie had had an operation on Saturday afternoon, the prognosis was good. On the Tuesday Riley called and told me he was awake and asking for me. I asked if he knew Krystal was dead. She told me I would have the pleasure of breaking the news.

The price of freedom I imagine.

I called the hospital and talked to a pleasant sounding nurse on his floor. She said my name was on the visitors' list. She also told me he was in excellent form for someone in his condition. She sounded a bit sweet on him. That was Charlie. I also phoned Bobby D and told him I was going visiting. He insisted on coming along. I said Charlie only wanted me. He insisted again. I gave in.

I arrived in the hospital car park around five. Bobby was already in situ. We went upstairs in the lift. There was a cop sitting outside a private room. I captured a nurse, and she told me Charlie was inside. I showed the cop my ID as did Bobby.

I went into the private room, Bobby D close behind. Charlie was lying in bed, some kind of metal meccano set holding his head steady. There was a cannula in his wrist with two bags of clear liquid on a drip stand, antibiotics and saline probably.

Hanging on the side of the bed was a piss bag half full of urine from a catheter. The room smells like death warmed up. His head doesn't turn but his eyes do. 'Nick,' he says, then sees Bobby. 'Who's that?'

'My lawyer.

If he could he would have shaken his head. 'No,' he says. 'Just you.'

'I should…' That was Bobby.

'No.' Charlie again.

'Bobby,' I said. 'Leave it. I'll be fine.'

'It's against my advice.'

'Duly noted.'

He shook his head, more in sorrow than in anger I think, and left closing the door behind him. I pulled up a chair. 'Well I don't have to ask how you are,' I said.

'A drop of water please mate,' said Charlie.

I held a plastic beaker complete with bendy straw next to his lips. He drank some, then gestured for me to take it away.

'Well, another fine mess you've got me into,' I said.

'Yeah, I'm sorry. I'm glad to see you mate.'

'Me too.' And it was the truth. 'Have you been charged?'

'I haven't done anything wrong.'

'Well, apart from Colin's money.'

'How do you know about that?'

'Simple. He wants it back. He wants me to get it back for him because you spread my cards far and wide. And if I don't I'll be in the next bed.'

'Sorry.'

'Don't keep saying that, Charlie, or I'll be tempted to give you a smack in the back of the head, and that might be fatal.'

He almost said sorry again, but thought better of it. 'You said cards.'

'You gave one to your girlfriend Krystal.'

'How do you know that?'

Now was time for the truth. No matter how much it hurt. I almost felt bad, but serves him right I thought as I said, 'I hate to be the bearer of more bad news, but she's dead, mate. Murdered in my flat by her pimp. McIntyre.' I described what had happened.

I thought he might have a relapse at that news. His face went whiter than the pillow his head was resting on. 'Christ,' he said. 'She was a good girl, no matter what she did for a living. She was good to me. She didn't deserve that.'

'She fooled me,' I said.

'You met her?'

'Once. She told me she was your daughter.'

'Fucking hell. What else have I missed?'

'We lost the last test match.'

'Funny.'

'You told her about me. Told her she could trust me. So why did she go through that rigmarole. Why not tell me the truth?'

'She was a whore Nick. She had a bad time. She was fucked up.' He swallowed, and there were tears in his eyes. 'We were going away to start over.'

'And you wrote the name on your fake passport on the card. I don't get it. Didn't you trust her, if she was so good to you? And you two were off.'

'With a million and a half at stake and that bastard McIntyre on the plot. He would have got it all out of her. He had his ways.'

'And she wasn't at the hotel with you. This is all upside down.'

'She was too scared to leave him. He had her almost a prisoner.'

'So why didn't you run straight away?'

'She didn't have a bleedin' passport. Poor cow. McIntyre kept hers so she needed a fake. That was what the ten grand was for.'

'Christ, that's a lot.'

'The geezer doing it was a Van Gogh of fake paperwork. A fucking Picasso.'

'Well I hope he didn't do the photo.'

'Fuck off, you know what I mean.'

'So, what about Colin's dough? The cops won't be guarding you forever. He knows where you are. He knows almost everything except where the money actually is.'

'And you want me to tell you.'

'Yes. You know you can trust me.'

'I know, Nick.'

He knew alright. He knew he could trust me because the one thing I hadn't told Riley and Ward, hadn't told anyone for a lot of years was because I'd allowed Charlie Barnett to get away with murder. He'd had a sister then. Back ten years or more. Julia. Lovely Girl. But she'd got in with bad company. In particular one bad boy with flash suits, flash address, flash motors, and lots of flash cash. His name was Vincent. Almost a bloody cliché. He was a dealer, she was a sweetheart who fell for him in the worst way. It had to end badly, and did when he smashed up one of his motors and he walked away without a scratch. Julia didn't. She hadn't been wearing a seat belt. Flash boy was over the limit and full of coke. Somehow the evidence got corrupted and he walked out of court with a fine. Three months later Charlie called me up one night. He needed a favour. I found him in a lock up garage in Bromley with a dead body. You can guess who.

I was Job. He was a snout. A villain too. I didn't give a shit. I'd met Julia, and she was a diamond. 24 caret. We loaded the body into the boot of Vincent's motor. Charlie drove, I followed on. There's a lagoon in Crystal Palace Park where folks go fishing. The fish have an extra companion now. Now with a load of old heavy metal tied to his legs. Never heard a word about it since. I suppose the body is still down there. At least he was doing some good feeding those fishes.

'If he does for you, he'll have to do for me,' I said. 'I'll leave a letter with my solicitor, only to be opened at the time of my death. I'm sure he'll listen to reason. He didn't seem so bad as it happens.'

'He's not. Nick, I was in love.'

That can bring out the worst in us.

Or the best.

I wish.

'OK,' he said. 'There's a boozer round the corner from my gaff in Battersea. The Hanging Judge And Usher. Most just call it the Usher. It's right by the court funnily enough. Everyone from the court and the Bill drink there. Safest place for miles. Guv'nor's called Nigel. Lovely bloke. Bent as a nine bob note. He keeps things for me behind the jump. There's an envelope with your name on it. Inside is a ticket for the left luggage at Waterloo Eurostar. Paid up for months, inside are two bags. Cash inside. Not the full Monty. I've spent some. Colin will have to swallow that. Nigel will expect a back hander. A ton should do, and I expect he'll front you a bevvy. Give him my regards. Get it back to Colin, and let the cards fall as they may. And what about Jack Robber? He'll make himself busy you bet your life.'

'The original sleeping policeman. He'll be fine as long as

he gets his bungs. Which he always does. He must have a pot somewhere.'

'You wouldn't think so the way he dresses.'

'He won't know a dickey bird 'til Colin gets the cash back. Then it's up to them. We'll be out of the picture.'

'I hope it's going to be that simple.'

'Trust me.' I hoped I was as confident as I sounded.

'Last thing,' I said. 'How come you had my cards?'

'You gave me a handful when you started out private. I still had some. I reckoned they'd get back to you.'

'Thanks again mate.'

I got up to leave as there wasn't much more to say.

'Thanks Nick,' he said. 'I'm real sorry it came to this. I'll make it up to you. No danger.'

'I'd like to say it was all a pleasure, but it wasn't,' I said and left. The cop was still outside.

I went out to the car park as the evening was turning to night, and the moon was creeping up behind the building, and went towards my motor, when I heard a voice I didn't recognise from behind say 'scuse me', and I turned and the moon went out and night fell like a dark, velvet curtain.

Later that same evening, or some bloody evening, the sun came out I woke up with blood in my mouth and a bright light in my eyes.

'You're back,' said the voice I didn't recognise.

'Light,' I said through a dry, thick throat.

The light went off but my eyes were still full of stars. 'Who are you?' I slurred.

'Name's McIntyre.'

'The pimp.'

I got a slap for that.

I was in a kitchen. Not flash, just a suburban kitchen. I was sitting on a kitchen chair, my wrists bound in front of me with what looked like speaker wire. On the table next to me was an automatic pistol with gaffa tape round the butt. Next to it was a Stanley knife with the blade open. Nasty things, Stanley knives in the wrong hands.

'Any chance of a drink of water?' I asked.

'If you behave.'

'Not much chance of me doing anything else.'

He ran a tap, then put a mug to my lips and I slurped thirstily. 'What d'you say?'

Christ, I thought. He thinks he's my mum. 'Thanks,' I said. I tested the wire, but it was tight. Too tight for me to stretch it unless I had hours to myself. Didn't look to me that was going to happen. 'Why'd you kill her?' I asked.

'She was going to leave me for that fucker.'

That fucker and a million and a half quid, I thought but said nothing.

'The money,' he said. 'Where is it?'

'What money?'

Another slap.

'You know.'

'Charlie didn't tell me.'

'Then I'll kill you and go and ask him myself.'

'There's cops all round him.'

'Not forever.'

Just what I'd said.

'So, the money?' And he picked up the knife.

I don't know if I'd've given the dough up or not. It wasn't mine and never would be, so what did I care? But I can be stubborn, even though the razor sharp blade of that knife would do a lot of damage before I talked or died. But I'd never know, because from the front of the house there was a crash loud enough to wake the dead, and suddenly the room was full of men but in black suits and helmets holding long guns. McIntyre grabbed me and stuck the knife into my neck and punctured the skin so I felt blood running into my shirt collar. The cops were shouting, And the knife went deeper and then one fired and the knife and McIntyre hit the floor in tandem. I was expecting to be covered in claret, but when I turned my head to look he was flat out but still breathing. My ears were concussed by the shot, but when I looked at the cop who had fired, he said, 'Bean bag. We like them to stand trial.'

I was cut loose and led out to the street.

Outside it was like the TV again with two ambulances and various police cars and vans wasting their batteries strobing their light bars. Bobby D was leaning against his Beemer with a supercilious look on his face. 'Was it you?' I asked.

'You bet.'

'How?'

'I was doing a bit of paperwork in the car after you dispensed with my services rather rudely.'

'Not me. Charlie.'

'Whatever. Anyway, I saw you come out and was about to suggest a drink and a bit of supper when this other bloke walks up and smacks you in the head.'

'I'm getting slack in my old age.'

'Anyway,' he went on. 'He bundles you into yours, picks up your keys and heads out. He was fast, and I couldn't get out of my car quickly enough, and I didn't want to lose him and stand there with my dick in my hand.'

'A wonderful thought,' I said.

'So I follow and when he gets here I call the law. Then I call your friend Riley. Like you said, better one of the untouchables is around to keep you safe.'

'Cheers.'

'She's over there.' He pointed in the direction of the flashing blues. 'Go and have a word. I think she likes you.'

I nodded. 'Well thanks again, Bobby, I won't forget this.'

'I won't let you, and I'm still billing you for my time. So *au revoir* and don't do anything I wouldn't. Lunch next week?'

I nodded, and he got into his car and drove off leaving me to nurse my sore head and hold a tissue to the cut in my neck.

Riley was standing by one of the ambulances. 'I don't need it,' I said.

'McIntyre does.'

'Lucky he doesn't need a hearse.'

'Always good to end things without bloodshed.'

'Tell that to Charlie and Krystal. And me.' I showed her the tissue and she tutted, but not in a sympathetic way.

'Yeah.'

'What's your favourite musical?' I asked.

She looked bemused. '*Les Mis*,' she said. 'Yours?'

'*The Music Man.*'

'Really?'

'Really. Old school.'

'You can say that again.'

'Maybe we could get together some evening. Have a drink. Compare musical scores. What do you say?'

'Could do. Give me a call.'

I did and we did. But that's another story. And the dough? Well, I went to the pub in Battersea, met Nigel, slipped him a hundred quid and was given a large G&T on the house, and the envelope with my name on it. Inside was the left luggage ticket, which I exchanged for two hefty bags at Waterloo station, gave them to Colin, and never took a penny. I prized my skin too much. I explained Charlie had spent some of the cash, and after all the trouble I had been to, I expected no comebacks for either of us. Colin nodded, then reached into one of the bags and hauled out a handful of cash. 'For your favourite charity,' he said. Later, I took the money into Li's and put it in the donkey jar. A promise is a promise.

Charlie spent a month in hospital and now and then I'd

turn up with some grapes and a few magazines. And even now we occasionally get together for a Ruby and a chat about old times.

Oh, and I still love 'Bags' Groove', and listen to it all the time.

UPTOWN TOP RANKIN'

It all started, as it often did, with me sitting in my office smoking a cigarette, listening to Otis and reading a paperback novel. This time it was a Lee Child I'd read before. So it was no hardship when I saw a silhouette behind the glass door, followed by a hard knock, before the door burst open and trouble walked in, although I didn't know that at the time. My cigarette continued burning, Otis kept on singing about the pain in his heart. I sympathised, and Jack Reacher could wait. Anyway, like I said I'd read it before, but it was still worth a second go. But I always wondered how a bloke who only changed his clothes about once a week got so much sex. And it was always marvellous. Not like real life at all.

Trouble stood in the doorway with the sun behind her, then walked properly into view. She was tall, dark haired, red lipsticked and all neat in black from head to toe as far as I could see, and I liked the view.

'Are you Nick Sharman?' she asked.

'That's what would be written on the door if I could've afforded ninety quid for a sign writer,' I replied.

'Funny. I heard you were funny.'

'No charge for jokes,' I said. 'Anything else is two hundred and fifty quid a day plus reasonable expenses.'

'Then you could have a sign written.'

'Good point. Come in, sit down, take the weight off. I assume you want dragons slayed.'

'You're astute,' she said. 'I'm Trubbel.'

'Say again.'

'Lisa Trubbel. Lisa with an S, Trubbel with double Bs, one L.'

I stood. It was the least I could do. 'Lisa,' I said, pointing to one of my clients' chairs. 'Coffee?'

'Does it come free with the two hundred and fifty?'

'No charge. How do you take it?'

'Black and strong,' she said. 'Unfortunately, like the man I want you to find.'

'Tell me all,' I said as I poured her a cup from my complicated caffeine machine. 'Don't leave out a thing.'

'Are you flirting with me?'

'As if.'

'Anyway, race isn't the issue. A thief is what he is, and I need you to find the little bastard.'

I wondered if she kissed with that dirty mouth. I imagined she must. Made that old heart of mine almost skip a beat. 'And what did he do to deserve that expletive?'

'He took something that belongs to me.'

'There was copper across the road by the pub a minute ago,' I said, delivering her cup. 'I could give him a shout. Get this all over in a second.'

She made a noise like a tire deflating. 'No police,' she said, then stuck her hand into her bag and pulled out a box full of Sobranie Black Russian cigarettes with gold tips, and a shiny black and gold Dunhill lighter. She offered me the pack, but I declined. Too strong for my blood. I preferred my Silk Cut. She sneered in my face, lit up, and the smoke lay thick and dark in the air.

'So, this item,' I said sinking back in my chair with a coffee of my own, this one with a dash of milk. I'm a wimp when it comes to coffee, just like cigarettes. 'A family heirloom, a *billet doux* from a famous person, an irreplaceable piece of art?'

'Shut up. What it is doesn't matter. Who it is, is all that does. Find him, and you'll find it, and I'll take care of the rest.'

'So, you're hiring me to find something, but won't tell me what.'

She nodded.

'Which may lead to a kidnap, which, when I last looked was against the law. Sounds like trouble with one B,' I said.

'Does it matter?'

'Depends.'

'Of course it does. You've broken the law before, I understand, and I'm the client and I pay the bills. You're a crook, Mr Sharman, and you're a sucker for guns, money and love. Guns are down to you. Money I have plenty. Love...' She shrugged. 'Maybe we can talk about that later over dinner. On me. How about it?'

'I'm also a sucker for Mr Chow,' I said. 'How about that?'

'That can be arranged. I'll pick you up at your home at seven.'

'You know where I live?' '

'And your phone number, and a lot of other things too tiresome to mention. I always research my staff.'

That was bit rude. That was also a bit worrying. But I let it go. What the hell. Like she'd said, she was a client, and clients paid the bills. Plus I hadn't been able to afford Mr Chow's prices for quite a while.

She got up then, and I did too, and saw her out of the office. Just down the street was an eighties stretched black Cadillac limousine polished to perfection with its chrome gleaming in the sun. As she walked towards it, the driver's door opened and a liveried chauffeur as big as a horse got out and opened the back door. She climbed in the back, he climbed in behind the wheel, the car started, then drifted off towards the corner. Not a word was said, not a move was wasted. Perfect synchronisation. I wondered then what I was letting myself in for, and what it was she'd lost. Then I mentally shrugged and looked forward to a free go at Mr Chows.

I went home then, and thought about my new client. Trubbel by name, trouble by nature I guessed. As I thought I played a reggae compilation. Perfect for a warm summer's afternoon.

When 'Uptown Top Rankin'' came on I played it on repeat a couple of times. Althea and Donna. I loved those ladies. 'Nah pop, nah style.' I don't think so.

For my dinner date I chose an Italian navy mohair suit, black slip ons, a pale blue cotton tab collar shirt, and a plain navy blue knitted silk tie. Sharp, or what?

At precisely seven pm, the Caddy drew up outside my flat. I was already in the front garden waiting. Somehow I knew she would be dead on time, and I was right.

Harry the horse got out of his door and opened the back door on the pavement side. I thanked him and ducked in. Lisa was sitting by the opposite door. She had changed into a black evening gown. Short, over black stockings. 'Good evening Mr Sharman,' she said.

'You're punctual. I thought you would be.'

'The politeness of princes, or in my case princesses.'

I just smiled, as Harry took his place back behind the wheel and we took off gently just like a good chauffeur should.

'A drink,' she said, and pulled open a drawer in the centre of the seats and produced a silver cocktail shaker and two glasses. 'Black Russian suit you?'

'To a tee.' Same colour cigarettes and booze. I could live with that.

She expertly poured the drink over ice without spilling a drop and passed one to me. We clinked glasses and drank. Perfect. Cold as Christmas and strong as Harry the horse. Then she reached into her handbag and pulled out a blunt and her Dunhill. She touched a button by her head and the glass partition between us and the driver's cab slowly closed, she fired up the joint and passed it to me. Heavy duty. 'Sensi,' she said, and pressed another button and the cabin was filled with music as sweet as the grass. 'Chet Baker,' I said, when the vocal began.

'I heard you were a jazz buff. Chet Baker singing. Beautiful.

And what a beautiful boy. People said he couldn't sing. What arseholes. He had the most gorgeous voice. Shame he was a stupid junkie who got his teeth kicked in so he lost his lip and couldn't play properly anymore. Still, let's grab the moment and pretend none of that shit happened to him.'

'I'll drink to that,' I said, and I did.

The Cadillac cruised through south London heading for Knightsbridge. The engine purred like a tiger cub and it seemed to float exactly like the big old boat it was. Of course the sensi helped. As did the Black Russians.

Outside Chows, the driver stopped, holding up traffic as he opened the left hand rear door. I exited by myself, then he helped Lisa onto the pavement. We created quite a stir, like a pair of rock stars. One pap even took a couple of shots, and she played up to the camera. Then she took my arm as the *maître'd'* opened the restaurant door and greeted her with extravagant air kisses, led us upstairs and parked us at a window table. Obviously I wasn't the only one who liked Chows.

'I took the liberty of ordering in advance,' she said when we were seated. 'I hope you don't mind.'

'Fine by me,' I said as a bottle of white wine was delivered, and a glass of something pale amber was put in front of her. It could have been cold tea but I doubted it. Wine was poured for me and dishes of steaming Chinese cuisine covered the table. I devoured plenty. She never touched a bite. I didn't care. I was starving. Of course the sensi helped. I finished the bottle of wine and she inhaled glass after glass of the amber liquid without any discernible results. Perhaps it was cold tea after all.

When the dishes were rescued by the staff she put her handbag on the table and pulled out a photo. It was a handsome young black guy maybe twenty five, maybe younger. A bit young for her, that was for sure.

'That's him?' I asked.

'I can see why you're a detective.'

'Thanks.'

'Don't mention it.'

'His name is Tyler.'

'And he's where?'

Out came a page from a notebook. It smelled of her perfume. 'He was last seen at a squat in King's Cross. That's the address.'

I picked up the paper and just avoided running it under my nose.

And finally, as if an encore, came a fat brown envelope. 'There's a grand in there, she said. 'Four days' pay. Any expenses I'll pay, but don't take the piss.'

'As if,' I said.

She gave me a dirty look.

'Why haven't you got your driver to do all this? He's big enough,' I asked.

'What, Alfred? He's afraid of spiders. Are you afraid of spiders, Mr Sharman?'

'No. But I don't like them much. My old mum tried to save one in the bath, tripped and broke her hip. It was the beginning of her decline.'

'Sad,' she said, but obviously didn't give a toss. Why should she?

'Actually I thought you were the type of woman who could take care of things for herself,' I said.

'I am. I have a twenty two pistol in one garter and a flick knife from Sorrento in the other. Italians make very good knives.'

I didn't know if she was joking, but I doubted if she was, and I wondered if I'd ever find out for myself. Though I doubt if I would. I was staff after all.

'I live alone in the penthouse of a block of flats Lambeth council sold me cheap because of the many and various ethnic sitting tenants who were *in situ*. Believe me, they didn't last long, and when I got rid of the scum I knocked through six flats on the top floor into a tasty apartment, and made myself very comfortable.'

Charming, I thought. But once again she was paying the bills.

After she finished speaking, she pulled out her phone and pressed a button. 'Now I have places to be, people to see. The boss here will call you a cab. I'll be in touch.' With that she got up and left without another word, leaving me unable to politely stand and wish her a good night. No kiss on the cheek, not even a handshake. Instead I sat like a flounder until she was gone. A few minutes later the *maître d'* told me that my taxi was at the door. No mention was made of payment. Obviously she'd taken care of that as neatly as she'd taken care of me.

So, fat and stupid after the feast, still a little bit stoned, and half in love, I got carried back to my lonely pad and an empty bed in a black London lobster. Not even a little spider to share my existence.

The next morning I woke up fresh as a new born lamb ready for the slaughter, surprisingly unhungover and ready to earn the thousand quid still sitting uncounted on my bedside table. I knew there would be exactly the amount she'd said. Lisa Trubbel was most precise. I went to the bathroom, abluted and emerged shaved and still pink from the shower and dressed in ancient jeans with torn knees, an ancient Blue Note t-shirt, an equally ancient leather jacket distressed to within an inch of its life, and similarly ancient monkey boots, the leather as soft as a virgin's kiss. My pants and socks were brand new. I had my standards, and eat your heart out Reacher.

I took the address and photo Lisa had given me and headed to King's Cross by bus and tube. I didn't need the aggro of a motor that early in my search, and it was a fine summer's day.

King's Cross was a shithouse those days. There was the station with beggars and thieves on every other corner, and on the other corners, ladies of the night were doing business although it was only eleven in the morning. Even in my scruffs I still had to fight off some of each.

I'd checked the street of the address in my A-Z before leaving home and headed towards it. It was in the boonies of the worst side of the area. Huge, empty buildings lined the roads, waiting for demolition or the gentrifying that almost certainly had to come to even this, the bad side of town, but not that day. The buildings seemed to loom together like lost souls. And even on this, the warmest of days, the walk was dismal and made me shiver slightly under my leather.

The address she'd given me was an old hotel, now not taking paying customers but graffitied up like a bad Andy Warhol. I'd bought a can of beer and a Ginsters pasty at a corner shop en route, and I sat on a low walk opposite the squat, peeled the pasty, opened the can and watched the front door. Didn't even try and see if it was open. Let the mountain come to me.

And, a few minutes later, after the pasty was gone, it did. Not exactly a mountain, but pretty large. A young woman. Girl really, with badly dyed red hair in a grown out Mohican, a leather jacket in worse shape than mine over a Sex Pistols t-shirt and leggings stretched to capacity tucked into a pair of Doc Martens. She saw me and headed over. 'Can I have a swig?' She asked.

I passed her the half full can. 'Finish it,' I said.

'Got any spare change?'

I nodded.

'Yeah?' she said with a question mark.

'Do something for me.'

Her face fell. 'It's too early for a blow job. I haven't completed my *toilette* or had my *petit dejeuner*.' All in a mock French accent. 'But maybe later, *monsieur*.'

I thought it must be tough to keep a sense of humour living in a horrible part of the city in a dump like that shithouse over the road.

'Quelle horreur,' I replied, and she laughed. 'You should eat breakfast – most important meal of the day,' I added. 'Just want to know if you know this bloke.'

I pulled out Tyler's photo. She knew him. You didn't have to be a detective to spot that change of expression. No laughing now. 'No,' she said.

'I think you do. A fiver says so.'

'A tenner would say more.'

This girl hadn't been born yesterday. 'OK,' I said. 'A tenner it is.'

'Show.'

Before I'd left home I'd popped single five pound notes into every pocket. Just for this sort of situation. Plus another ton in tenners in my wallet. I just didn't want to show anyone I was bribing the whole package. I reached into both front pockets of my jeans and pulled out two notes. 'Now you,' I said.

'His name is Tyler,' she said. 'Or so he says. He stays in the top rooms. It's like a separate flat. He's tough. But he's in Bristol at the moment. Or that's what he said. He told everyone he'd be back and not to go in his place.'

'And you wouldn't.'

'None of us would. He's got a gun.'

'Do what?'

'I'm not kidding. He says he was in the army.'

Christ, I thought That puts a different complexion on the job. 'Did he say when he'd be back?'

'That's the tenners worth.'

'Fair enough.' And I passed over the dough. 'When?'

She reached out her hand again. Another pocket, another Lady Godiver. 'Tomorrow,' she said. 'When he's done his business, whatever it is.'

I hoped she wasn't having me on as I parted with the third note. 'Thanks,' she said again, 'and how about that blow job?'

'Thanks yourself, but I'll take a rain check on that.'

'OK, but you don't know what you're missing,' and like a magician she reached into her mouth and pulled out a full set of dentures. 'See. Soft as,' she said exposing a set of pink gums

'Thanks again, but no.'

'If you change your mind, just ask for Gummo. I'm in second floor front,' she said.

'Tell you what,' I said, and pulled out one of my cards with my name and mobile phone number. I wrapped it in another two fivers. 'If he shows up, give me a call. On the QT. Not a word to him.'

'As if.'

She pocketed the lot and went back to the hotel. Maybe she'd call, maybe not, but it was worth a punt.

I headed home then by tube and bus, reversing my previous journey. I was back by two and ordered a super supreme pizza from Pizza Express and played some Miles Davis on vinyl. Afterwards I busted open a cold beer and worked out my options. If Gummo wasn't lying, Tyler was somewhere in Bristol on business. From what I knew of Bristol Saint Paul's I imagined he was selling something or other. Maybe what Lisa was missing. Maybe drugs, maybe something else. I was either too late or not. I wasn't about to head out to the Wild West to find out. It would be late before I could get there, and there definitely were monsters lurking, and not about to welcome a white man asking questions. And Gummo had said he was armed. Maybe he was, maybe he said it to keep his neighbours out of his digs.

Two choices. Go back before he was due, or wait until tomorrow, and maybe a call from Gummo. No choice really.

The night time was the right time, and tonight was alright by me.

This time I took the car. A nice dull Ford saloon, dirty blue, but with enough poke to make a quick escape. And it was all perfectly street legal. The only thing that wasn't, was the automatic I was carrying, fully loaded for bear.

It wasn't such a comfortable journey up to town as it had been in the Caddy, but I got to King's Cross in one piece. By night the area was even worse, junkies, drunks and whores roamed the pavements looking for cash or kind. I parked the car on an empty meter a quarter mile or so from the squat, donned tight leather gloves and checked my trusty Colt 1911, fully loaded and heavy as the lead it carried.

There were lights on all over the squat. Some were bright, some were dim. Some candles, some electric, probably illegally hooked up to the electric company. Too bad. They could afford it if my electric bill was anything to go by. Nothing on the top floor. Obviously when Tyler talked, people listened.

I tried the front door of the old hotel and it swung open easily. There were several bulbs in the foyer, some worked, some busted, but just enough light to see the dead, open lift and a wide flight of uncarpeted stairs. Littered about was the usual detritus of urban communal living. Bikes padlocked to anything nailed down, flyers from more take-outs than seemed possible. All cuisines, all prices. Loads of other flyers of every description, and letters in dozens of names. Bills mostly, but sadly declined.

I took the stairs, there were lots of them. Many floors. Some lit, some dark. There was music everywhere. All sorts, but mostly heavy on the bass. That suited me. Noise, when I wanted to be quiet. There was no music on the top floor and no lights. I used the small Maglite I'd brought with me. The one door had a hasp and a padlock. Tyler did want to be alone. Did I tell you I pick locks? Well I do, and I practise a lot. I can do it in the dark and I did. The padlock looked strong, but was a piece of shit. I had it open in a few seconds. I carry my picks in the barrel of what looks like an innocent ballpoint pen. Like hide in plain sight, and no questions asked. No drop, no foul. Of course the pistol was harder to explain.

Inside was neat. Army, Gummo had said. There were three rooms. One was a sort of kitchen, one was a bedroom, one was a living room. And there was a bathroom with an old fashioned tub in the middle and a toilet that was clean but with no water. This had to be servants' quarters from when the hotel was live.

There was power up here and I used it, I didn't think anyone apart from me was going to visit Tyler's den that night. And if they did I was armed and extremely dangerous. My only worry might be that he came home early.

I found nothing. No swag. No gun. There was a massive boom box with a stack of CDs. A mobile clothes horse hung with smart clothes. Too smart for this gaff. I imagined Lisa had paid the bills before he skipped, taking threads and whatever else. There was a set of bookcases made with planks and bricks. Lots of books, all well read. A couple of Reachers as a matter of fact. We obviously had similar tastes in literature and women. I flicked through a couple of the books and out fell a piece of lined paper. On it was scribbled RINGO and a phone number. A clue. My word, that was a stroke of luck. I diligently copied down the name and number in my own note book. Couldn't hurt.

I left after half an hour. Lights off, padlock on, and away. And I never saw another soul the whole time.

When I got home the second thing I did was phone my old friend Detective Inspector Jack Robber, my go to geezer for things lawful, or maybe not exactly. The first thing I did was to pour myself a hefty glass of red wine. Housebreaking was thirsty work.

He answered quickly. 'What time do you call this?' He demanded.

'Nice to talk to you too Jack. Time to earn your corn. What does the name Ringo mean to you?'

'The Beatles. Always preferred the Stones myself.'

'Funny. I mean in our line of business.'

'Not a lot.'

'Can you ask around?'

'How hard?'

'Well don't kick any doors in.'

'I mean dosh-wise.'

'The usual.'

'Sounds important.'

'It is. Alright, a monkey. I'm on expenses.'

'Doors beware, and the kebabs are on you.'

'Fair enough.'

'I'll be in touch.' And he hung up with not as much as a fuck you very much. Well, that was an interesting improvement.

Next I called Lisa.

'Well?'

I cut straight to the chase. 'What does the name Ringo mean to you?'

'The Beatles. I always preferred the Stones.'

'Everyone says that.'

'Did you find him? Tyler?' She demanded.

'I found his gaff. Just like you said. He wasn't home, but he'll be back. All his stuff was there.'

'So keep trying.'

'I will.'

'And let me know when you've earned your money.' And she hung up without a fuck you very much as well.

I finished the wine, got undressed and went to bed wondering why I bothered.

The next morning I breakfasted on two poached eggs on

two slices of toasted Warburtons Danish sliced white with butter and Marmite. The breakfast of champions!

I was thinking about heading back to King's Cross when my mobile rang. I'd not had it long and not many people had the number. It was a big, ugly thing, but everyone said they were here to stay. I answered and a female voice, a little quavery asked, 'Is that Nick?'

'Speaking.'

'It's Gummo. You remember?'

'Of course. What's up?'

'Everything. The boy you were asking about. I think he's dead.'

'Do what?'

'He must've come back late last night. Anyway, first thing this morning there was a lot of shouting upstairs, and a big bang, then some people ran away. We went upstairs and he was lying there covered in blood. Someone called an ambulance and the police. They took him away and the cops slung everybody out. Locked the place up.'

'So, where are you?'

'Waterloo. I'm going home.'

'Where's that?'

'Guildford. And before you say it, I know the only decent thing about Guildford is the A3 to London.'

'Got your fare?'

'Yeah. That money you gave me.'

'So why did you phone?'

'Because I liked you. You gave me cash and didn't want anything back. Some blokes would just take the blow job and fuck me off. You were decent.'

'Thanks for that. And what's your proper name? I hate what you called yourself.'

'Nancy.'

'OK Nancy. Have a safe journey, and keep the card. If

you're ever in trouble bell me, yeah?'

'Yeah. And Nick…'

'Yeah.'

'Take care yourself. There's some bad people out there.'

'I'll remember that,' I said, and we both hung up.

I called Lisa next. 'You find him?' She demanded.

'Yes.'

'Well!'

'Not good news.'

'Why? How is he?' A strange thing to say I thought, about the bastard as she called him who'd just ripped her off.

'If you want to know you should try the local hospitals or the mortuary.'

Silence.

'Lisa?'

'What did you do.'

'To him. Nothing. Someone got there first with a gun.'

'Christ. I'll be in touch, stay where you are,' and she hung up.

She was back in twenty minutes. 'He's alive,' she said. 'At the London Hospital. In ICU under police guard. Are you home?'

'Yes.'

'I'll pick you up in ten minutes. You'd better be armed. We'll go see him.'

'They won't just let anyone in.'

'They'll let me.'

'Why?'

'I'm his bloody mother, and I've got the papers to prove it.'

There wasn't much to say to that, so I said nothing. After a moment the phone went dead, and I collected my Colt, tucked it into a pancake holster in the back of my jeans and went downstairs and waited for the Cadillac.

It purred up a few minutes later and pulled up to the kerb.

I dived into the back where Lisa was sitting looking ten years older. 'Why didn't you tell me?' I demanded.

'You didn't need to know.'

There was no answer to that, and no Black Russians or spliffs this time round.

The drive to the London took about thirty minutes and we were in the ICU five minutes later. Tyler Trubbel as I now knew him was in a single bed ward with a cop on a chair outside. We lassoed a nurse, Lisa showed some papers, the nurse whispered to the cop and we went inside.

Tyler was linked up to tubes and monitors, but he was breathing and all seemed OK. Minutes later an Asian doctor came and pulled Lisa outside. I watched through the window, and she smiled and grabbed the geezer and gave him a big, fat kiss. Looked like all was copacetic.

Then she came back to me. 'He's going to live,' she said. 'They got him just in time.'

'So, what now?'

'Now we go and celebrate.'

'What about his dad?

'Sod his dad. He's in Argentina raising beef with someone younger and blonder.'

'Fair enough,' I said. 'Let's celebrate then.'

So we did.

Arnold drove us west into Soho, where he pulled up in Poland Street and helped Lisa out of the car, but left me to my own devices. He'd parked outside a plain green wooden door with a camera pointing down, and a single bell in the centre of the wood. Lisa walked towards it, and the door opened before she rang. She never ceased to amaze me. She led me down a narrow corridor that opened into a dimly lit bar, behind which stood a grey haired party with a big smile on his face. 'Hello stranger,' he said, the smile widening. 'Long time.'

'Things happen,' she said. 'I've missed the place.'

'Still here. Still standing.'

'This is Nick,' she said. 'A helping hand. Nick, Django with a D.'

'Nick,' he said to me. 'Pleased to meetcha. Any friend of Lisa's is always welcome.' Then back to her. 'Something wrong love? You don't seem yourself.'

'Life gets worse with age. People get hurt.'

'Never a truer word. So what's it to be?'

'Champagne. Your best brandy and a lump of sugar, twice.'

Django turned and shouted back through a serving hatch in the wall. 'Janice. Two champagne cocktails. Large size.'

And that's when the evening started to get fuzzy.

I woke up to bright sunshine coming through massive, uncurtained windows in a massive room on a massive leather sofa opposite a massive TV screen under a blanket, fully dressed but for my shoes, Lisa was standing over me with a mug in her hand. 'Coffee?' she asked.

I grunted something from a mouth that felt like the inside of a budgie's cage. Thank God she took it as a yes, and she plopped the mug into my hand. 'Ouch,' I said, and copped for the handle. 'Hot.' I took a luxurious sip and sighed. 'Beautiful. Where am I?'

'In my lair.'

I looked round and remembered she'd knocked six flats into one. It was quite something. 'Nice digs,' I said, sitting up, and only regretting it for a moment until my equilibrium settled. 'How did I get here?'

'Alfred carried you.'

'Are you serious?'

'Deadly.'

'It must've been something I ate'

Another dirty look.

'Sorry about that,' I said.

'We did mix our drinks.'

'Like?'

'Champagne cocktails, Brandy Alexanders, espresso martinis, blahdy, blahdy, blah.'

'What was that place called by the way? That bar?'

She shrugged. 'Don't ask me.'

'Well thanks for getting me home safe.'

'You were good company until you nodded off.'

'Christ.'

'No problem. But you still have my money to earn. I'll get Alfred to take you home for a shower.'

Which is exactly what he did.

Her building was just off the Brixton Road. Five stories high if it was an inch. There was a huge underground car park, empty but for the Cadillac, a concrete ramp, and an over and under metal door that worked on a remote from the motor's dashboard. Very high tech.

When I got dropped off at home I stood under alternate hot and cold water until my head felt a bit better, scrubbed my teeth hard and shaved as close a nun's habit. At least all that made me feel a bit more human. A large Bloody Mary made me feel even more so. I sat and looked out of my window as I drank it and I played more Miles at very low volume. It was a pretty day outside, and eventually I spoiled it by answering the phone. It was Jack Robber. 'Got a bite,' he said. 'On your Ringo.'

'Yeah?'

'Let's meet.'

'Where?'

'Yours.'

Thank God, not the Dog pub. 'You've not been banned out of your favourite boozer have you?

'Maurice gets the hump.' Maurice was the landord. A very strange individual.

'You two should get married. Or at least live in sin.'

'Fuck off.'

'That's just denial.'

'And that just cost you an extra oner.'

'Like I said I'm on expenses.'

'Fish and chips?'

'Not 'alf.'

'Got beers in?'

'A fridge full.

'Half an hour.'

And he was true to his word. The chips came from the good shop in Herne Hill. Pure white cod, batter crisp, but not tough. Lovely soft chips and mushy peas. A pickle and a small gherkin each. I supplied the ketchup and vinegar, and of course the lager. We ate straight out of the paper off the tiny table in my tiny kitchen. The food was perfect for the way I felt. Not much had been eaten the night before as I remembered. A green olive or two. Maybe a cocktail sausage on a stick or even some cheese and pineapple. Real old school, the club with no name. When every scrap was gone I shoved the greaseproof into my bin and we took more beers to my living room. We'd said nothing about his visit over dinner, or was it a late lunch? But before he'd arrived I'd counted out six hundred smackers from the cash Lisa has given me and when we were comfy I handed it over.

'Sweet,' he said as he counted it slowly. He never trusted my count did Jack.

'So,' I said, when all was merry and bright. 'Ringo.'

He took a small leather bound note book from inside his jacket. 'Ringo,' he repeated. 'Also known as Richard Stark, aka Big Ricky. Fat cunt. Comes from up north somewhere. Too many chip butties.' Thus spoke a man who'd just chowed down a double portion of fried Maris Pipers with his battered cod. 'Drug dealer, enforcer, gun for hire. Muscle the same or similar. This bloke would definitely favour the Rolling Stones, although he dresses like one of the Beatles.'

'Record?'

'Pretty light. Some assaults as a lad. Thing is, witnesses seem to take a powder when it comes to court. He's webbed up with a nasty face, goes by the name of the Walrus. Long streak of piss. Wears a syrup. Both on the list of interest to the police. So, what's your interest?'

'Client confidentiality.'

'Fair enough.' He tore the page from his book and gave it to me, finished his beer and got up to leave. 'Just be careful Nick. These blokes have a very bad rep. And you're not getting any younger.'

'Thanks for that.'

'Much as I don't like you, I'd miss you if you were gone. And of course there's the occasional sweetener.' He patted his pocket and left. Left me to my own devices.

So Ringo was the bad man. But had he got what he wanted from Tyler? If so, why shoot him? A done deal and everybody happy. But obviously not. And if he hadn't, once again why shoot him? A conundrum tied up with an enigma. I looked at the page from his notebook Robber had given to me. An address in the Elephant and Castle. Time to take a look see. Tomorrow morning would do. People like Ringo liked their kip. So did I. So I took the remains of my all day hangover to bed.

I felt much better after a good night's sleep and breakfasted on fried egg, bacon, beans, fried tomatoes and a slice of Warburton's Danish, washed down with builder's tea. I didn't shave and dressed scruffy again. I mentally tossed a coin whether or not to drive. But as it was just a recce I didn't need the aggro of parking. And besides, I was sure I'd end up in some boozer or other, and I needed my licence. I left my gun at home too.

So, happy as Larry on another beautiful London summer's day, I headed north by London transport Routemaster. The address Robber had given me was a lock-up shop securely locked up. Or so it looked. Fortuitously there was a greasy spoon almost opposite, and I grabbed a *Daily Mirror* from a corner shop and a window seat in the cafe, and ordered a cup of tea and a bath bun which I really didn't need, but was good camouflage.

But, as so often happened on a surveillance operation, nothing happened. No one came or went, and there's only so many cups of thick, brown tea one man can drink, and only so many times he can re-read the *Daily Mirror* before something gives. Either the capacity of his bladder or his mental capacity to ingest bullshit.

I was home by mid-afternoon and popped a can of lager and popped a King Curtis album on the deck. Minutes later my mobile rang. It was Lisa with an S.

'What are you up to?' she asked.

'Just detecting.'

'Are you in a hairdresser's?'

'Why?'

'That music.'

'That music as you call it is the late, great King Curtis in his pomp.'

'OK.' I should've saved my breath.

'How's Tyler?' I asked.

'Much better. That's why I phoned. Still out of it, but less tubes and monitors.'

'Good news.'

'Sometimes I wonder with that boy. You have a daughter.'

'You did research me. Yes. But I don't see her as often as I'd like.'

'That's tough.' Almost human, I thought. 'So I thought a celebration was in order.'

'I'm still recovering from the other night. I don't think I could take another go round in the bar with no name.'

'No. There's a Thai restaurant down the road who do take-outs. Arnold could fetch dinner, and we could crash a bottle of wine.'

'Why me? What about Arnold?'

'Like most food, Thai gives him wind, so we don't want to go there. He survives mostly on dry biscuits and water.'

'Bad luck. Spiders and food don't agree with him. Tough life.'

'He survives. And I enjoy your company. Didn't think I would.'

'Me being staff and all.'

'Exactly. Then he can head downstairs to his apartment and we could shoot shit, or shoot pool.'

'You have a pool table?'

'A pool table, pin ball machines, a juke box. A proper games room.'

'Some place you got there. And we should talk about this Ringo character. He probably shot Tyler. Have you told the cops?'

'No.'

'Why?'

'I'll wait until Ty wakes up, and he can tell them himself. Besides I don't like police. I wash my own dirty knickers.' Sweet thought.

'And if he hadn't woken up?' I asked.

'That would be a white horse of another colour.'

'Nice turn of phrase.'

'You remember my place?'

'Once seen, never forgotten.'

'Seven o'clock.'

'On the dot.' And that was that.

I got prettied up in a pair of shiny black Tony Lama needle

toed shit-kicker boots, a black H Bar C Rancher shirt with an appliquéd black and white rose motif and five studs on each cuff, faded Wrangler boot cut jeans. The boots were decorated with silver chains that jingle-jangled as I walked. I'd thought about buying a pair of spurs, but as I didn't have a horse or a pick-up truck I thought it was going a bit far. The chains worked for me anyway. I added a black silk jacket that covered my gun in the pancake holster down the back of my jeans. I don't know why I took it, I just did.

I drove my old Ford to Brixton and found the open door to the car park under Lisa's block that I remembered from the other night. Arnold was standing by the Cadillac in the dim lights in the ceiling and I parked next to it. I got out and he wished me a good evening. I wished him one back, and realised that was the first time I'd heard him speak. He showed me to the lift that I remembered too, pressed the top floor button and left me alone.

When the lift doors opened I was in the penthouse and Lisa was waiting for me looking fantastic in an outfit with a wide net skirt, a tight bustier which pushed her breasts up, and black, high heeled, lace-up boots. She looked a bit like a black haired version of the blonde bird in Fleetwood Mac, although that wasn't my kind of Musak, she was worth looking at. Lisa had a cigarette in one hand and an old fashioned cocktail shaker in the other. 'Hello cowboy,' she said.

'Hello cowgirl,' I replied.

She smiled as I took off my jacket, tossed my pistol onto a chair by the dining table that was set for two, and the jacket on top.

'I like your shirt,' she said.

'Thanks.' I didn't mention her top.

'Black Russian?' she asked.

Here we go again, I thought and nodded.

She poured, and we both drank and she told me about her

visit to Tyler and how he was improving. The lift door pinged and Arnold came in looking unhappy carrying a white carrier bag in each hand which had to contain our supper, then he got shoved in the back and two blokes came in too, both carrying handguns.

'I'm sorry, miss Lisa. I left the door open and they ambushed me.'

Lisa shook her head. 'Not your fault.'

The two intruders looked like half a Beatles tribute band, or possibly a quarter of two Beatles tribute bands. One very tall, one very fat. Fatty pushed past Arnold who stood, still carrying the bags with an ever more hangdog expression than usual. 'Shut up,' Fatty hissed at Arnold as he came. He had long dark hair, a black suit with a velvet collar strained to the max and a white tab collared shirt, and skinny black tie that looked like it was strangling him. The fingers of both hands covered in rings. Silver, gold, with stones that twinkled as he moved. Ringo, as I lived and breathed. The bloke behind looked like he was almost seven feet tall in his Cuban heeled Chelsea boots. His suit was black too and hung on him like a shroud on a coat hanger. He was as skinny as Ringo was fat, but his hands were huge and made the nickel plated pistol he held look like a toy. On his head was the syrup as Robber had called it. Long and black, and just a little bit crooked like he'd put it on in a hurry. This pair would have been funny, if their intent wasn't obviously serious.

'Who's the boyfriend?' Ringo demanded. I imagine he meant me.

'Get fucked,' said Lisa. Maybe not the best thing to say when guns were in the room.

'Put those glasses down and keep your hands in sight,' ordered Ringo. He had some weird northern accent, half Liverpool, half fuck knows where.

We did as we were told.

'Where is it?' he asked, but not in a friendly way.

'What?' Lisa again.

'My money or my drugs.'

'Non comprende.'

Christ I thought, don't keep bugging the guy.

'Walrus,' said Ringo. 'Shoot the goon in the knee.' I guessed he meant Arnold, who really hadn't done anything but get supper.

'Hold on,' I said. 'Sorry. I don't understand what's going on here.'

'None of your fucking business,' said Ringo.

'Looks like it is from where I'm standing, looking down the wrong end of a gun.'

'Your boy, missus,' back at Lisa, blanking me. 'He took a lot of money from me on a promise. Not enough to change my life, but enough to piss me off. The money must be here. It wasn't at that dirty squat.'

'Ringo, or whatever you call yourself,' said Lisa. 'My son takes after his father. He's a liar and a cheat, but he's still my son. If there is any money here I don't know where it is. He's roamed this place since he was a boy. He knows every hidey-hole where he could stash money. More than me. He used to hide away when he was bunking school and I could never find him. But, I know he owed some very nasty bastards in Bristol, and my friend Nick here was told that's where he was a couple of nights ago, before he ended up in hospital.'

'That was unfortunate. A mistake.' It didn't sound like it.

Suddenly Arnold piped up. 'Can I put these down please, they're getting heavy.'

'Do it, you stupid old fool,' said Ringo, and Arnold gently put the food down. Then with an agility I'd never noticed, he suddenly turned into Harry the horse and caught the Walrus's pistol arm and dislocated it with a crack and caught his gun as he dropped it.

'Fuck,' said Ringo, and his gun pointed to the floor, as I knocked my jacket off the chair and pulled my .45 from its holster and pointed it at him. 'Keep it down,' I said, and he obeyed.

'Now, gently on the floor with it.'

He obeyed again, and the whole deal had changed to the good guys' advantage.

'What happened there?' I said.

'I didn't tell you,' said Lisa. 'Arnold was a close combat instructor in the marines.'

'Respect,' I said, and Arnold nodded.

The Walrus was lying on the floor making a keening noise, and Arnold kicked him in the ribs. 'Shut up,' he said, 'or I'll really hurt you. That boy was as close as family to me.' Walrus did as he was told.

'Now what?' said Lisa.

'Now I make a call, and we wait for some nice policemen,' I said.

'No,' she said, and walked over to Ringo, kicked his gun away, then pulled back her skirt and produced a little double barrelled belly gun. She pulled back both hammers with a sound as loud as a factory closing down, in the warm, triple glazed silence of her penthouse.

'No, Lisa,' I said gently.

'Yes, Lisa,' she said back. Then to Ringo, 'Tyler's a crook and a conman. But he's my son and you shot him. You're a mug. There never were any drugs. I have my fingers in all sorts of mysterious businesses, but the most dope I'm involved in is the occasional spliff. He took your money and paid back the brethren in Bristol, and I'm glad.'

'Don't shoot him, Lisa,' I said. 'This can all be worked out. I have a mate on the force.'

She shook her head, then pulled back her skirt again with her left hand, and pulled out the flick knife she'd told me about. She clicked it open and the steel in the blade twinkled in the light. She pushed the point against Ringo's neck, where a vein bulged and a thin trickle of blood ran down his collar. Then she moved back and let the hammers of her pistol down, 'OK, Nick,' she said. 'We'll do it your way.'

I think everyone in the room but her let their breath out at that.

We got Ringo and the Walrus on one of Lisa's sofas, Walrus still complaining about his arm, but only under his breath, when Arnold gave him the evil eye. Lisa's and my weapons were stashed away in one of those hidey-holes she'd mentioned and I kept hold of the bad guys' guns and called Robber whilst I chewed on a warm vegetarian pancake roll.

I told him as much of the story as he needed to know and he promised reinforcements and an ambulance ASAP. When I told him about guns, he warned me they'd come in hard and they did. We all ended up face down on the foot until Jack sashayed in and allowed Arnold, Lisa and me back on our feet.

It all ended up with Ringo and the Walrus carted off to Brixton nick and Jack and a couple of uniforms slurping down beef and noodles, and chicken satay with peanut and chilli sauce whilst we made our statements.

And that's pretty much all she wrote.

Ringo and the Walrus got fifteen years each. Tyler recovered, left hospital, got a job in the city, where I understand he's made a small fortune. Lisa still has her fingers in several mysterious business pies that are none of my business. We still keep in touch and every so often she treats me to a meal at Mr Chows, and an evening at the club with no name. Arnold still drives the Cadillac and takes care of her. Robber gets nearer retirement with every month, but still gives me the occasional heads-up in exchange for cash. Nancy's dad paid for teeth implants, and she went to college to study home economics. And as for me, I still do a bit of detecting when I can find someone to pay the piper.

ON A RAGGA TIP

Two blokes walk into a bar.

It's after three on a gloomy, wet weekday afternoon. Apart from them, there are three people in situ. A young guy behind the jump, gay as a parakeet, a customer sitting at the bar chewing on what looks and smells like chilli chicken wings, washed down by a bottle of Becks, and me at a table with the remains of a club sandwich, an empty coffee cup, a bottle of Rolling Rock and my new Nokia. I've got a *Telegraph* folded at the crossword and a Staedtler fine black pen in my hand. I'd been doing a half hearted investigation on the husband of a half hearted payer, and when it started to rain I'd ducked into the bar for lunch, as I'd caught a bus up to Waterloo as anyone would with parking like it was there during the week. I'd stayed for a beer or two because I didn't have a coat, and it was a five minute hoof to the bus stop. Just enough time to get a soaking and sit for the journey home smelling like a wet dog. I'd been in worse places, the beer was cold, and apart from the fact Sade was on the stereo it was good to be warm and dry indoors. Sade! I ask you. How eighties was that?

The two blokes felt wrong. Cop instinct, and once a cop, always a cop. They were dressed alike. Long leather coats, Gestapo style. With matching gloves. Hoods underneath, both up, and Docs. Shiny black. One pair with yellow laces, one pair, red. Although they had their backs to me I just had a feeling they were a salt and pepper team. Don't ask me why, but I was proved to be right. The barman smiled and asked their pleasure. Their pleasure was the contents of the till, and to underline the request they both pulled out sawn-off shotguns with the stocks cut down to pistol grips. The barman cried a little cry and the bloke at the bar unwisely decided to be a hero. He stood and was about to speak when red laces gave him a good clout with the barrels of his gun right on his eyebrow. Boy, that smarts.

Yellow laces demanded the cash from the till again, and of course the boy was so scared he couldn't open the damned thing, and he started to cry. I knew how he felt. Yellow laces had to go behind the bar and open it himself. I'd been in the gaff for a couple of hours and it had been a slow day from what I could see. The burgers and fries hadn't exactly been flying out of the kitchen, so the till wouldn't have been brim full of dough. Red laces glances over to me and the bottom of his face was covered by one of those scarves Arabs wear, red and white, with white tassels, but there was enough of his face exposed to let me see he was black. When yellow laces had emptied the till he gave me a squint too, same sort of scarf, this time a white boat. He came out from behind the counter and headed my way. The Nokia went in his side pocket. 'Wallet,' he demanded. I gave it up. There was maybe twenty quid inside. And a photo. Screw the money, but I asked. 'Can I have the photo back please?' Polite as can be.

He snorted and put the wallet in his pocket too, when he noticed my watch. 'Watch,' he said.

Not the Rolex. Not the value, but it had been a gift from the woman in the photo. Someone who loved me, then poof, was gone.

'No,' I said, but he stuck the shotgun into my face and I did the wise thing and gave it up too.

Meanwhile, the customer who'd got a smack decides to get back into the action and red laces shoots him in the chest. No reason really. Just because he could. The customer, half dazed anyway from the blow to his head was no danger. Fuck, that gun was loud. Loud enough to bring someone out from the kitchen, if there was anyone there, but later it transpired both the cook and the washer-up had gone outside for a smoke in the rain.

Now was the moment when anything could happen. There were just two witnesses left. Me, and the barman, and the robbers had three full barrels between them. It would've been easy to blow us both away.

Instead, yellow laces pocketed my watch and without a word the pair legged it outside and into a waiting navy blue S-reg, what I thought was five series BMW, and away, leaving just an empty till, a weeping boy and a brave but stupid punter bleeding out all over the floor. And me of course. On the way yellow laces grabbed the phone off the bar and threw it hard against the wall where it smashed into a dozen pieces.

'Get a towel,' I yelled at the barman. He did. I put it over the wound. 'Hold it tight,' I said. 'Don't leave him.'

The phone was a bust so I ran outside. On the right was a deli, on the left a mod men's shop. I hit the deli door hard. Behind the counter was a young boy in a long white apron. They certainly seemed to be making staff younger these days. 'Phone,' I yelled, 'there's been a shooting.'

'Is that what I heard,' he gargled. I saw a telephone on the wall, grabbed it, dialled three nines and called for an ambulance. 'Someone's been shot,' I said.

'Where?'

'What's that place called?' I said to the kid. 'The bar?'

'Jake's.'

'Jake's,' I echoed. 'The Cut. What number?' To the kid again.

'Sixty-six.'

I passed the information on and went back to the bar. The boy was still holding the cloth to the customer's chest. I felt for a pulse through the blood on his neck. Nothing. 'You can stop now son,' I said. The kid was covered in blood and still weeping and I felt like joining him again.

The ambulance arrived, followed shortly by the cops. I made a statement, told the officer who questioned me everything including the registration number of the BMW. The only thing I didn't share was the colour of their shoe laces. He gave me a crime number to tell my insurance company. I didn't know or care if my watch was insured. I intended to find it for myself.

The cop offered me a ride home which I declined. It had stopped raining and I fancied a walk to clear my head. I washed the last of the blood off my hands in the bar sink and wished the barman, who was sitting head in hands covered with a silver blanket, the best of luck. He didn't reply. I expected he'd be looking for a new, safer job soon.

I strolled through the early evening streets towards Waterloo station. The temperature seemed to have risen and I took my time. When I got close I popped into what looked like a decent pub and had a pint. I had just enough change left in my pocket, and my Oyster for the bus ride home. It didn't matter what I did. There was no one waiting at home. No one cared what I did. Whether I came or went, lived or died like that poor fucker in the bar. Maybe if I'd been sitting where he'd been and him at my table, perhaps I'd be on my way to the bone orchard now.

When I got to my flat I phoned the bank's twenty four hour call centre and cancelled my bank card. It took a while as the line was crap and the individual at the other end didn't have English as his first language. I didn't do the same with my credit card. It only had a few hundred quid credit left as business, as usual, was spotty. I sat in front of my switched off TV and wondered how come I'd ended up like this.

I stayed low for the next few days. The London news had featured the murder of the man in the bar. His name had been John Thompson. He had been a pharmacist on his day off, up to London for a day that was to include a night at The Old Vic which was showing a Shakespeare season. He'd been single. He'd made a bad choice for lunch. Me too.

First thing I did before I got busy was to replace my phone.

Secondly I let my credit card company know my card had been stolen. Once again the call centre was somewhere east of Eden, but the bloke I got to talk to was most amenable even though he gave me a bit of a scolding for my tardiness. Finally I discovered the card had been used at John Coffey's supermarket in Brixton at the back of the town hall, at a record shop in the market, a restaurant in Atlantic Road and a clothes shop, once again in the market. Then it had maxed out and had been refused at a record shop in Soho. I got the times and dates, and thanked the bloke for his time and he promised a new card would be heading my way shortly.

Now, by coincidence, John Coffey had used me and an associate to capture some shoplifters a few years before and we'd kept in touch. I called him up at his office in the building and he invited me to lunch. We met at his favourite pizza shop in the market. He was bigger, older, and his nappy hair had more grey, but his grin was as big as ever. We exchanged news and I told him the whole story. 'Christ,' he said. 'That's big news. And you were there?'

'Right there.'

'And your card was used at the shop. I really must improve the staff training.'

After lunch we went to the shop and he took me through to the back where the CCTV cameras were kept. I told the computer bloke the date and time of the transaction and he pulled up the video. The camera on the checkout showed a big white bloke who was probably yellow laces, and a blonde woman with him, in charge of a four wheeled baby buggy, buying up the shop. When he signed my name on the receipt with a flourish, his left hand jacket sleeve pulled up and there large as life was my Rolex, or a double. The video outside showed him in jeans, leather jacket and Docs. The video was monochrome but the laces were light in colour. Probably yellow. The car was a BMW, same series as the getaway car in Waterloo. I didn't get the reg. I didn't need it. I thanked John and left.

I went back to the market then and found the record shop. Nothing much more than a hole in the wall with a counter, racks of CDs and vinyl and two big fat speakers which pumped out reggae at a volume I'm sure was illegal. Behind the jump was a white boy with dreads. As the tune finished I asked him about the sale that had been made with my credit card, he spoke a cockney version of Jamaican patois and denied all knowledge, but I knew he was lying. I thanked him and left. Closing time for the shop was eight I saw from a sign in the window. Plenty of time to get home, have something to eat and get back to continue our conversation.

Eight pm found me outside the market at the entrance closest to the shop. Just as I hoped, dreadlocks appeared pushing an expensive looking racing bike. It was dark by then, and as he was fiddling with the light on the bike I grabbed him and shook him hard enough to make his teeth rattle.

'You told me lies,' I whispered in his ear. 'You know who I was asking about.'

I felt his skinny shoulders through his sweater. 'No,' he said. The patois had vanished. Just a frightened cockney boy now.

'Just tell me, and I'll go away. I don't want to hurt you.'

'Chaucer house. Chaucer estate. Don't know the number, but you can't miss it. Ground floor party central. He's always there. But they'll eat you mon.'

'Name?'

'They call him Trojan.'

'If you're lying, or if you tell him I'll beat you son.' And with that I shook him again, but gently and let him go. He climbed onto his bike and wobbled off into the night.

I knew the Chaucer estate of old. LCC flats. Open walkways. No lifts. Condemned, but not executed. Squats, junkie hangouts, drug factories, needle parks, zombie dorms, lovely. But no cops, which was just what I wanted.

I went home then and went to bed. Tomorrow could be a long day.

I had a gun then, and a licence and belonged to a gun club before it was confiscated by the government. I haven't voted since. Anyway, whoever you vote for you always get a politician. It was a Colt 1911 seven shot. If you were greedy, you could always put one in the pipe and pop another shell into the bottom of the clip. If you couldn't get what you wanted with eight .45 bullets you might as well stay at home and make babies.

I took it out of the safe it was kept in the next morning, broke it down, cleaned it with Hoppe's, put Humpty back together again, and hung around my flat waiting for darkness to fall. When I left, I attached the gun with gaffa tape under the dash of the anonymous Japanese crap motor I was driving at the time. I didn't want any nosy police checking me out so I drove well within the speed limit and made all the correct turn signals on the way to the Chaucer.

In the back of the car was my Louisville slugger. I had plans for Trojan.

The Chaucer stood, as it had stood since just after WW2 I reckoned. Once it had been the borough's pride, but now it just reeked of the end of an era. I slid the car through the open break in the wall of the estate and let it drift down, lights off. There were a number of cars parked in the front of the six houses that made up the estate. All bangers much like mine. I slid the car to a halt and surveyed the scene. Most of the estate was in darkness, just a few dim lights showing signs of life, except for one flat on the ground floor of what I assumed was Chaucer house. Inside was brightly lit and the sound of reggae burst out of every window. I hunkered down and waited for something to happen. I didn't have to wait long before a BMW five series drove down and parked up not far from my car. A big black geezer got out. Trojan no doubt. In the light from the flat I saw that the laces on his Doc Martens were coloured red.

He strolled across to the flat like he owned the place. I waited until he was inside before I left my car. As I went I pulled on skintight black leather gloves and retrieved the gun and the bat.

Next to the BMW was a rusty Transit van up on blocks. I stayed close and waited for Godot.

He was inside for close to an hour getting his rocks off on something or someone. I didn't worry. I had nowhere to go. Eventually he came back out alone, as the music boomed on.

He walked to the BMW driver's door and was busy with the keys when I stepped out from behind the van and said, 'Trojan?'

He turned, and as he did I was already spinning the bat above my head and it crashed into his eyebrow just like he'd crashed into the eyebrow of poor dead pharmacist. He went down like a giant Redwood being felled and I finished the job by swinging the bat into his left knee cap. He cried out then, but 'On A Ragga Tip' was on the sound system inside, and he might as well have stayed silent. 'Your mate,' I said. 'Where?'

'Who?'

'Waterloo. Jake's Bar. Remember?'

He squinted up at me and remembered. 'Yellow laces,' I said. Keeping one eye on the flat.

'Fuck off.'

I took up the Colt, pulled back the hammer and stuck it up his nose. 'No one will hear,' I said.

He thought about it for a moment, then good judgement prevailed. 'Jacko,' he said. 'Jacko Smith.'

'Where?'

He gave me an address, I had no way of knowing if it was kosher, but it was time to go. I left him lying there, one leg at an odd angle. Oh, bollocks, I thought, went back and smashed his other knee. I rescued my car and found a phone box that worked after four that didn't, and called an ambulance on him. And the cops. It was the least I could do.

The address Trojan had given was just south of Stockwell tube station. Big houses, but split. This was just before gentrification dared creep into those mean south London streets. I drove up late morning. In my experience, the criminal classes kept bankers hours. Even those with babies in buggies. Parked outside the house in question was another five series BMW. Same colour, but different plates to the getaway car, but I'd bet my flat it belonged to Jacko, aka yellow laces. Boy, these fuckers loved their Beemers. Anyway, I noted down the registration in my notebook.

Sure enough, as a nearby clock struck twelve, Jacko and his bird, buggy and all came out of the house door carrying bags and boxes, put them in the boot of the BMW and headed off. I wondered if I was too late. Only one way to find out.

I gave them a minute and, with my gun in my belt, left my car and headed over to the house.

There were half a dozen bells by the door. The slip of paper next to FLAT 1 read Smith. The front door was unlocked and I pushed in. Inside were a couple of bikes, a load of uncollected junk mail and a bunch of dead flies. Par for the course for a cheap multi dwelling. Flat one was on the ground floor down the hall. I'd become quite proficient with my lock picks and I had the cheap lock done in a minute. Inside, in the hall were four large suitcases and a sports bag. Seems like they were coming back. Inside the bag were a load of wallets and credit and bank cards held by a rubber band. My wallet complete with photo was amongst them. Result! I creeped the rest of the tiny flat good. Someone was an excellent housekeeper. There wasn't a dirty cup or ashtray to be found. Nothing else either. When I'd finished I sat in the living room facing the door, my gun in my hand, safety catch off.

I didn't have to wait long. I heard a key in the lock and Smith and the blonde pushing the baby buggy came into the room. He was still wearing the Docs with yellow laces.

'What the...?'

I pulled back the hammer of the Colt. 'My watch.' I said.

'Fuck,' said the blonde, who wasn't half bad looking up close. Her hair was spiky and black at the roots. 'I told you to ditch that thing. With his name on the back. Bad luck.'

'I liked it,' said Smith

'Gimme,' I said.

He pulled it off and tossed it to me. I caught it left handed never taking my eyes off him. 'And I got my wallet,' I said.

'How'd you find us anyway?' said Smith.

'You and your friend. You should've stuck to black laces,' I said.

He looked bemused. Not the brightest knife in the rack I figured.

'I told you we should've gone just now,' said the blonde.

'We need stuff. And I had to fill up the car. And we needed another one for all your junk.'

'We could've done that on the way. And we didn't need another car.'

Before the conversation turned into a proper domestic I intervened. 'Sorry about your situation. But now I think I should call the cops.'

Blonde looked down at the buggy. 'Can I see to baby?' she asked.

'Sure,' I said.

She leaned over and came out with the sawn off Smith had held at the bar, or a reasonable facsimile of, pulled back both hammers, and pointed it at my head. Smith saw the move and smiled. 'Isn't this what they call a Mexican standoff?' He said.

Blimey, what kind of mug was I?

The two barrels of the gun looked as wide as two Channel tunnels from where I was sitting. 'Be careful with that thing,' I said.

'I am,' came the reply. 'I'm not just some dizzy Essex blonde tart.'

'This pistol has got a hair trigger,' I said. Which it hadn't. 'That thing goes off, and so does mine. And it's pointed straight between his eyes.'

'Then what?' Her again.

'Then let me go. I've got what I want. No hard feelings.'

'And then you call the cops.' I saw her finger white on the triggers. She wanted to use that bloody thing. This bitch was a couple of fries short of a happy meal, that was for sure. And I'd bet she was the stoppo driver on the robbery.

'No. I'm reaching for my phone.' I took out my new Nokia gently with my left hand and tossed onto the couch. 'No phone. You'll be long gone before I could find a phone box that works round here.'

'Let him go, Sylv,' said Smith. 'That fucking thing is pointed at me.'

'I should let him shoot you,' she said. 'You fucking div.'

Christ, fancy being webbed up with this cow.

She came closer gun still at on me. 'Go on,' she said to Smith. 'Let him through.'

So awkwardly I got up and still with the gun on Smith I left the room, then the flat, backing slowly down the hall. Outside I parked the gun inside my belt at the back and went down the front steps. Suddenly I was grabbed, and forced down onto the cold pavement by a bloke in a leather and jeans until I was breathing in grit. I felt a gun at the side of my head and cuffs clicked tightly on to my wrists. Another bloke frisked me and whispered into a collar mic. 'Gun, I have a gun here.'

'It's legal,' I said.

'Not loaded.' He had a point.

'You're after Jacko Smith and his missus,' I said.

He said nothing.

'She's got a loaded shotgun in the baby buggy.'

The cop passed that on.

Smith and Sylv came out then, and more men in plain clothes surrounded them and they ended up on the ground too. Served them right. Especially her. I'd nearly wet myself when she pointed that gun at me with that look on her face. As it turned out there was no baby in the buggy. No baby at all. But it was a good way to carry the shotgun around. They were both found guilty along with Trojan and are still inside as far as I know.

Me. I ended up in the choky again. My gun was confiscated and I ended up with a fine from the court. After all I had done for the guardians of law and order. Sometimes life isn't fair.

And the last time I was in The Cut, Jake's Bar was gone, replaced by Rooney's Fish And Chip Plaice. See the clever way they spelled that. One thing I've discovered is of course life goes on.

Thanks to Michael Connelly for letting me plunder his Lincoln Lawyer novels for Bobby D, the Beemer Brief. Cheers mate! A copy of the book is on its way.

To be the first to hear about new books and exclusive deals
sign up to our newsletters:

crimeandmysteryclub.co.uk/newsletter